Stay For Me

Tam DeRudder Jackson

What readers are saying about the Balefire Series:

Play For Me

"This is a fast read with everything you want from a steamy romance novel. Good chemistry between the characters, intense love you can feel, and great banter."
– Brooke Gillespie-Trout, author of *The Art of Zen*

Sing For Me

"I loved every second of this read! Blu and Ash are a fantastic couple, and every second of their story had me either laughing, crying, yelling, or sighing." –Amazon reviewer

Wild For Me

"This book is full of steam, lies, trust and betrayal, and gave me the HEA I was hoping for." –Doris S., Amazon Reviewer

Hot For Me

"The chemistry in this book was palpable whether it be between Adam and Cristy or bandmates and the fans. I feel like the whole storyline had a great energy that kept me invested from start to finish." –Britney Wall, Amazon Reviewer

To learn more about my books and what is coming next, please sign up for my newsletter at:

https://www.tamderudderjackson.com

Books by Tam DeRudder Jackson

The Talisman Series
Tracker (prequel novella)
Talisman
Warrior
Prophetess (novella)
Bard
Druid
Rogue

The Balefire Series
Play For Me
Sing For Me
Wild For Me
Hot For Me
Stay For Me

CHAPTER ONE

Olivia

SEEING HIM AGAIN was inevitable.

I just didn't expect it to hurt this much.

Ten years ago, Garrett Phillips made a decision. Fine. Maybe I helped him make that decision, but that's beside the point. He chose to go with "his boys" and leave me in the dust of a ratty old tour bus. The memory gripped my heart, sharp pain lancing through it, and I gasped in a breath. Curling my hands over the back of my chair, I stared at the man on the screen in front of me. There he was, looking ridiculously hot in an Armani suit that fit him like he owned the company. Unlike "his boys" who showed up on the red carpet—again—wearing cheap T-shirts beneath their five thousand dollar suits, he actually wore a silk dress shirt and a tie. He'd cut his hair since the last time I Googled him. Short looked good on him.

Who was I kidding? I'd liked his hair any way he wore it. Sometimes, like now, I could still feel his thick, coarse mane sliding through my fingers. On cue, that thought led to what we'd been doing the last time I had my fingers in his hair, and my body flashed fire.

"You okay, boss? You look a little flushed," Jeremy Rowland, my assistant said. "Would you like me to grab you a water?"

I blinked, and the world righted itself again. Wrapping my hand around my mic, I nodded. "That would be great. Thanks."

Blowing out a long breath, I willed myself to let go of the past. Garrett Phillips managed Balefire, the biggest rock band on the planet, but tonight, it was my job to make sure the bad boys of rock 'n' roll behaved on live television. Or, at least, I could control the narrative with quick, creative editing if the situation called for it. Judging from what I'd seen when I studied previous Grammy productions in preparation for directing this one, Balefire could, and likely would, cause a ruckus at some point in the show. I needed to be ready.

If life were different, I might have coordinated with Garrett, had his help in making sure his boys played nice for national TV. I might have had *him*.

Squeezing my eyes shut, I willed my mind to focus, to stay on point for the task at hand. I was well aware that landing the job of directing the Grammys—a woman at thirty-three—was a monumental deal. I landed the gig because I was a rock star director and producer in my own right, something I needed to remember. If I wanted to run a large studio someday, which had always been the goal, I couldn't blow my first big chance. Especially not for a man who couldn't wait to start his dream, even if it meant leaving love behind.

"Here you go, boss." Jeremy handed me my water and glanced at the screen in front of me. "Wow! Is that Balefire?" The awe in his voice revealed a true fan.

"All four of them with their ladies."

"No doubt they're going home with hardware tonight. They're legit!"

Arching a brow, I reminded him where we were and what he was supposed to be doing.

"Sorry, Olivia. Sorry." A sheepish smile slipped over his features. "It's just—it's Balefire."

Like that explained everything.

Which it did. Damn it.

It was difficult to hear my colleague over the screaming fans lining the red carpet. Staring at the screen and listening to the commentary through my headphones told me all about what an incredible job Garrett had done as a manager, making Balefire into a household name all over the world. The band sold out arenas wherever they played. Every one of their albums had gone platinum, except for their first one, which only hit gold. No doubt, the players were stunningly talented musicians and song writers in their own right, but they never would have come this far without the shrewd management of one man. To my disgust, my eyes strayed back to Garrett.

Though each member of Balefire escorted a beautiful woman, no one was holding onto Garrett's arm. Somehow, being on his own made him even more dangerous. Somehow, it would have been easier to see him again in person for the first time in ten years if he'd been with someone. Questions swirled through my head. Was he with someone but choosing to go solo tonight? Was he single? Was he still anything like the excited and exciting young man with stars in his eyes who left me behind to chase a different dream? Google never divulged these details, which left me to speculate.

"Zoom in on Cristy Valor and Adam Tron, please," I directed into my mic. Immediately, all the feeds switched from the entire band to the bass player and the pop diva who'd joined Balefire during their last tour. With Tron's tall, dark good looks and Cristy's blond pixie cut and delicate features, the two made a stunning couple. Add to that the story of how her Be Valorous Foundation to put an end to child marriage came to be, and the two of them would be a massive draw during the ceremonies.

On cue, our red carpet commentator stepped over to them.

"Thank you, Natasha, for asking," Cristy said. "It's the goal of the foundation to make it illegal for any girl younger than age eighteen to marry for any reason in any state in the US. Since only adults eighteen and older can divorce, it seems only right that only adults can marry. Anyone can help our cause by joining the Be Valorous Foundation."

Natasha turned her mic to Tron. "I understand Balefire is part of the foundation?"

"One hundred percent."

He stared into Cristy's eyes with his heart in his.

"Hold the camera on them. We need this," I said into my mic.

When Cristy turned away from Tron's stare, I instructed the camerawoman and Natasha to move on to Parker Malone and Jennifer Hartwell, two major movie stars who attended the Grammys as presenters, more so to be seen than anything else. We gave them two seconds and moved on to Lady Gaga who put on a show as only she could. The woman was every director's dream.

On it went until all the stars took their seats in the cavernous space of the Crypto.com Arena, more widely known as the Staples Center. I hadn't seen Garrett during rehearsals, which wasn't exactly a surprise. The band didn't need their manager with them when they rehearsed, I supposed. Balefire would play their song with Cristy Valor, the one currently tearing up the charts, as one of the first songs to open the show. Later on in the production, they'd be playing their number one hit, "Fire Me Up," one of their other songs with several nominations. The band was a musical juggernaut. As Jeremy rightly speculated, they'd win multiple awards tonight, no doubt.

Another certainty popped into my head. Garrett would be at the after-parties, the ones that, as director of the show, I was expected to attend. Any other time, I'd relish the opportunity to hang out with so many major musicians. But the idea of seeing Garrett again left a Gordian knot of gargantuan proportions twisting in my stomach.

Knowing this would be my only moment of calm for the next three hours, I finished off my water in one long swig when we cut to commercial and opening credits. Pulling in a long breath, I held it, pasted on my best smile, and spoke into my mic. "Okay, folks, this is where shit gets real. Let's make this one the most memorable events of the season."

♪

"That's not the song they rehearsed, boss," my assistant director communicated as Balefire took the stage for their second song.

"I can hear that. I can also hear how incredible this song is. Seems like they're debuting something new, and we're recording it first. Do not—I repeat—do not cut the sound. Set the timer back one second for censoring if we have to, but keep that feed rolling."

As Balefire antics went, debuting a new song live on the Grammys was tame. I had to hand it to them; it was a hell of a statement. The rumors of the band breaking up had run rampant since Cristy Valor joined their tour last summer and again when it came out that she and Adam Tron were an item. But this anthem to the importance of brotherhood and the strong bond the band enjoyed shot down all the rumors. Not that I believed journalists in the tabs would be deterred from spreading them. The band probably didn't believe one song would end the rumors either.

Afterward, Parker Malone and Jennifer Hartwell stepped out onstage together to announce the vocal event of the year. I doubt anyone was surprised when they opened the envelope and said, "Balefire with special guest Cristy Valor."

"Did you like that little tune we played just now?" Blu Connolly asked as he held his Grammy statue up. "This kick-ass lady"—he pointed at Cristy Valor—"is a blast to work with. But she's not breaking up Balefire."

"Thank you guys for inviting me to your party," Cristy said. "And thank you for supporting me and the Be Valorous Foundation."

Adam Tron pulled her in for a one-armed hug and a lingering kiss to the side of her temple. Like every other woman watching, I imagine, I couldn't help but swoon a little at the casual way he showed the world how much Cristy meant to him.

Garrett used to be sweet like that too.

As soon as that thought intruded, I shook my head to send it packing. The days of caring affection from my college sweetheart were long past. I had a job to do, one I was determined would make me a sought-after director for every music-related production in Hollywood. I couldn't let a long-ago love distract me from the ultimate goal.

♪

More than anything, I wanted to slide into a chair, put my feet up, and let the final applause wash over me. Of course, that wasn't an option.

"That's a wrap. Great work, everyone. Thank you."

"Nice job, boss." Natasha's voice was the first I heard in my headset, followed by Jeremy, several members of the camera crew, and the team sitting in front of the monitors in front of me in the control room. When the final credits rolled, we shut off our mics, took off our headsets, and let out an unprofessional whoop! Not since my days as a member of the crew for our college theater productions had I done that.

Like lifting a lead cape off my shoulders, the pressure released, and I could breathe for the first time in months. Closing my eyes, I absorbed the good will of my team. Then the thought of ratings intruded, and the pressure dropped on me again. At least I could breathe for a minute.

"Olivia, the car is waiting outside. Time to bask in the glow of your success," Jeremy said with a smile.

Nodding to the rest of my team, I followed my assistant out of the studio to the waiting town car. The first stop was the producers' party. As the biggest party of the night, it stood to reason that Balefire would be there, which meant Garrett would be there as well.

Time to face the music.

Chapter Two

Garrett

LUCKY FOR ME, the band had won three Grammys this year. Quite a feat for a rock 'n' roll outfit in a genre that filled stadiums but didn't wow critics. Didn't mean I wasn't still on probation with them. Ten years of managing these boys to the heights of fame and fortune, and they wanted to jettison me. For what? For love? They had all the women in the world at their feet. What could possibly be the draw of settling down with one?

I snagged a flute of champagne from a passing waiter and made my way over to the band where they were posing for photos, their hands full of statues.

"Get in here, Garrett. Show off with us," Blu said, a big grin on his face.

I stepped over to where they stood in front of a screen and looped my arm over Blu Connolly's shoulders. Out of the original members of the band, surprisingly, Blu had been the most forgiving. After everything that went down, I'm not sure I deserved that, but I'd take it.

Right as the camera's flash went off, I turned my eyes to my guys and raised my glass to them. The move was deliberate, of course, immortalizing my devotion—and my pride—in their accomplishments. When the pics hit the tabs and the band saw them, they'd have to see that everything I'd ever done had been for them.

After the photographer had his fill of Balefire, he motioned to his assistant who scurried off in the direction of Bruno Mars. Taking that cue, I carefully herded the band, now numbering eight with all their women, to a spot where we could talk for a minute without having to shout at each other over the din of the party revving into overdrive.

"You guys want to pack around that hardware all night?" I indicated their awards. "Or do you want me to see to it that they end up in your car?"

"Maybe we should grab one of those trolleys"—Dakota nodded at a nearby drinks cart where waitstaff were busy filling glasses with champagne—"and push our statues around with us." He laughed uproariously at his idea while Jack Whitehorse rolled his eyes. Jack seemed to be the only person who was able to simultaneously jerk Dakota Perri's chain and calm him down. It was fascinating to watch.

Ever the steady one, Adam Tron said, "Let's put the bling in the car."

With a nod in his direction, I pulled out my cell and shot off a quick text. Things hadn't quite turned out the way I envisioned when we took on our first intern. Annabelle Stewart had been an incredible asset—and someone I'd wanted to know much better—yet now she sported a monster diamond on her left hand courtesy of Dakota Perri and no longer worked for Balefire. But she showed me how great it can be to have someone on the road with us to handle all the minutiae while I concentrated on the big picture. As if by magic, Landon Berg, our new intern, stood beside me.

"What do you need, sir?"

"I need you to take the band's hardware out to the town car." He nodded.

"And stop calling me 'sir.'"

"Sir Garrett, the wonder manager," Dakota said. His tone was playful, but his eyes, as always these days, were watchful.

With a shrug and smirk in his direction, I returned my attention to my assistant. "You'll have to figure out a system for ferrying the bling in and out of parties since I imagine this bunch will want to show off everywhere we go."

"Damn straight we will," Blu said. "We aren't Grammy virgins, but somehow, these feel even bigger than the first one we won." He hugged his fiancée, Ashleigh Baker, close to his side and smacked a kiss on her cheek, making it obvious what he was on about.

As I watched his antics, the champagne in my stomach soured.

Right there. That was the problem. My boys were no longer mine.

For now, I still managed the band, but their women managed each of them. With the exception of Jack's wife Clio, I'd made mistakes with all of those women, mistakes the guys were still making me pay for. Somehow, I'd never found the words to convince them that everything I did had been for them, for their success. Because without them, where did I belong?

♪

Celebrities crowded around the band, Parker Malone and Jennifer Hartwell being among the hangers-on. Jennifer had made it no secret she wanted Balefire to write a song for their upcoming movie. Guess she thought if she hung around the band enough and brought it up every time she saw them, she'd get her way. There had been a time when I would have suggested they do as she wanted, and they would have listened to me. Now they ran everything by their women first. I had the distinct impression that Clio and Ashleigh didn't like Jennifer much, so the jury was still out about a song for the soundtrack. Didn't seem to deter Jennifer in the slightest.

"You know, after all your success tonight, boys, it wouldn't be a surprise if the song you write for our movie ends up nominated for an Oscar," she said, eyeing each Balefire member in turn. "Something to think about." She tipped her flute of champagne up and took a delicate sip.

"We'll talk shop later, babe," Dakota said. "Right now, it's time to par-tay!" He wrapped his arms around Annabelle, lifted her, and swung her around, making a spectacle as usual. When he smacked a kiss on his lady's lips, I rolled my eyes and turned my head.

That's when I saw her.

Olivia Carter.

All the activity in the room slammed to a halt as I worked to breathe.

Ten years spun away as I took in the understated silver sheath dress that showed off her long, lithe body to perfection. There had been a time when I'd loved exploring that body with my lips and tongue, listening to her soft moans of pleasure. Her chestnut hair was piled on top of her head in some sort of loose braided affair that left a few tendrils to kiss her neck. Lucky curls. Though she listened attentively to whatever the suit she was with was saying, she held herself slightly aloof. Olivia never did let herself get too close to anyone—not even me. Not even after she told me once that she loved me.

Reality slithered over me. She didn't love me. Or at least not enough to come along for the thrill ride that the band and I made into Balefire. The thought put the brakes on my libido.

This business ran on gossip, and I'd heard at various times over the years that she'd gone into directing and producing. Looked like she made good since she'd directed tonight's major event. Before I could walk over to say hello, she excused herself from the suit and wandered over to chat with Chris Stapleton, lifting her glass to his success at the show tonight. While I tried to figure out a polite way to interrupt them, Blu waved his hand in front of my face.

"Hey dude, you can pick up a lady later. Right now, we have a producer to see."

"I thought you guys said you weren't talking shop tonight."

"The idea of an Oscar changed our minds." He smirked. "Come on, 'sir,'" he mimicked my intern. "Let's go make a deal."

Wrapping me in a headlock, he tugged me along with the rest of the band.

Away from Olivia.

Away from the past.

♪

At some point during the night, the parties all blurred together. Too many glasses of champagne, too many shots of Jameson, and my five-hundred-dollar silk tie ended up around the neck of some B-list actress. The wannabe I left in my bed this morning said something about being in commercials, but I was paying more attention to her rack. Crass and caveman, I know, but she was the one who kept drawing attention to it, sticking her tits up in my face, leaning them against my arm, running her finger along the edge of her dress where it rested a breath above her nipples. Being young and definitely single, I took advantage of what was on offer. It's one of the perks of my job. Sue me.

A visual of an elegant brunette flashed in my mind, hauling me up short. There was a time when the only woman I wanted in my bed was Olivia Carter. Seeing her for a minute at that first party reminded me why. No, she wasn't stacked like the girl I left snoring between my sheets this morning. And she didn't scream like a damn banshee when I made her come. She stretched that long body like a beautiful cat and purred when I touched her. She wrapped her endlessly long legs around my waist and arched up into me, commanding me to love her with everything I had. Even now, I could almost feel her low sounds of pleasure humming through my chest, urging me on while she gave me mind-blowing orgasms I'd never experienced with anyone else.

She demanded my respect, and I was only too happy to give it to her.

Guilt washed through me at the way I left the girl in my bed. Pulling out my cell, I made a quick call to the front desk of the hotel. I couldn't help my latest one-night stand with her Hollywood dreams, but hopefully, the simple gold bracelet and the words on the card would make her feel special.

The next item of business was business. As though I'd summoned him with my thoughts, Landon Berg appeared at my table.

"The hardware is packed for easy transport to the press conference, sir. Also, Bailey advised me to have pitchers of a special concoction sent to each of the members of the band, so I've done that." He stopped and stared at the drink in my hand. "You already did that?"

"Not yet. Since I usually roll out of the sack a couple hours ahead of the boys, I have a smoothie made up for me at the bar." I took a sip of the vile green creation our head roadie, Bailey Saunders, introduced us to years ago and wondered at how the sour, earthy taste of the stuff had started to grow on me.

"It smells terrible. Sorta slimy like pond scum. What's in it?" Landon asked.

"I have no idea, but it works wonders on a hangover. Twenty minutes after finishing a glass of this, and you feel like a million damn dollars." I grinned. "Now about the press conference. Did you send over the list of off-limits questions?"

"I did, sir. I got the impression the tabs are going to ask them first."

His fidgeting made me laugh.

At his quizzical expression, I said, "That's your first lesson in managing a press conference. Dangle something they interpret as juicy in front of the tabs and let the boys take care of themselves."

"You set them up on purpose?" His cartoonish stare cracked me up again.

"Not at all. We decided on those questions together, so the band knows exactly what's coming. Since you took care of them with the hangover cure, they'll be on top of their game." I winked over the top of the glass and took another pull of my smoothie. "The press conference will be another Balefire show."

Landon nodded as he pulled out his iPad and tapped in a few notes. The guy was always taking notes. I liked that about him, how he studied the business, studied how I managed the band. The only exception I noticed was that he stayed on the fringes at the parties. He drank Cokes like water and never left a party with a girl—or a guy.

"So what's the deal with you?" I asked.

He glanced up from his iPad. "Sir?"

"You're twenty-three years old, college educated, and normal, as far as I can tell. You're good-looking enough to draw attention from people at the after-parties, but you never take advantage of what's on offer." I leaned back in my chair. "You're working for a rock 'n' roll outfit. The parties and the people who attend them are some of the perks."

Red tinged his high cheekbones, and he cleared his throat a couple of times. "I'm married, sir. Happily and totally committed."

I arched a brow at his naked left hand.

"We, my wife and I, decided that me wearing my ring while I worked for the band might make things awkward, so she's got it at home." He glanced at his hand, drawing my attention there as well. Now that I studied it, I saw the faint tan line where a ring had been. "But since all the members of Balefire are married or engaged or whatever, it seems that was an unnecessary precaution."

I snorted. All my boys being mothered up was a sore spot for me. Rationally, I knew it was bound to happen at some point. But the longest any of the original members had been with a woman was once about eight years ago when Blu picked up a groupie in Houston and she crisscrossed the country with us for a month before he encouraged her to stay behind in Chicago. Otherwise, in a decade of touring, it had been an ongoing stream of parties and women, and I wasn't ready for it to end. Discovering my new intern was married landed a blow I didn't anticipate.

"So, uh, how long you been married?"

Landon smiled the same smile I'd seen on Jack's, Blu's, Dakota's, and most recently, Tron's faces. A man in love. Suddenly, Bailey's magic green smoothie wasn't doing its job so well.

"High school sweethearts. We married at the end of our freshman year of college." He pulled up a photo on his phone of a pretty brown-skinned woman with braids clear to her ass. "She's in graduate school studying to be a physician's assistant. Since she's putting in wicked-long hours, we thought it would be a good time for me to do this internship."

He scrolled through his photos and held up his phone to show me the two of them at their college graduation. They made a striking couple, he, a tall Scandinavian and she, a Black woman almost matching him in height. Together, the two of them would turn heads wherever they went.

"This business is hard on marriages. I hope you know that."

Landon grinned. "Izzy and I are solid. It was actually her idea that I go without my ring on this internship. She got a kick out of some of the videos I shared with her last night." He gazed fondly at the pic on his phone then shoved it back in his pocket. "After the press conference, we pack up and head back to Denver. Is that correct?"

"Yeah, that's the plan." I finished off my hangover cure and tried to figure out when I'd lost confidence in myself. At one point, when I wasn't much older than Landon, I believed I could rule the world. I could keep the girl and live the rock 'n' roll life: if not like a rock star, then at least like the next best thing. Somewhere along the line, though, that changed. How the hell had that happened?

CHAPTER THREE

Six months later
Olivia

I RAN THE NUMBERS again, sat back in my chair, and groaned. Then I slapped my hand over my mouth and checked to see that my office door was firmly shut. It wouldn't do me any favors if anyone, even my assistant, discovered exactly how red the bottom line of my fledgling production company was. If I didn't find a cash infusion ASAP, my company was going to take a digger and maybe stay buried—another Hollywood dream turned from stardust to ash.

After my huge success directing the Grammys, I thought I'd finally made it, that work would come calling. Not that I was so naïve that I wasn't out there hustling, taking meetings, picking up the tab at obscenely expensive lunches, attending cocktail parties in heels that threatened to leave my calves in permanent spasms and my toes in a perpetual state of numb. Yet I'd only managed to score a couple of independent music videos for some midlist players, nothing that would get me noticed by directors who could make my career. I knew when I chose this business what I was letting myself in for. But after nearly ten years, I thought I'd be several rungs farther up the ladder.

That glaring blank on my accounts receivables page where a payment should have been mocked me, and I jabbed my finger down hard on the keyboard to close the program. For several minutes, I stared at the framed photo of my favorite getaway back in Colorado. I'd always thought someday I'd own that mountain cabin and the ten acres of forest surrounding it. A derisive laugh slipped out of me. I'd thought I'd own that cabin already and be a studio head by now. The trajectory I set for myself should have put me on the pinnacle of movie success. Yet here I was, still scrambling to make music videos for B- and C-list musicians. Turns out, those didn't pay the bills any better now than they did when I first started in the business. I needed a big break, and I needed it now.

A hard rap on my office door was my only warning before my assistant, Jeremy Rowland, breezed through. I flipped the page to a blank document right as he stepped in front of my desk.

"Hey boss, I got something for you."

He handed me a printout of an email with an unmistakable flame logo at the top. The way he sort of caressed it as he let it go twitched a smirk from my lips.

"You could have just forwarded it, you know."

"But Olivia, it's from *Balefire*."

"You think I should frame it or something?"

From the look on his face, I shouldn't have let that giggle escape. Sometimes I forgot exactly how big the band had become. Then I remembered the way Jeremy fan-girled all over them the night of the Grammys and I composed myself.

"Thank you, Jeremy."

Instead of his usual efficient exit, he waited expectantly in front of my desk. When I raised a brow in question, he gave me the universal hand gesture for "go on," and I figured out he wanted me to read the email right then, which meant he'd already read it.

As I scanned down the page, the words stopped making sense. I laid the page on my desk and ran my finger under the lines, forcing myself to slow down and read every single word. Balefire wanted to make a video for the theme song for Parker Malone and Jennifer Hartwell's new movie. Balefire wanted to make the video with my production company. The caveat was that it had to be done during the next month while they were on hiatus from touring—and Garrett Phillips was to have a hand in writing it.

What the hell?

I read that last part a third time and the sign-off at the end. The email came directly from Garrett himself. No cc to him from an assistant. A fourth read confirmed what the first three times through already told me as I heard his voice in my head. Though the words on the page said he wanted to collaborate with me on a music video, his voice said that after all these years, he wanted to spend time with me, which made no sense. My heart dropping into my stomach to do the backstroke at his words made even less sense.

"So? We're doing this, right?" Jeremy bounced on the balls of his feet like an overeager puppy waiting for his mistress to throw his favorite toy. "We're going to make a video with Balefire?"

"I don't know, Jeremy," I hedged.

He cleared his throat. "Um, boss, it's not like we've been making videos on an hourly basis here." The expression on his face made me cringe.

Guess I hadn't been hiding the issues with my company as well as I thought. *But after everything that happened at the end of our relationship, how can I even entertain working with Garrett?* Involuntarily, my gaze slid to my computer where those awful numbers seemed to glare at me from the blank screen like some cartoon version of doom, and I knew what I had to do.

"Do you want me to email Balefire that we're in?"

Guess I hadn't hidden my response to my predicament well either.

I folded the page and slid it into a file in my desk. When I glanced up, I burst out laughing at the look of horror on my assistant's features. "What?"

His finger shook as he pointed to where the email had disappeared into my desk. "Th-that's from *Balefire*. And you *mangled* it."

"If you're going to be any help to me at all with this project, you're going to have to figure out how to deal with the band without freaking out over every little detail related to them. Are you up for that?"

He shot a fist in the air. "Yes! I knew you couldn't pass this one up. I knew it!"

"Answer the question, Jeremy."

With a shrug, he tugged at the cuffs of his shirt and ran a hand over his hair, like *that* would make him look cool and in control. "Sure, sure. I'm totally up for keeping my shit together around the band." The flaming red tips of his ears said otherwise.

I bit down on my lips to hold in my first response. "I'll have to take your word for it, I guess." Waking up my computer, I opened my email to a new document. "I've got this, Jeremy." At his dejected expression, I added, "If you could contact Hartwell Studio to request the usual information about the movie and let them know we're working with Balefire on their video, that would be super."

With a marginal improvement in his disposition, he nodded and walked out of my office, leaving it to me to stand and close my door.

Instead of sitting down at my computer again, I stared out at the city below, cars moving at walking speed, people coming and going into the bistro across the street, clouds obscuring the horizon. My thoughts wandered to the last time I'd seen Garrett. Not on the red carpet or onstage at the Grammys, but the last time I'd spent time with him. We were walking the pavement at Venice Beach, laughing at the antics of street performers. All the while, we both tried to figure out how to make our life together work while the impossibility of that grew into a gulf between us that rivaled the Pacific gently lapping at the shoreline.

I'd been accepted into Pepperdine's law school, and Garrett had signed a five-year contract with Balefire. He'd booked shows for them at midsize venues all along the West Coast for a three-month tour. On paper, that should have worked for us. I met him on multiple weekends wherever the band was playing. But I fell behind in my studies, and by the end of the tour, I wasn't meeting up with him on the weekends.

Until they hit LA and I flew down to see him.

Those first months on the road with the band changed him, made him happy in a way I'd never seen him. Gone were the suits he hated, replaced by jeans, T-shirts, and leather vests. Gone were the designer shoes, replaced with lace-up boots—steel-toed boots, he told me, to protect his feet when they were loading and unloading equipment from the bus. Gone was the ill-fitting corporate sheen, replaced with a carefree excitement that vibrated off him. If anything, hitting the road with Balefire released the inner Garrett, showing me a man I wanted even more than the one I met in a coffee shop a lifetime before.

But I had a dream too.

When he booked the band for a six-month tour through the Midwest and Mid-Atlantic states, I knew we were at a crossroads. I couldn't take that much time off from school, and he couldn't fly out to see me even when the band was traveling between shows. Plus, I'd seen the groupies at the venues Balefire played. Those women were determined to be with the band, including Garrett. When they discovered he was the manager, some of them zeroed in on him even more than they did on Dave Brubaker—the original drummer, Blu, Tron, and Dakota. He assured me he had no interest whatsoever in those women, but he was hot, and his charisma attracted people to him. I'd be lying if I said I didn't worry about being replaced—at least for a night or two—while he was on the road.

Then came the video Dakota sent me. He thought it was a lark, but there was nothing funny about the smile on Garrett's face before a woman giving him a lap dance poured champagne down his throat. Dakota said they'd packed a small venue of about five thousand people and someone from Attitude Records saw them. After their celebration, and a detour back to Denver to stow the tour bus, they were flying to LA to sign the papers. Balefire was on their way to the big time, and it was all because Garrett knew exactly how to manage the band. Wasn't I proud?

That feeling of my heart swimming in my stomach hit me then because I knew Garrett and I were over.

Today, I had to decide what that feeling meant and how I was going to work closely with Garrett Phillips over the next month. They say you never really get over your first love, but for the sake of my company—and my sanity—somehow, I had to make sure I'd extinguished that old flame for good.

♪

The eyewatering sum the band offered my production company for their video should have been my first clue something was up. It was roughly the equivalent of five music videos with full orchestras and a raft of professional dancers. Even if Heart Strings Productions had been running in the black for years, I would have been a fool to pass up that kind of money, let alone the opportunity to work with the biggest rock band on the planet.

Still, something about how the contract seemed to show up out of the blue with its short time frame and big budget had my Spidey senses tingling. There was more to this video than the band wanting to work with the team that created the best Grammys production in the last five years. Though my interactions with Jeremy told me I hadn't been as circumspect at work as I'd thought concerning the financial health of my company, I knew no one outside of it had any idea I was floundering. After all, business credit cards took care of spendy lunches with the music execs who loved them. Maybe the reason behind Balefire's sudden interest in working with me was some sort of payback for taking Garrett from me back in the day? But why now? I'd started Heart Strings Productions two years ago and sent information to all the major bands—including Balefire—about our music video interests and capabilities, but they didn't bite—until now. Something weird was up.

Then I remembered hearing about a scandal with the band recently. Pulling up Google, I scanned through the archives of TMZ, and there it was: the Cristy Valor-Adam Tron story. But as I read through the articles and watched a few of the videos, it was obvious there wasn't anything scandalous about the band, or at least nothing more scandalous than their usual antics. After all, they had a reputation as the rowdy boys of rock 'n' roll, a reputation I knew from firsthand experience they'd cultivated with hard partying and women. They might have found their sound from listening to Godsmack, Shinedown, and Metallica, but they found their touring persona in Mötley Crüe.

If anything, the articles were trending toward the guys in the band settling down, a trend that started when Jack Whitehorse replaced Dave Brubaker on the drums. From what I could see, each of the band members was married, engaged, or in a serious relationship. And they were all in for supporting the Be Valorous Foundation, Cristy Valor's organization committed to ending child marriage in the US. No scandal there.

Still, my skin tightened when I reread the contract. Even though the terms were fair, the work 100 percent in our wheelhouse, and the time frame doable considering our current wide-open schedule, I couldn't quit the feeling something about it wasn't on the up-and-up.

A light rap on my door alerted me to Jeremy a second before he poked his head into my office. "I thought you could use a pick-me-up. Here." He handed me a venti go-cup. With a smile, I popped the lid off and let the heavenly smell of dark, rich coffee waft over me. As I let the first sip of hot Americano with the perfect amount of cream slide over my tongue, he said, "You've been hard at it for hours. Anything I can help you with?"

I sipped more coffee, replaced the lid on the cup, and set it aside. Turning my computer screen toward him, I said, "This seems perfectly legit. But something about it is bothering me."

Jeremy inclined his head. With his brows somewhere near his hairline, he couldn't have made his opinion of my worry any more clear. Still, he pulled up the chair opposite me and settled in to read. He might have been a production assistant, but he was whip-smart, and I trusted him. It was this contract with Balefire—or more honestly—with Garrett that had me second-guessing myself. I sat back and left him to it as I savored my coffee and sifted through my memories to figure out what I was missing in this scenario with Balefire.

I was halfway through my Americano when Jeremy glanced up from my screen. "I'm not a lawyer, but I don't see anything in this contract that's different from any other contract you've agreed to since you brought me on board." He glanced back at the screen and set the cursor to highlight a section. "Except for this part where you're required to work with the band's manager on the script and the preproduction. That's a bit weird."

With a shrug, I said, "Balefire's a megaband. Apparently, they want to control as much of the production as possible." I turned the screen to face me again. "But you're right. That part is a little strange. Maybe that's what was bugging me."

No *maybe* about it. Per the terms in the contract, I had to work closely with Garrett to produce the video. The way my heart hitched at seeing him on the red carpet at the Grammys and again when I read the initial email that started this project told me he was the center of my trepidation about working with Balefire. *Why is it necessary for me to work with him at all beyond agreeing to the contract to produce a music video?* He was their manager, not their dad, for crap's sake.

"Olivia?"

I finished off my coffee and tossed the cup in the trash can beside my desk. "Time to go to a preliminary movie screening." Pasting a smile on my face, I shut down my computer and grabbed my messenger bag and phone. Holding my office door open, I matched Jeremy's raised brow with a superior one of my own and followed him out of my office.

CHAPTER FOUR

Garrett

"IT'S GOING TO be fun seeing Olivia again. Wonder if she was airbrushed in those party pics we saw or if she's really aged that well?" Dakota shot a shit-eating grin my way as he settled the strap of his axe over his shoulder. "'Cause that woman is *smokin'* hot."

Some idiot took a photo of me staring at Olivia at a Grammy after-party the night Balefire won. Ever since, the guys would not let up about hot she was. But Dakota's assholery about her was the worst. In all the years the band and I had been together, I'd never had a clue the guy could hold a grudge the way Dakota Perri held one.

So I'd royally fucked things up for him with Annabelle for a while. After everything settled down and was sorted out, I owned it. A year later, they were still together. Hell, they were engaged, damn it. No long-term harm done.

"How long till you lose the attitude, Dakota?"

"Tsk, tsk, tsk. You're a bit touchy today. Been a while since you got any?" The unholy gleam in his eyes had me grinding my back teeth.

"This last tour was your biggest one yet. Packed stadiums all over Asia. Again." I crossed my ankle over my knee and picked up my iPad from where I'd set it beside me on the comfy suede couch. "You're welcome, by the way."

Of all the amenities the boys had added to their home base studio in Denver, the couches along the walls of the practice space were my favorite. Except for right now, when Dakota was glaring down at me and I had to remain seated to hold on to a shred of dignity. And my temper. Honestly, he'd punished me long enough, I thought.

"Let it go, Dakota," Tron said as he grabbed his bass from a rack beside Jack's massive drum kit. "Garrett's always been a stud when it comes to managing us." He shot me a warning look. "At least when he confines his efforts to the business part of this rock 'n' roll rodeo."

"Jesus, Tron. How many fundraisers for the Be Valorous Foundation do I have to organize for you to believe that I'm sorry?" I returned my attention to my iPad but couldn't help adding under my breath, "I bet Cristy doesn't put Gretchen through this every day."

"What was that, Garrett?"

"Nothing."

I hadn't been the only manager to get in the way of my star's love life. Gretchen Hoff had done her own number on Tron and Cristy's relationship before the two of them figured it out without us.

"Hey, guys. Sorry I'm late. Angel's in the terrible twos or some shit. Anyway, she threw one hell of a tantrum when I tried to leave. Took a minute for Clio to pry her off my leg so I could get out of the house." While explaining, Jack kept moving. In one leap, he hopped up on the platform where his drums waited. "I can't believe we'll have another one this time next year."

He tossed off that little nugget of info like it was no big deal. But *what the fuck?* It wasn't enough that he *married* his baby mama, but now they were adding to their brood? Despite what they all assured me in Orlando last year, this rock 'n' roll party we'd been on for the last decade was quickly devolving into the goddamn Brady Bunch. Pretty soon, none of them would want to go out on the road anymore, and where the fuck did that leave me?

"You knocked Clio up again? Congratulations!" Blu had been standing off to the side, warming up his vocal cords when Jack rolled in. "Ash and I have been talking about it. When I tell her your news, bet we do more than talk about it." He waggled his brows suggestively, and Jack cracked up.

I sank lower into the cushions of the couch. More kids? At least Blu and Ashleigh weren't married. Yet.

"Maybe we should plan a double wedding," Dakota piped up. Then he glanced over at Tron. "Make that a triple wedding. Wouldn't that be a kick?" He emphasized his words with a wicked guitar lick I hadn't heard before.

"For shit's sakes, you all sound like fucking groupies at an after-party. 'Ooh, I wouldn't say no if Dakota asked me to marry him.' 'I'd love to have Jack's babies.' 'We could have a double wedding when I marry Blu and you marry Tron,'" I mimicked with my best falsetto. Over the years, I'd heard some variation of this same conversation among the groupies at nearly every party the band threw after their shows. My stomach threatened to heave up my bacon and eggs breakfast at hearing the guys talk like this.

"Nope, Garrett hasn't been laid in a while. Probably not since we got off the road last month." Dakota cackled like he'd cracked the world's funniest joke, but I wasn't laughing.

Truth was, I'd barely taken advantage of all the first-class pussy on offer during the last tour. That was bugging the shit out of me too. But at least the boys hadn't noticed.

"Nah. I think it was seeing Olivia again after the Grammys." Tron played a "boom-chick-a-wow-wow" bass riff. "And the prospect of seeing her again." The second boom-chick-a-wow-wow riff he followed that comment with had me white-knuckling my grip on my iPad.

Over the years, I'd figured out how damn observant Tron was. But I thought he kept his eyes focused on the other guys in the band. Discovering that he watched me too didn't sit well, and my tenuous hold on my temper snapped. "Fuck off, already."

The guys guffawed like a pack of hyenas.

I flipped them the bird, which only made them laugh harder.

"All right, already." I gifted them with an epic eye roll. "Are you guys going to run stuff I can record today or what?"

Tron's laughter dropped to a chuckle. "Sure, *sir*."

That sent the guys into gales of laughter again. Landon was an excellent assistant—I'd hired him before our last tour—but I had yet to break him of dropping that honorific on me, usually at inopportune moments in front of the band.

Four pairs of dancing eyes stared at me. I smirked. "That's better."

"Yep, he definitely needs to get laid," Blu whispered to the rest of the band—through his mic.

Shaking my head, I cued up the page on my iPad where Olivia and I had fleshed out some preliminary scenes for the video. She'd insisted on doing the work via email rather than over Zoom or even FaceTime, which irritated the shit out of me even more than the guys making fun of me by calling me *sir*. She agreed to work with me, but she'd made it clear she damn sure didn't want to see me. Wasn't that another kick in the nuts?

I was living a lifetime of penance and for what? For trying to keep the band together? "Brothers since before we started." The line from "Brothers" flashed through my mind, and I popped an antacid. The newest Balefire hit, the one they debuted during the Grammys, the one they'd kept secret even from me, reminded me they were a unit. The women—and now the babies, apparently—weren't going to break them up. Even though I remained a part of them, though they said they'd forgiven me for doing what I did to keep them together, I was more on the outside than I'd ever been.

For a few minutes, they dicked around doing their own thing.

Then, as if to reiterate the point of "Brothers," Jack suddenly smacked his sticks together four times, and they launched into "Dangerous Life," the new song for the video, like they'd been rehearsing it for hours rather than playing it together for maybe the third time. Jack and Blu wrote the song during hiatus after the Grammys, and Dakota and Tron picked it up like they'd been in on the composition from the get-go. If anything, the events of the last two years had pulled the guys closer together, their synchronicity and sound tighter than it had ever been. When I glanced up from my iPad, all four of them were grinning, playing together for the pure joy of it.

That was the problem.

They had enough money. They had enough fame. They didn't need to hustle and tour anymore to draw in the fans. If they wanted to, they could park the bus and the plane and never tour again. Just hang out here in their studio and make music together. Go home at night to their wives and kids and live boring, suburban lives similar to the ones they'd come from. Like the one I came from. Closing my eyes, I pulled a long breath in through my nose and let it out slowly. This video was the next big thing for the band. For me. It had to be.

When they finished playing the song through the first time, I stood up. "I know the Academy doesn't like awarding Oscars for rock songs any more than the Grammys like to give album of the year to rock bands, but day-um. 'Dangerous Life' is an undeniable winner." I grinned. "If we do this right, we're not only going to help your friends sell their movie. We're going to make a case for you winning more hardware for the trophy case." I tossed a glance over my shoulder to the hallway that led into the cavernous space of the practice area. The gold and platinum records lining the walls in that hallway were a testament to the rock god prowess of my boys, something I was as proud of as they were.

For once, when he looked at me, Dakota's smile lit up his eyes. "Oh, hell yeah!"

"That riff you added to the bridge needs special attention when the cameras are rolling, I think." I made a note on the scene where the bridge fell. When I looked up, Dakota's expression was as close to the old days as I'd seen it in forever. But it wouldn't do to let any of them see how my chest warmed at his response.

"Of course it does. It's fucking awesome." He punctuated his enthusiasm for his own skill with a blistering version of the riff in question. The rest of the band shook their heads, but each of them sported a grin. Dakota accused Blu of being the diva of the band, but everyone knew it was Dakota. The man needed all the attention all the time. But he made everyone laugh, so it was easy to put up with him.

Usually.

"Right. So how do you guys feel about playing in a flight simulator?"

Tron pumped his fist. "Fuckin' A! I've always wanted to try one of those."

"Good to know you haven't lost your gamer edge with all that HGTV you watch these days, Tron," Blu teased.

"Which explains why I kicked your ass in COD just last night, Master Gardener."

"What-the-fuck-ever." Blu dismissed him with his middle finger.

Ever the pragmatist, Jack asked, "Exactly how do you propose I drum in a flight simulator?"

"Don't worry. We have a plan." I grinned at him. "Can you play that drum riff that leads into the chorus again?"

The band had pitched the music video to Parker Malone and Jennifer Hartwell as a way to drum up interest in their new action movie coming out at the end of the year. Marketing efforts were well under way, but dropping the theme song as a music video a couple of months ahead of the premiere would go a long way toward building a buzz. Though she never said it in so many words, this video had always been Jennifer's aim, I think, when she pitched the boys the idea of writing the movie's theme song. She'd approached me about having them write the entire soundtrack, but with their Asia tour already scheduled, that was never going to happen. The fact she weaseled a hit song out of them was a testament to her persuasion skills and the band's ego. The video was a bonus.

When the boys agreed to work with Olivia's music video company instead of Hartwell Studios, Jennifer's dad's movie company, they told me two things: one, they wanted control over their own work, and two, they were in a forgiving mood. This was the first suggestion I'd made that they'd agreed to since the press conference clarifying the rumors about Cristy Valor and announcing her foundation for stopping child marriage. I understood I had something to prove to them. What they didn't get was that I'd been proving myself to them since I pitched them my services after I watched their show in a college bar in Grand Junction a decade ago.

Like he knew exactly what was going through my head, Tron nodded, speculation in his expression. I rolled my shoulders and settled my iPad more securely in my left hand while I scrolled unseeingly through my notes.

The band was not letting up on me about seeing Olivia again after all this time, and I'd be lying if I said it didn't grate on my nerves. I refused to acknowledge that picture that kept flashing in the back of my mind. Not the one the photographer took that night, but the one I took with my own eyes—Olivia Carter, all sleek and perfect in a silver-blue gown that clung to her curves the way I wanted to. Instead, I clung to my story: we were working with Olivia's company because she rocked the Grammys, directing the best iteration of the event in years. My history with Olivia Carter had fuck-all to do with it.

Maybe if I kept telling myself that, I'd believe me too.

♪

A couple of hours later, the heavenly smells of something spicy and delicious wafting from the state-of-the-art kitchen at the back of the studio forced a break. Chef Jeff never had to call us to lunch or dinner. He just let his food do all the work. I'd tossed out ideas throughout the rehearsal, some of them mine, some of them Olivia's, some the two of us had come up with together. The band liked nearly all of them—shocker. It had been more than a minute since they'd taken even a suggestion from me beyond the five-star hotels I booked them into on tour.

Arrows and highlights and notes in the margins covered the screen on my iPad. I had at least three or four hours of work ahead of me after we broke for the day, and we were only half done. Exhilaration coursed through me at the thought. For today at least, I was back. For today at least, my boys and I were together like in the old days before they decided sex, booze, and rock 'n' roll weren't enough.

A picture of Olivia flashed through my mind. Not the sleek goddess tipping up a flute of champagne for a ladylike sip at the Grammys after-party. Nope. The shy college student with the killer body and whip-smart brain floated through my thoughts, closely followed by a hollowed-out feeling of guilt and regret. Back then, I couldn't understand how she didn't share my dreams of the two of us working as a team—my business acumen coupled with her sharp legal mind. We could have toured the world together, built the Balefire brand together. Hell, we might have even created a management company that took care of more than the biggest rock band in the world.

I shook those thoughts right out of my head. She'd made her choices and I'd made mine.

"What's on the menu today, Jeff?" I called out as I entered the kitchen.

Standing in front of the island separating the cooking area from the eating area, Jeff Scott, the band's private chef, was plating something that looked like sandwiches and smelled like heaven.

"Steak bahn mi."

"Say again?"

"Vietnamese skirt steak sandwiches paired with a salad of baby greens, pears, and leeks with a lemon balsamic vinaigrette." He handed a plate across the counter to me. "Dessert is homemade strawberry sorbet with my specialty Limoncello syrup." His brows waggled playfully when he delivered that last part. Jeff's strawberry sorbet was my personal favorite, and he knew it. I glanced past his shoulder at the massive stainless steel side-by-side refrigerator-freezer, and he laughed. "Yes, I made extra."

I grinned back. "Good to know."

The guys sat around the big table, another improvement from the last time we met at the studio to work. Clearly, I wouldn't have to sit with Jeff at the island and pretend everything was great while the band sat at a four-top, proving that things obviously weren't great between us. I set my iPad on the table beside my plate and pulled out the chair next to Jack. Last fall when things went south with Cristy Valor and Annabelle Stewart and the band wanted to fire me, Jack was the one who spoke up for giving me another chance. I'd never forget it.

So I swallowed my attitude and said, "Another kid, huh?"

He grinned around a bite of sandwich, chewed, swallowed, and said, "If I'm really lucky, we're having another girl."

My brows shot up. "How is that lucky?"

"None of my brothers are married yet. As long as Clio and I keep popping out little girls, I keep being the favorite son." He threw back a swig of his beer. "I like being Mom's favorite."

The smirk on his face cracked me up in spite of the fact that he and Clio had clearly planned their new addition. Damn it.

Dakota butted in. "I like being Annabelle's mom's favorite."

"Jesus, is everything with you two a competition?" Tron rolled his eyes, but laughter colored his tone.

I cleared my throat. "From what I can see, you're all mamas' boys." Pretending innocence, I took a big bite of my sandwich and let the flavors of succulent beef, spicy sriracha, carrots, cucumbers, and buttery home-baked bread fill my mouth.

From somewhere behind me, I caught Jeff's soft chuckle. "Right there with you, Garrett."

"Yet here you are," Blu said while Tron pulled off a tiny crust of bread and chucked it at Jeff.

Tron's antics deflected the sarcasm in Blu's tone, but I'd been reminded all the same. They may have let me sit at the table, but they weren't quite ready to let me join them again.

"Besides the flight simulator, what do you guys think of going out on location? I thought I'd ask Ashleigh about finding a garden, something lush where we can have some fun with creating suspense like the pivotal scene in the middle of the movie."

I'd had the thought smack on the heels of Blu's comment, but as the guys eyed me, the better I liked it.

"It'll have to be somewhere in LA or nearby, though. You all might be rolling in cash, but we're still working with a budget." I set my sandwich aside and added a note on my iPad.

"Flight simulator, a jungle garden, the studio, and whatever Olivia's got lined up," Jack began. "Looks like you'd better book suites for a month in LA." He popped the last of his sandwich in his mouth and watched me with a speculative expression.

I knew what he was really saying. "Guess so. What kind of bed does Angel need?"

"If it's all the same to you, Cristy and I will be crashing at her place," Tron said, glancing around the table at the rest of the band.

Dakota nodded at Tron. "I talked to Parker, and he'll be out of town working on his next movie. Annie and I are staying at his place."

Though I tried to keep the scowl off my face, it came out in my tone. "Jesus. I didn't say you were strapped for cash. I only said we were shooting this video with a budget."

"It's not about money, Garrett," Tron said. "It's about privacy."

There it was again. The band didn't want me to know what was going on in their personal lives. Time was when they came to me for advice—or to rescue them from a potential mess—with a woman. Now they were all coupled up and wanted their privacy. It was enough to give me a headache.

"Right." I cleared my throat. "Blu? Jack? What's the plan for you? Do you want me to book you at the usual place?"

"Works for me," Jack said. "In answer to your other question, we need a toddler bed for Angel. It will need to be in the same room with Clio's and my bed. And an adjoining room for the nanny." He finished off his beer. "Now that I think about it, prolly ought to have a second toddler bed in the nanny's room too."

He gave me his list without an ounce of irony, a dad looking out for his kid. The thought gave me a pinch right in my solar plexus.

"Ash and I will stay at the hotel too with the usual amenities. A room with a nice big Jacuzzi tub. My girl can use some pampering." Blu shot a grin at Dakota who rolled his eyes.

I wanted to roll my eyes too, but I made a note on my iPad instead. It wasn't necessary. As soon as I told Emory in the office where Jack, Blu, the rest of the crew, and I were staying, she'd make the arrangements to their exact specifications. But taking notes allowed me to keep my feelings to myself.

"How 'bout you, Garrett? You planning to bunk with Olivia?" Blu asked, batting his lashes at his joke.

I spared him a glare and turned my attention to Chef Jeff who chose that opportune moment to set dessert in the middle of the table.

CHAPTER FIVE

Olivia

I MUST HAVE CHANGED outfits fifteen times before I settled on a floaty lemon-yellow camisole beneath a turquoise linen jacket over a pair of white capris. After I slipped on a pair of Manolo Blahnik sandals that matched my camisole, I took another turn in front of my mirror and decided this would have to do. It was the first day of working with Balefire in person, but damn. They were only men, not gods, no matter how the media portrayed them. And I knew them when none of them were old enough to drink in a bar.

The image in the mirror shot me an *uh-huh* look, and I rolled my eyes at her. No matter how hard I tried, I couldn't fool myself. That mess on the bed behind me wasn't about Balefire. At. All. It was about one Garrett Phillips, the man I'd put off seeing in person for the last few weeks.

He'd wanted me to fly to Denver, work with him at Balefire's home studios. Dangling the carrot of using our time together as a working vacation, during which I could spend time with my parents and see old friends, didn't incentivize me to return to the scene of the crime though. As it was, too many memories of the death of a long-ago love flooded my brain in the deep dark of the night. I didn't need to be geographically smack in the middle of where all the action had taken place. I didn't need to relive old times that reminded me of what we had before both of us killed it.

Whether or not Garrett had reliving old times in mind didn't matter. Going home meant facing the choices we'd both made, and I'd moved on. Firmly telling myself that had become a mantra. I laughed as I thought of my yoga instructor's face if I asked to use it in my next class.

The buzzing of my phone told me I couldn't procrastinate this day any longer. Grabbing it off the charger beside my bed, I grimaced at the tangled mess of discarded outfits and answered Jeremy on my way out the door.

"Hey, boss. Should I grab a few bottles of Jameson on my way to the office?"

I sighed into my phone. "We're meeting them at ten *this morning*. They're not on tour. Coffee and soft drinks will be fine." Knowing my assistant as well as I did, I could almost hear his fidgeting on the other end of the call. "Out with it."

"Well, um, when I called their people to see what they like, they said the band likes to party when they're working. This video is work, ergo, I thought maybe we should have their go-to beverage ready." He cleared his throat. "Just in case."

Again, Wonder Kid reminded me how he'd made himself indispensable in the short time he'd worked for me.

"Yeah, sure. Go ahead and pick up a couple bottles of whiskey. The high-end stuff. Charge it to the company."

The advance for the video would come through after this first meeting, but I was expensing every dime we spent on alcohol to the band. It was only fair since they would be the ones drinking it. Breakfast was on me, though. I'd had it specially catered from my favorite bistro—the one directly across the street from my building. I smirked. The food there was fantastic, but because the owners weirdly had no pretensions of landing their own cooking show, I could afford it. I'd ordered fresh fruit and my favorite quinoa bowls. Because I, too, had asked Balefire's office manager, a lovely-sounding woman named Emory Murakami, what the band preferred, I'd added extra bacon and steak to the menu along with an assortment of the bistro's specialty pastries. Merely thinking of their signature cinnamon rolls made the waistband of my pants feel a bit snug.

Snagging my messenger bag from the back of the kitchen chair where I'd dropped it the night before, I checked for my laptop and keys and the folder of notes I'd made. Everything was where it was supposed to be, so I slung the bag over my shoulder, locked up my cozy studio apartment, and headed out for my six-block commute to work. On my way down in the elevator, my phone buzzed in my pocket, and I shut off my alarm. Damn it. I'd pushed my morning as far as I could, and now I'd be lucky if I squeaked in to the office thirty seconds before Balefire was due to arrive.

♪

The bad boys of rock 'n' roll had earned their party reputation, but from the beginning, Garrett had drilled into them the value of professionalism. Which meant arriving to meetings on time. I could have used a little more of the party and a little less of the professionalism today. Luckily, when I arrived at the office at 9:30, Wonder Kid was already there directing the caterers where to set up the food in our tiny conference room.

From the way he was wired, I wondered if Jeremy had slept at all the night before.

"Did you spend the night here?"

"Ha. Ha." A sheepish grin slid over his features before he turned to help a caterer find an outlet for the food warmers.

The heavenly smells of warm, buttery croissants and savory meat wafted through the door as people brought in the food and arranged it in the warmers. My stomach gave away the fact that I hadn't eaten since sometime yesterday afternoon.

"Was that you, Boss?" Jeremy's eyes danced.

"Never mind about me."

He snagged a cinnamon roll from the pastry plate and a napkin and handed both to me.

With I laugh, I waved him away "I can wait."

"We can't." With a meaningful raised brow, he pushed the food toward me. Jeremy might have seen me with low blood sugar once or twice in the past. Honestly, it couldn't have been that bad. "Olivia." His tone said it was worse than that bad.

I threw my hands in the air. "Fine. I'll eat something now."

Right as I sank my teeth into fluffy, buttery, cinnamon and sugar deliciousness, raucous laughter rang out in the hall. Though I tried to chew fast, there I stood with a monster pastry in my hand and my mouth full when the entirety of Balefire walked into the conference room.

"Hey, Olivia. Lookin' sweet." Dakota's eyes danced as he greeted me.

Swallowing hard, I set my treat aside.

"Nice"—I had to clear my throat when a few grains of cinnamon tickled it—"nice to see you too." I extended my hand to him. "I hear congratulations are in order."

He tilted his head in question.

"On your engagement."

At my clarification, his whole body lit up. "Fuckin' A. Annabelle's awesome. Wait till you meet her."

"Did I hear the two of you are also engaged?" I asked, glancing between Blu and Tron.

Their megawatt smiles overwhelmed the fluorescent lights in the room.

"We are," Blu said. "To two incredible women."

Zeroing in on Tron, I said, "I've met Cristy Valor. She's more down-to-earth in person than you'd expect from her public persona."

"Aren't we all?" Tron said with a smirk.

"Hello, Olivia." The voice that had haunted my dreams for years sent a ripple of nerves through me.

Garrett stood behind the band, his presence solid compared to their lightness. When I'd talked to him a few times over the computer—and all the times over the years that I'd Googled him—he'd appeared to have aged well. In person, he was even more handsome at thirty-six than he'd been at twenty-six. Laugh lines bracketed his gray eyes, and his dimples had lengthened in that way that made some men even more gorgeous as they aged. His lips were stretched into the gentle smile I remembered from when I first met him on the other side of the counter in the coffee shop where I'd worked during college. Those same butterflies I remembered from that first meeting arrived en masse, and I was glad I'd only had one bite of prebreakfast before the band showed up.

Other than his professional haircut that swept back that thick lock of blond hair that always wanted to fall over his forehead, the rest of him looked the same. Same broad shoulders, same trim hips, same powerful thighs. The thing he had going on with the leather vest paired with a T-shirt over expensive dress pants was new. Maybe he only worked with a stylist for awards shows? But that wasn't why I couldn't look away from him.

A throat clearing beside me reminded me I'd been staring. "Hello, Garrett." Switching my attention to the man standing beside him, I stretched out my hand. "You must be Jack. I'm Olivia Carter, and this is my assistant, Jeremy Rowland." I indicated my erstwhile Wonder Kid who was all but bouncing on his toes beside me.

"Pleasure to meet you!" Jeremy's effusiveness extended to his handshake. Seeming to remember himself, he shook Garrett's hand then Blu's, Tron's, and Dakota's. "I'm a huge fan."

"Understatement of the year," I muttered under my breath.

"What was that, Olivia?" Garrett asked.

"Jeremy's been looking forward to this project since three seconds after you proposed it." I playfully knocked my shoulder into my assistant's and laughed as the tops of his ears flared pink. "Wait till you see all the cool things he's helped to line up for the shoot." If anything, my praise intensified the color of his ears.

"What about you, Olivia? You looking forward to working with us?" There was something dark in Dakota's eyes even as the tone of his question was playful.

"It's a big deal to work with the world's most famous rock band." With a smile, I added, "Speaking of work, best not to do it on an empty stomach. Grab something from the buffet and we'll get started."

I hid a smile as I watched Dakota step forward, first in line to grab a plate. Good to know some things never changed. When it was Garrett's turn, he motioned to me to precede him, and we danced around each other until I stepped past him. "Go ahead. This is my treat to you."

I couldn't quite read the expression on his face, but I had the distinct impression he wanted something else from me.

Dakota interrupted our little standoff. "Yes! Check it out!" He held a bottle of Jameson Black Barrel above his head.

"Good call," I mouthed to my assistant who grinned back at me.

Assuming the role of bartender, Dakota wasted no time pouring generous shots of whiskey. Starting the morning with shots had not been on my radar, but when each of the members of the band raised their glasses for a toast, I had no choice but to join them.

"To an Oscar-worthy video!" Dakota's eyes danced.

"Or at least something that gets an MTV award," Blu added, laughing.

The whiskey burned going down, and Jeremy slapped his hand on my back.

"Guess some things never change, Olivia," Blu said. "You

couldn't hold your whiskey back in the day either." With a laugh, he held his glass out to Dakota who splashed more Jameson into it.

The rest of the band followed suit except for Garrett who grabbed a coffee mug and set it beneath the Keurig. That, too, was new. Usually, he was right in the middle of whatever the guys in the band were doing. Perhaps age was mellowing him.

I seated myself at the head of the table with Jeremy to my right. Dakota grabbed the place to my left, with the rest of the guys filing in on either side of the table beside them, which left the place at the end opposite me for Garrett. His eyes remained on mine as he seated himself with his full plate of breakfast. But it was Blu who started things.

"I looked you up, Olivia. You keep a low profile. Which begs the question: which Hollywood hotshot are you dating?"

My second bite of heavenly pastry stuck in my throat, and Jeremey pounded on my back. After a couple of swallows, the bite made its way down, leaving behind a stream of tears that no doubt turned my carefully made-up face into something resembling the characters in *Suicide Squad*.

"That top-secret, huh?" Blu laughed. "Now you have no choice but to tell us who it is."

With my napkin, I took my time dabbing at my face as I contemplated telling the biggest lie of my life. "Studio heads stay behind the scenes and let their projects do their publicity work for them. I think I'll follow my guy's lead on that."

Jeremey's eyes saucered, but mercifully, he didn't say anything. The band interpreted his response as me being indiscreet, which was a bonus.

"You're with some big-time studio head? Who is it?" Dakota asked, but weirdly, his gaze slid to the other end of the table. Garrett's single-minded attention centered on cutting his steak into teeny-tiny strips and stirring it around in his quinoa. But I noticed the way his Adam's apple bobbed when he swallowed hard at Dakota's question.

"Telling you would break the code, wouldn't it?" I asked with what I hoped was a saucy grin. When I smoothed my napkin back in my lap, relief flooded through me at the evidence that my makeup hadn't morphed my looks into something clownish.

"Well, we're glad your important studio head boyfriend could spare you to make our little video." Blu waved his fork loaded with quinoa clinging to steak and eggs over his bowl. "Because we like all the cool ideas you have for this shoot. Especially the flight simulator." His eyes danced as he slid his fork into his mouth.

"Oh, yeah. I'm all over that flight simulator," Tron chimed in.

Mercifully, the conversation turned to the ideas we had for the shoot, leaving my lie about dating some anonymous studio head hanging. But I couldn't help the way my eyes kept straying to Garrett to notice the studious way he avoided looking at me.

Chapter Six

Garrett

WE'D BARELY SEATED ourselves in the town car after leaving Olivia's offices when Dakota started in. "Olivia didn't need us in order to move on to the big time, eh, Garrett?" He leaned back against the plush leather seats and crossed his ankle over his knee. "Surprised the hell out of me she's dating some studio head. But you've been coordinating with her ever since you hired her, so maybe you already knew that." More than anything, I wanted to punch the self-satisfied smirk off his face.

"I don't know what she thought she was hiding under that jacket, but whenever she turned just right, you couldn't help but see a shadow of sweet cleavage beneath that thin top she had on. Isn't that right, Garrett?" Blu asked, mischief gleaming in his eyes.

Of course I noticed what Olivia was wearing—and how she smelled, like jasmine and musk—and how she moved with easy grace and confidence even as her body tensed when we stood next to each other.

"She's not that shy college girl who hung out with us in the early days, that's for sure."

What the hell? Tron too?

"I had a clue you had some history with the lady, but from the familiar way you all talked to each other from the get-go, there's a story. Care to share with the rest of the class?" Jack asked as he turned sideways on the seat next to me. The movement served to put me even farther in the corner by the door than the usual place the guys had relegated me after shit hit the fan with Ashleigh Baker in Dallas a couple of tours ago. She and Blu were happily engaged now. In fact, the entire band was all engaged now—or worse—married, so why couldn't they cut me some slack?

His laser focus on me drew out the truth. "For a minute when Balefire was starting out, Olivia and I dated. But I wanted to represent the band, and she—" Memories of our last conversation a decade ago threatened to swamp me. Uncapping my water bottle, I took a long pull and willed them back into their box. "Olivia had dreams of being a studio boss from the first time we met. Guess she's well on her way, especially after you all agreed to make the video with her production company."

"Yeah, that's why we did it. As a favor to your old flame." Dakota huffed out a mirthless laugh. "With her dating someone in the industry, she probably doesn't need us."

Blu smacked the back of his hand over Dakota's bicep. "That's a shitty thing to say. Don't be an ass."

Dakota reared back away from Blu. "Ouch." He rubbed a hand up and down his arm. "That's not what I meant at all. I meant if she's moving in those circles, she's doing us a favor by taking time out of her busy schedule to make us look good."

"Better," Blu said.

Tron leaned forward and grabbed a bottle of water from the mini fridge between Dakota and Blu. "Dakota's probably right. Lucky us," he said with a salute of his drink. "Having a kick-ass music video can't hurt our song's chances at an Oscar nomination, yeah?" After swigging back a drink, he chuckled. "'Cause winning hardware is what it's all about."

The rest of the guys laughed with him, and I bared my teeth.

Over the last decade, I'd managed Balefire into a household name around the world. The band and all their associates, from Emory running the show from the studios, to Bailey taking care of logistics on the road, to every roadie and tech employed by Balefire, was awash in cash. None of them had one damn thing to complain about as far as how I'd taken care of the business side of this rock 'n' roll circus—including this latest gig. They were still sore about some of what had gone down with their women. Everything was fine now, so maybe it was time for the lot of them to get over it.

"I didn't hear any of you offering to return those Grammys you won this year." I aimed my sarcasm at Tron, but I meant it for the whole damn band. Beside me, Jack sat up straighter, giving me some room. "Jennifer Hartwell might have talked you guys into writing 'Dangerous Life,' but she had nothing to do with the quality of the song." My gaze took a tour of the men riding in the car with me. "Releasing it as a video is going to create the kind of buzz that wins Oscars. Bet you won't want to return yours when you win it, either."

For a long, silent moment, I shifted my gaze to the blocks of concrete buildings passing outside the window of the car. In a conversational tone, I added, "At some point, you're going to have to acknowledge that I put you guys and your careers first—always." I glanced back to the band. "Along the way, I made sacrifices too, something I didn't feel the need to advertise, but maybe I should have."

♪

I hissed in a breath as the coffee burned my tongue. "Shit!" At that second, my assistant let himself in to my suite.

"Sir? Are you all right?"

"Might have scalded my tongue on the coffee. Sorry. Say, Landon, do you have those rewrites handy?"

"You mean the ones we worked on right before we flew out, correct?"

"Yeah." I blew on my coffee again and set it aside.

"Got 'em right here." He laid his messenger bag on the table and pulled out a bound copy of the "Dangerous Life" script.

Sliding into the chair opposite me, he asked, "What's up? Does the producer want to change something?"

"No." I glanced up from where I paged through the script. "I do."

Like magic, Landon dropped a pen into my open palm on the table, and I started scribbling over a section of the script. Tron's fascination with the flight simulator, combined with Dakota's penchant for flying hydraulics during the band's last tour, had given me an idea, one I hoped would return me to the guys' good graces—and maybe impress a certain video producer.

Sure, Olivia might be involved with some studio head, but she didn't have a ring on her finger.

Mentally smacking my palm on my forehead, I hauled myself up short. Olivia and I had gone our separate ways because we had vastly different dreams. Even though I'd engineered an opportunity for us to work together, it didn't mean those dreams had changed or that we could make things work between us even if she was free.

Apparently, she wasn't.

Damn it.

During our initial meeting yesterday, she'd handled the band like she'd managed them for the last decade rather than I. Bantering with Dakota and Blu, drawing Tron into the plan with her flight simulator idea, quizzing Jack about the genesis of the song for the video, she masterfully ingratiated herself with my boys, and all the years fell away.

Olivia had meshed with Balefire from the first time I introduced her to them. Though she was a prelaw student when we met, she'd minored in music production in college. She had an incredible ear and picked up nuances in Balefire's sound she suggested they amplify, and she'd been right. When they acted on her advice, their sound subtly changed from bar band to arena rock, and the rest—as they say—is history.

More than once over the years, I'd wished for a different history with Olivia. Somehow, I should have found a way to make it all work instead of letting myself get lost in the rock star life right out of the gate. The photo she saw—the one that ended us—wasn't even real. I'd had nothing to do with that girl that night. How someone caught a shot of the fleeting second she'd landed on my lap when I was tipping back that bottle of Jack was a mystery I'd never solve.

But that was in the past. The here and now was all that mattered.

During her production of the Grammys, Olivia's ear for music was on full display. If she didn't win an Emmy for that show, there truly was no justice in the world. My chest warmed at how proud of her I was—not that I was in any position to express that pride.

Our music video could be another opportunity for her to shine in her own right rather than as a behind-the-scenes genius producer. After all my years on the road with the band, I knew a thing or two about how to showcase their sound too. Between Olivia and me, we could create a video that cemented Balefire as a household name like the Beatles or the Rolling Stones, bands even people who didn't listen to rock knew. In the process, Olivia could set herself up as the premiere music producer everyone wanted to work with. She would never need to know my part in it, how I vetted her production company and saw how much she needed the work.

"See what you think."

I handed the script to my assistant and swigged back hot—but no longer scalding—coffee.

Landon's brow furrowed, and for a second I thought I might have gone too far. Then his face lit up, and he handed the script back to me. "Holy shit, sir! If we can pull this off, I bet the studio will include it as a trailer for the movie."

We shared a grin.

"What I need you to do is figure out where we can access

materials that won't break Olivia's"—I cleared my throat—"Miss Carter's budget. The band can afford this, but she's the producer. We don't want her to freak out and toss the idea aside before we can show her how well it's going to work."

"On it, sir." He pulled out his laptop.

"And for the love of Christ, stop calling me sir."

"Of course—Mr. Phillips."

I thought I saw a grin ghost over his face as he pulled up a page on his computer, and I let an exasperated breath escape. Landon was a kick-ass assistant—nearly as good as Emory Murakami back at the band's studio—but with his insistence on using manners that left me feeling ancient, the kid seriously tested my patience.

As his fingers flew over the keyboard, I noticed he wore his wedding ring, and my coffee soured in my stomach. Queen's "Another One Bites the Dust" played on a loop in my head, and I had to stand up and move around. Why every man associated with the band thought he needed to be in a committed relationship tested my patience on an entirely different scale.

A picture of Olivia flashed through my head. Not the sophisticated version in the pretty blue jacket, the one she wore at our meeting. The one that left room for a man's imagination with what was hidden beneath that pale yellow camisole and those formfitting pants. No, the Olivia that invaded my head was the gorgeous barista in the company T-shirt and apron who didn't have a clue how she made every man's mouth water, wondering at the taste of her full lips. Wondering at the feel of her generous rack pressed against his chest. Wondering how her perfectly rounded hips would fill his hands. That Olivia had made appearances in my head far too many times over the last ten years no matter how hard I tried to block her out.

Because I knew exactly how she tasted—darkly feminine with a hint of the cinnamon gum she chewed to cover her coffee-drinking habit. I knew how perfectly her hips filled my palms when she invited me into her apartment and the first thing I did was put my hands on her on my way to kissing her. I knew exactly the plush softness of her breasts flattened against my chest, how her pebbled nipples rubbed against my pecs when I pulled her close in bed.

After years of never hearing it, her sultry alto on the phone sent memories cascading over me. She didn't want any face-to-face meetings, even over Zoom, but those phone conversations only intensified what I'd always known to be true of her—her damn sexy brain came in a package that would test a saint. More than once, I'd have to ask her to repeat something because my thoughts had wandered somewhere unprofessional. After we hung up, I'd have to count back from a hundred to force my dick to relax—or give in and jack off.

When I saw her again yesterday for the first time since that Grammys after-party, my thoughts went somewhere they never needed to go. For the first time since our breakup a decade ago, I wondered if I'd made a mistake in walking away from her. Following close on that thought was speculation about my sudden disinterest in the twenty-something groupies who followed Balefire like it was their job. Why was it I got hard from only talking on the phone with an old flame, but my dick showed no interest in young women who were all about having a good time and wanted that good time with me?

Landon interrupted my thoughts. "What sort of budget did you have in mind, Mr. Phillips?"

His perfect timing at pulling me away from where my thoughts were headed meant I couldn't twist off about his insistence on calling me "Mr. Phillips."

"For now, let's aim for the low end of the usual Balefire scale. After I pitch my idea to the producer, we might be able to talk her into raising the production costs."

He nodded, made a few more notes on his laptop, and shoved it into his messenger bag. Checking his watch, he said, "Perfect timing, s—Mr. Phillips. The town car should be here when we hit the lobby." That smirk from earlier ghosted over his features again, making me wonder what was going on with him. Before I could call him out though, he'd crossed my suite and stood with the door open, waiting for me.

I slipped the amended script into my own messenger bag, slid the strap over my shoulder, and sauntered out of my room ahead of my assistant. We were quiet in the elevator, which was odd. Usually, Landon had a million questions for me. The kid's drive to learn absolutely everything about managing a massive enterprise like Balefire alternately amused and confounded me. His silence, today, annoyed me. Something was off, and I hated that I couldn't put my finger on it.

CHAPTER SEVEN

Olivia

FOR THE FIRST time since he walked away from me all those years ago, I was meeting Garrett alone. Well, not alone, alone. Our assistants would be in the room with us. But the two of them wouldn't be much of a buffer for the feelings that surged over the dam I'd spent years building. All this time, I'd convinced myself I was over him. He was a first love, a college fling, my first heartbreak—all things adults move on from. Yet sitting across the conference table from him over breakfast yesterday surfaced all the feelings I thought I'd successfully pushed to the bottom of my heart and locked up tight. The intense expression in those gray eyes when he focused on me made me remember the quiet, private times we'd spent together before our dreams split us apart. The dangerous waves of those memories threatened to swamp my resolve.

Nope. I was over him. I'd been over him for years.

If I kept telling myself that, it might be the truth.

A watchful, contemplative professional had replaced the cocky, overly enthusiastic rock fan who couldn't wait for me to hear "our future" in a smoky bar in the heart of Denver. Spending the last decade on the road with rock music's bad boys, the self-proclaimed stars of sex, booze, and rock 'n' roll, should have aged him beyond recognition. Instead, he was sexier now than when we split up a lifetime ago. The rasp of his voice had deepened, laugh lines intensified his gray eyes, and his strange fashion choices highlighted how he'd maintained his body. His clothes were quite awful, but the leather vest and cut-off T-shirt showed off the definition of his arms, the breadth of his shoulders. The fitted designer dress pants revealed his trim waist and powerful thighs. A woman would have to be dead not to notice that Garrett was a man in his prime.

As I sat at the table in our conference room, glancing over the script we'd agreed on, a thought scratched at the back of my mind. When we'd met with the entire band, Dakota and Blu did most of the talking rather than Garrett, which was odd. As their manager, he should have led the negotiations. A current of hostility hummed right below the surface of several of the comments the guys aimed Garrett's way too. Over the last year or so, starting about the time Cristy Valor joined Balefire as their guest on their last tour, there had been rumors in the tabs about trouble in the band. Most of what I'd dismissed as gossip centered around Cristy and Tron's relationship and how she was out to break Balefire up. After meeting with the band to discuss the video, I had no doubt those rumors were pure BS. But I wondered if something else was going on, something between the band and their manager.

Before I could ponder that further, Jeremy breezed through the door of the conference room with a tray of coffees from my favorite coffee shop. My mouth watered when the rich aroma hit my nose.

"Wonder Kid, you are my hero," I said as he set my steaming Americano in front of me then arranged the other coffees around the table before he handed me a tiny pitcher with exactly the right amount of cream. I smiled up at him and went to work doctoring my coffee.

"Just another service I offer." His straight face couldn't hide the smile in his voice.

He set the leather folder he'd tucked under his arm on the table beside his coffee and took his seat to my right. "I still can't believe you never let on you've known Balefire almost since they started."

Now, in addition to the band, he was fan-girling *me*?

"Here's your lesson for today: it's good to keep it on the down-low when you build relationships with people in this business. It maintains a level of trust." I shot him a stern look over the rim of my coffee. After blowing on the scalding brew, I took a sip, savored it, and replaced the lid on my cup. "Besides, they're just people, no more special than we are."

At my off-hand comment, his eyes almost bugged out of his head.

The low hum of two male voices grew in volume until our guests walked through the door of the conference room, effectively ending today's lesson for my assistant. Garrett gave the room a second's once-over and walked directly to the end of the table where I sat facing the door. He claimed the seat directly to my left and turned to the super-tall white-blond man trailing him. "Landon, would you grab those coffees and join us here please?" He indicated the two go-cups Jeremey had set at the opposite end of the table. "Good morning, Olivia." Nodding at my assistant, he added, "Jeremy."

The tips of Jeremy's ears flamed, and I shot him a warning side-eye.

Jeremy swallowed and stood, extending his hand. "Sir."

Garrett threw up his hands. "Aw, not you too." He grasped Jeremy's outstretched hand and said, "It's Garrett, okay? Not 'sir.'"

His assistant let out a snort that he deftly covered with a cough. Seating himself beside Garrett, he said, "Here's your coffee, Mr. Phillips."

"When it comes to assistants, you're the bomb, Landon. But if you don't stop with the honorifics, I'm going to fire you." His words lacked heat, and I watched in fascination as a ghost of a smile flitted over his assistant's features before he turned his attention to the messenger bag he slipped off his shoulder and laid on the table beside Garrett's.

Turning to me, Garrett said, "Olivia, this is my assistant—at least for today." He shot the white-blond man a glare. "Landon Berg. Landon, Olivia Carter and her assistant Jeremy Rowland."

With the weirdness of the introductions over, we all sat again, and I worked not to suck in a massive lungful of Garrett's delicious smell. Back when we were dating, he'd preferred Drakkar Noir cologne, which I'd always loved. But he'd changed his cologne to something that reminded me of the ocean with some sort of fresh, citrusy top note, and all I wanted to do was bury my face in his neck and breathe him in.

He'd shown up to this meeting in a Balefire T-shirt and well-worn jeans that hugged his ass and legs like they'd been molded to him. His clothes said roadie rather than manager, which threw me off. A relaxed Garrett was a dangerous Garrett, so I determined to set the tone of the meeting—and our relationship—to strictly business.

Clearing my throat, I said, "We have the flight simulator on loan from Hartwell Studio, but only for a couple of days, so we'll need to shoot that part of the video first."

Garrett sipped his coffee, his eyes intense on my face. "No, 'Hey, how are you? You settling in all right?' Just jump right into work."

"Work is what we're here to do, correct?" I raised a brow and hoped I sounded aloof rather than snarky. I caught Jeremy's quick intake of break and mentally smacked myself for coming across as a bitch. Uncrossing my legs beneath the table, I leaned forward, resting my forearms on the edge of it. "Did I misunderstand? Balefire hired my production company to do a job. I thought we all were here because we want to create a kick-ass video."

"Agreed. But it might be easier to accomplish that goal if we're more relaxed working together." For a second, his eyes slid to where I'd folded my hands together on the table then back to my face.

Without looking away from him, I slowly unclasped my fingers where I'd subconsciously held my hands together so tight, I'd left marks on my skin.

Trying to regain the upper hand, I glanced toward his assistant. "Tell me, Landon. What's it like working for Balefire? Don't make it sound too glamorous, though. I don't want Jeremy jumping ship." I slid a smile at my assistant and wondered why the tips of his ears turned pink again.

"The short tour the band took through Asia for a few weeks was outstanding—more fun than I anticipated it would be. The office staff and Mr. Phillips are top-notch pros. I've learned more in a few months with them than in the previous four years of college." I caught a hint of mischief playing in Landon's eyes as Garrett ground his teeth at Landon's use of the honorific again.

"No doubt that's true. I've always admired Garrett's financial acumen, even when he wasn't so impressed with it himself." A little grin escaped me as the memory of Garrett's distaste for his first profession in finance flashed through my head.

"What about you, Jeremy? What's it like working for Olivia?" Garrett asked, putting the focus on me. The tiny smirk tilting the corner of his mouth said he remembered how much I hated the spotlight.

"Working with Olivia is the bomb! She has so many great ideas, but she's open to everyone else's too. She makes all of us feel like a team." Now the back of my assistant's neck matched the tips of his ears. Obviously, we had a ways to go in helping him control his enthusiasm around celebrities.

Everyone in the business knew who Garrett was and credited as much of Balefire's success to him as to the musical prowess and wild reputation of the band. That thought led to other, darker thoughts about his reputation with the band's groupies, and I stared hard at the tabletop to dispel it.

"Still uncomfortable with praise, Olivia?" Garrett's tone was teasing, but when my eyes flashed to his, I saw curiosity there—and something warmer.

"The goal is always the quality of the production, not the ego of the producer. In the end, it should never be about me." I shot Jeremy a grimace.

"That's kind of perfect for an idea we have, right, sir?"

It seemed both of our assistants weren't clued in to the undercurrents running between Garrett and me. Hearing those compliments from each other came with a price for each of us, judging from the tension in Garrett's shoulders and the cramps in my legs where I squeezed them together to keep myself seated. If not for the money this gig would bring into my company so the team Jeremy referenced could continue to function with steady paychecks, I'd be on my way out the door right now.

Garrett pulled in a breath, let it out slowly, sipped his coffee, and reached for his messenger bag. Taking his time, he extracted a bound copy of the script for the video and flipped it open to page three. "I had an idea for the flight simulator scene." He slid his chair around the corner of the table, seating himself right beside me. "Give this a read and see what you think." He pulled the script between us and pointed to the notes he'd made in the margins.

I struggled to make sense of the lines on the page, not because I couldn't read his exceptionally neat handwriting but because I could feel his eyes on my profile as the heavenly scent of his cologne tickled my nose. The intensity of his stare robbed me of my concentration. Closing my eyes for a second, I willed myself to ignore him, even as the phantom heat from his laser focus warmed my skin. Keeping my eyes on the script, at last the words on the page penetrated my brain.

"You want to use hydraulics with the flight simulator? You want to lift Dakota into the sky as he plays the bridge solo?" A quick calculation in my head, and I forcefully shoved the script to the middle of the table. "Not possible. My company doesn't have access to the kind of hydraulics needed for your idea." *And I can't afford to buy or rent them either.* But I didn't say the words aloud.

"I asked Landon to do some research, so we're aware the sound-stage you use isn't equipped for this." He paused. "But Balefire is."

At my raised brow, he continued. "I don't know if you've watched any Balefire videos. We use a couple of different types of hydraulic stages on the live tour. It won't be a problem to incorporate one of them into the video." His matter-of-fact tone made it sound like the changes were a done deal.

They were not.

I didn't have access to the kind of soundstage his idea required even if Balefire supplied the hydraulics.

Pinching the bridge of my nose, I worked to summon the requisite patience I needed to redirect Garrett. Our history wasn't on my side. If I'd been able to redirect him ten years ago, we might have remained together. This project might have been only one of dozens we'd created with each other. Instead, this project was my lifeline, but I couldn't do it on his terms. Not if I wanted to make enough money to pay my staff, let alone set aside enough to keep the studio afloat until I scored another paying project. I had a few lined up, contracts signed on two of them even, but if we made this one right, the Balefire video would draw attention from other big-name bands. It had the potential to launch my studio—if Garrett's big ideas didn't cause me to stumble and fall right out of the gate.

"Our soundstage can accommodate the flight simulator and a stage. We can fly the band using conventional means, but we don't have room for your massive hydraulics."

"What about setting up the band's hydraulic stages somewhere outside and filming in front of a green screen?" Landon asked, his enthusiastic gaze trained on his boss.

Garrett sat back in his chair and folded his arms over his chest. To anyone else, it appeared he was giving his assistant's idea a great deal of thought. But once upon a time, I'd known him intimately. That lift of the corner of his mouth acknowledging Landon's suggestion told me this little song and dance had been rehearsed. Garrett had anticipated I'd balk, and he'd made plans to preempt me.

How much did he know about the state of my business? And why, with that knowledge, did the band still decide to work with my studio?

During this exchange, Jeremy helped himself to the amended script. In a split second, he morphed from Wonder Kid to Benedict Arnold. "This is such a cool idea. We could do this at the Rose Bowl." His enthusiastic smile had me fisting my hands. Then another thought struck him. "Or at the Griffith Observatory. Several bands have performed televised concerts there recently." He flipped ahead to page five, his finger tapping the middle of the scene. "We could film this part of the video up there too and save money on a starlight simulator."

Garrett steepled his fingers under his chin. "Great ideas, Jeremy." Turning to me, he added, "I can see why you think so highly of this one." He winked.

He had the fucking audacity to *wink* at me. Like the boys had done all the heavy lifting, and now all I had to do was sign off on their ideas and step out of their way.

I knocked back half of my coffee, carefully set the cup back on the table, tugged the script away from my assistant, and flipped it to the last page where Garrett had bound in a copy of our contract. Uncapping my favorite fountain pen, the one I kept loaded with purple ink, the one I always carried but rarely used, I made a show of circling the agreed-upon end for this project.

"You see this date? It presents all sorts of problems for the big ideas you boys are tossing around." Yes, I was petty enough to emphasize the word 'boys.' "If you expect us to complete this project on time, you're going to have to content yourselves with the original script we all signed off on—including the band. Speaking of which, nowhere in our conversation today have I heard the band is on board with the use of their concert equipment for this video.

I might remind you bringing in their equipment adds zeros to the price tag and time to the project since you'll have to haul it in from wherever you store it when Balefire comes off the road." I stared at each man in turn. "Plus, there's the tiny detail of scheduling with either venue. They aren't sitting around waiting for us and our 'big ideas.'" I directed that last bit at Landon who had the good grace to glance away.

To my right, I sensed Jeremy deflate and willed away the feeling that I'd kicked a puppy. Part of running a successful studio involved negotiating for everyone's benefit. Now was a good time for my assistant to learn that lesson. Landon's dropped shoulders were Garrett's problem.

"Olivia, you've heard the demo of the song. 'Dangerous Life' has the potential to win the band an Oscar for best original song. The way we produce this video could go a long way toward helping them achieve that hardware. Creating something original—" He put up one finger when I started to interrupt. "Creating something original, which your flight simulator idea already gives us"—he shot me a long intense stare—"and making it over the top, means everyone will be talking about the song as much as the movie. 'Dangerous Life' will be at the top of the Academy's attention at the critical time for nominations. After that, it's pretty much a done deal."

"Cocky much?" Sarcasm like battery acid dripped from my tone. This time, my finger went up at Garrett's attempt to interrupt me. "'Dangerous Life' is a great song. It's definitely Grammy-worthy. Maybe it's Oscar-worthy too, which is going to come from its musical merits and the way the director uses it in the film, not from this video. Using the flight simulator by itself is going to do the job and grab the attention you're seeking. Trust me."

Shooting a sharklike smile first at Jeremy then back at me, Garrett said, "But imagine the noise it will make in the recording industry if we combine our hydraulics ideas with your flight simulator idea and Jeremy's observatory location idea. This video could be next-level awesome, a bar-raising production to eclipse every other music video anyone's ever done." He angled his body toward me, caging me in with his eyes.

I wanted to smack him.

I wanted to stop the humiliation train bearing down on me.

I wanted to climb into his lap and let him tell me this plan was foolproof, the answer to saving my dream.

I did none of those things.

"Olivia?" Dana poked her head in the door. "Your 11:30 is early, but I thought you'd want to know they've arrived."

No doubt she heard how the men were ganging up on me with their big ideas—including Jeremy who should have known better. Her timely intrusion merited a raise—once I figured out how to save my studio.

"Thanks, Dana. We'll be finished in a few minutes."

Garrett narrowed his eyes.

Giving him my full attention, I preempted whatever he'd wanted to say. "You say we can use the band's hydraulics. How long will it take to get them here?"

"They're on their way as we speak." He sat back and folded his arms over his chest, drawing my attention to his sculpted biceps.

I wanted to scream. He was so sure of himself—and of me—but just in case, he was doubling down with his sexy display. "You didn't answer the question."

"Tomorrow. Day after, tops. We can start the production on time with the dancers scene then move on to flying the flight simulator with the band's hydraulics. Won't put us behind schedule at all." Though I think he tried to rein it in, a cocky grin played at the corner of his mouth.

"The band is in on this change." It wasn't a question.

"They were all over it after we proposed it to them." He included his assistant in his response. A nearly imperceptible shrug accompanied the sheepish smile Landon gifted me.

I didn't bother to hide the irritation in my tone. "There's still the little problem of our soundstage not being large enough to accommodate your equipment."

"Um, Landon reached out to me—"

When I whipped around to face him, the tips of Jeremy's ears and his neck bloomed together, but he didn't back away. "So I made a few calls, and we can get the observatory for a couple of days next week."

"I see." Returning my attention to Garrett, I said, "You went behind my back to work with my people without my input." He had the good sense to wipe the smile off his face, but it wasn't enough. "This is *my* company, *my* reputation, *my show*." I stood up. "We aren't in college anymore. I'm not the same girl who let you talk her into things that in the end served you better." On my way out the door I called over my shoulder, "Jeremy, my office. Now."

CHAPTER EIGHT

Garrett

RUNNING MY HANDS through my hair, I stared at the two men sitting with me in Olivia's conference room. "Well, that didn't go as planned. Hope I didn't cost you your job," I said to Jeremy.

"I still think the flying flight simulator is a good idea," the kid said, a note of despondency in his tone as he gathered empty coffee cups and chucked them in the trash on his way out the door.

Landon cleared his throat. "At the risk of pissing you off, I thought you said you had Olivia on board with our idea."

Pinching the bridge of my nose, I said, "I may have overestimated my influence." A long breath in, then I slapped my hands on my knees and pushed back from the table. "Time to regroup, figure out a new tactic." I shoved my script back into my messenger bag and headed for the door. "Let's grab some lunch and see what other ideas we come up with."

He cleared his throat again. "I have one."

I stopped and waited.

"Shoot the original script. Since Olivia cowrote it with you,

you know she's on board with it. She's the one who brought in the flight simulator in the first place. The guys were way more excited about that than all the additional bells and whistles we suggested."

A muscle jumped in my jaw as I clamped my mouth shut over the words that wanted to escape. Words that didn't need sharing with anyone, least of all with a brand-new assistant.

Of course, Landon was too observant for my own good. "Again, I'm not trying to piss you off. But she made a good point about the time frame for the shoot." He shouldered his messenger bag. "Unless you consider her refusal to make the changes a breach of contract. In which case, the video might be a wash."

We were quiet as we headed out of the studio, passing a group of suits sitting in the artfully understated waiting area. Of the many things I'd always admired about Olivia, her taste was definitely one of them.

Once we were in the town car headed back to the hotel, we resumed our conversation. "That's the thing. We don't have time to contract with another studio, not that the boys would consent to that anyway."

At Landon's big-eyed expression, I clarified, "Working with Olivia is their idea. After she had the good sense not to cut to commercial when they went off-script and played a new song during the Grammys, they decided she was the one to produce this video." *That, and they wanted to torture me by forcing me to work with her.*

Leaning my head back against the leather cushion of the seat, I closed my eyes and experienced another form of torture. Olivia during the meeting gazed back at me from front and center in my mind's eye. A half-carat diamond on a delicate gold chain winked from the hollow of her throat when she fidgeted in her chair, crossing and uncrossing her legs. The silk leopard-print blouse she'd buttoned up one button too many for my liking left a mystery I found myself wanting to solve. Her short black skirt clung to the perfect curve of her ass as she walked out of the conference room. All I wanted was a time machine so I could return to that minute and follow her back to her office, close the door, and figure out what the real problem was without the audience of our assistants. Or maybe remind her of our history together, the part that was always right between us.

No doubt, I got to her. But was it because of our past, the changes I'd suggested for our project, or something else?

Landon interrupted my thoughts. "So we go back to the original script?"

I turned my head and flicked my eyes open. "No."

His brow furrowed. "No?"

"The equipment is already en route, so we're putting it to work."

He cleared his throat, a habit I was starting to find annoying as it signaled he was about to say something I probably didn't want to hear. "We've seen Olivia's soundstage, sir. She's right. It's nowhere big enough to accommodate Balefire's hydraulic stages. Those things were built for stadiums and fifty-thousand-seat arenas."

"Yep." I closed my eyes again.

"Sir?"

Sitting up straight, I exploded. "For the last fuckin' time, stop calling me 'sir.'"

His throat worked beneath his wide-eyed stare. "I'm sorry, s—, Mr. Phillips."

Falling back against the seat, I glared at the ceiling and drew in a long breath. At last, I blew it out slowly. "It's been a long day, and it's not even lunchtime. I shouldn't have taken that out on you." Leveling my eyes on him, I added, "But the 'sir' thing stops now."

He acknowledged me with a long slow nod.

"As you may have guessed, Olivia and I have a history. It's not ugly. More sad than anything. But that lady is smart. She'll come around to our idea—all of it—and sooner rather than later. You'll see."

A plan formed in my head, and I waggled my brows and shot Landon a grin.

♪

"Happy to hear she's kept you on board, man," I said into my phone as I caught up with Jeremy later that same afternoon. I'd spent the time between our meeting and this call finalizing a plan to make it easy for Olivia's studio to set up, shoot, and tear down the video on the top of the LA skyline at the Griffith Observatory. It added some expense to the production, but I was pretty sure the band wouldn't care if we amended the contract.

"Yes, well, I don't think it's a good idea for me to take any more of your calls for a while, Mr. Phillips. Not if I want to continue to work for Olivia." A subdued assistant had replaced the enthusiastic kid from our meeting.

"Understood. Understood. But since you took this one, can you tell me what time your boss usually leaves work?"

He paused. "Seven or eight most nights unless we have a shoot."

"What time do you think she'll head out tonight?"

"Um, I really don't know."

Sounds in the background alerted me Jeremy might not be alone. Plus, there was something cagey in his tone, which said he knew exactly what time Olivia planned to knock off tonight.

"If you had to guess—"

"Probably around six. She has a date."

A date? Well, that shot my plan all to hell.

Or not.

"Thanks, man. Appreciate your help. By the way, the band loves your idea to shoot the video at the observatory. Inspired thinking, Jeremy. Talk to you soon."

I didn't give him a chance to say anything before I clicked off. If Olivia was in the room with him, she heard the entire conversation. If not, well, I might still have an ally in her camp despite this morning's fiasco.

Since this video shoot had begun as a casual affair, I'd left the expensive suit at home. My plan, however, called for dressing up, so I headed out to Rodeo Drive to fill what was left of the afternoon spending too much money on clothes I'd probably wear once. If my plan paid off, the extra outlay would be worth every penny. While I was in the clothes-buying mindset, I added a little something I hoped would soften up the lady in question enough to enjoy a "business" evening with me, one that would culminate with her agreement to our revised script.

I arrived at Heart Strings Productions at 5:45 p.m. dressed to impress, a fancy dress bag draped over my arm. Olivia's secretary's eyebrows disappeared into her hairline when I stepped over to her desk. "Is Miss Carter still in?"

"S-she is." It sounded like the woman had a frog in her throat. She coughed into her hand and said more forcefully, "She is, but I don't believe you have an appointment."

"It's on her private calendar, I imagine."

The secretary narrowed her eyes, and I added, "You know. The one she keeps on her private phone. The one that applies to her life rather than her business."

If anything, the woman's eyes narrowed into paper-thin slits. "I truly don't think she's expecting you."

I turned up the charm. "Olivia and I are old friends. It's why Balefire wanted her to have the shot at making their video." Surreptitiously glancing at the nameplate on her desk, I let my million-dollar smile loose. "Trust me, Dana, she's expecting me."

"I thought I heard voices." Olivia stepped out of her office and stopped short. "Garrett? What are you doing here?"

"I was just asking him the same thing," her assistant so helpfully chimed in.

Ignoring Dana, I locked my gaze on Olivia, her changeable eyes more gold than green today. I'd forgotten how much I loved watching the transformations of color in her hazel eyes—and being able to gauge her mood from those differences. "Hello, O. I thought

I'd make up for our rough start this morning, take you somewhere fancy for dinner."

Behind me, I heard the office door open, and her gaze slipped past my shoulder.

"Jason!" I'd only ever heard that fakey-bright tone in her voice one other time in my life. It wasn't a fond memory. "Let me grab my jacket, and I'll be right with you."

Angling my body to keep an eye on her office door, I caught sight of "Jason" and ground my back teeth together. *What the fuck is Jason Stahl doing here?*

"Garrett Phillips," he drawled. "Fancy seeing you here. It's been what? Eight, ten years since you bailed on the firm—and Olivia—to follow a bunch of kids playing guitars?" The edge in his voice said there might still be hard feelings.

"Guess that kinda worked out, yeah? That bunch of kids playing guitars won three Grammys this year—again. Now we're all working together—with Olivia." I let a pause and my raised brow in Olivia's direction say the rest. "What brings you to LA?"

"Work—and Olivia, obviously."

My hands itched to punch the smirk right off his face. Good thing one of them was currently occupied holding a dress bag.

The lady in question exited her office and closed the door. Her eyes darted between us, so I made the first move. "Jason here seems confused. Your assistant said you're dating another producer these days."

The deer-in-the-headlights expression flashed over her features only for a second before she drew herself up, straightening her shoulders even as she tugged her purse closer to her body. "My staff knows better than to gossip about anyone's private life, least of all mine." She stepped past me to join Jason Stahl, my old colleague from the financial firm I'd worked at before Balefire and I joined forces. "Was there something you needed?" she asked me.

"Yeah, I wanted to run something by you, but it can wait. I

guess." I rested my eyes on hers, willing her to walk away from Jason to hear what I had to say.

She shifted her attention to her administrative assistant. "Mr. Phillips is on the schedule for tomorrow at ten. If there's something else he needs, please take care of it Dana. Thanks."

"Will do." The dragon lady's smile showed nothing but teeth.

Olivia's innate good manners wouldn't let her leave me hanging. "See you tomorrow, Garrett. Have a nice evening."

The musky jasmine of her perfume hung in the air for several minutes after Jason closed the door behind them. His smirk left a bad taste in my mouth. Then the dragon's rasp assaulted my ears. "You heard the boss. Was there something you needed? Besides the ability to tell the truth, that is."

"You'd get along well with Balefire's administrative assistant. Emory and you have a lot in common." I gave her my own dragon smile. "Clearly, Olivia and I share the same taste in who we have running the store." I let that sink in for a few seconds. "There is something I'd appreciate. May I hang this in Olivia's office, please? It's a gift with absolutely no strings attached. You'll let her know that, of course."

Deliberately lifting the dress bag so Dana could see the name emblazoned over the front of it, I waited. On cue, her narrowed eyes widened a fraction. With a nearly imperceptible nod, she rose and led me into Olivia's inner sanctum.

The understated elegance of her office came as no surprise. My girl had always had class. An area rug in sand and sage tones shot through with a floral design in deep cherry took up the space beneath her desk and the two wooden chairs facing it. Leather dyed to match the floral design cushioned the blond wood, but those chairs didn't look all that comfortable. Not nearly as comfy as the mahogany brown leather arm chair neatly tucked in behind her desk.

She'd covered the sage-toned wall to my left with framed posters of projects with various bands, none of them A-listers. A low bookcase took up most of the sand-colored wall to my right. Various pieces of glass sculpture decorating the top of the bookshelves caught my attention, and I stepped closer. In the back corner near the wall, a tiny blown-glass figurine of a dancing unicorn hid behind a sculpture of vertical intertwined waves in otherworldly shades of blue. The larger sculpture would have overwhelmed that figurine, except that I alone understood its significance. Not only had she kept it, but she kept it in the place where she spent most of her time. My chest warmed as memories washed over me.

The dragon lady, a.k.a. Dana, dragged me back to the present. "This is Miss Carter's private space. Leave the dress and be on your way, Mr. Phillips."

Shining my best smile on her, I said, "The artistry of these pieces is remarkable. I can see why Olivia likes them." Glancing around at the rest of the room, I noted the floor-to-ceiling windows behind her desk were obscured by vertical blinds in the three colors she'd chosen, artfully topped with a runner in a geometric design. I walked around her desk, curiously devoid of any framed photos or mementos, and draped the dress bag over the back of her chair. With a nod to her assistant, I headed out the door, noticing the plush leather couch on my way out. *Wonder what my girl got up to there?*

I stopped short, and Dana nearly bulldozed me through the door. *My girl?* Shaking my head, I glanced over my shoulder at a scowling dragon lady and shrugged. "Enjoy your evening, miss. See you tomorrow."

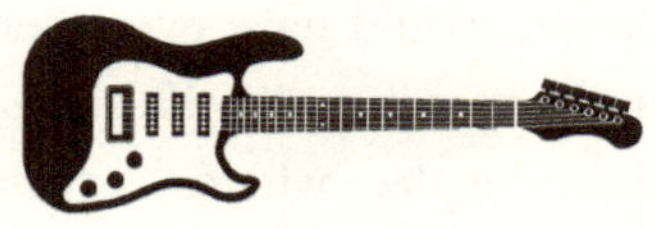

CHAPTER NINE

Olivia

MY MEETING WITH Jason Stahl told me everything I knew and didn't want to know. No matter how I worked things, I couldn't back out of the contract with Balefire regardless of what harebrained ideas Garrett and apparently everyone's assistants dreamed up. Since none of them knew my financial situation—that was info they'd only discover over my dead body—I had to play along with a smile on my face while I tossed back antacids like Skittles.

Jason's not-so-subtle come-ons all during dinner did nothing to improve my attitude. Newly divorced, the man was on the prowl, and Garrett's untimely appearance at my office only served to ratchet up Jason's dubious interest in me. When I'd let myself into my studio apartment at the end of a too-long day, I was still trying to figure out how I could have my account reassigned without pissing him off. The rest of my night I'd spent wrecking my bed as nightmares of losing my business and reputation warred with dreams of Garrett riding in on a white unicorn while I tilted at windmills on top of the massive sign symbolizing the hopes of far too many people.

A group of troubadours played Balefire's "Brothers" on a loop, and the song stuck in my head like a hangover headache after I woke up.

By the time I arrived at work, I needed a nap, five shots of espresso topped up with hot water and no cream, and a week at the beach—alone. Dana handed me my usual Americano as I walked past her desk, and I paused. It was our unwritten rule that my administrative assistant never grabbed me coffee.

Reaching for her offering as one trying to pet a rattlesnake without sustaining a bite, I said, "What's up with this?"

"Thought you might need it."

"Because…"

"It's going to be one of those days." My eyebrow shot up, and she continued, "Starting with what's waiting for you on the back of your chair." She nodded in the direction of my closed office.

My body, already tense from my short, restless night, coiled almost to the breaking point.

"Do I even want to know?"

"Probably not. But if you're not interested in Versace, I definitely am." Dana's habitual scowl relaxed a fraction, her only tell. The woman had me by fifteen years in age and a lifetime of experience. That second part is what made her so invaluable on my staff. But at the moment, she seemed to be deliberately ratcheting up my nerves when she had to know how much I needed to be Zen this morning.

Absently, I sipped my coffee, discovering it to be the perfect temperature with the exact right amount of cream. I leveled my gaze at her, but she merely shrugged and swung her attention back to her computer screen.

Sucking in a fortifying breath, I faced my office door.

"He said to tell you it comes with no strings attached." She snorted. "There's no such thing when it comes to expensive gifts. Remember that," she added without looking away from her work.

As warned, a garment bag was draped over the back of my chair with Versace's distinctive logo emblazoned over the front of it. Carefully, I set my coffee on the corner of my desk and let my messenger bag slide off my shoulder to land on the floor beside it. I'd seen the dress bag folded over Garrett's arm last night when I left him with Dana but hadn't thought much about it. In the dim glow of morning sunlight reflecting off the opposite building and through the slats in the blinds in my office, the gift mocked me from where it rested on the back of my chair.

Taking time I didn't have, I tugged the zipper down like pulling it through a slow-motion time warp and gently extracted the most beautiful cocktail dress on the planet from its hiding spot inside the bag. Sleeveless with a plunging neckline, the paisley print in a subdued shade of red, the dress exuded elegance. Echoing the neckline, a deep vee arrowed down the back. In spite of myself, I held it up against me, noting the hem of the sassy flair of the skirt landed somewhere south of my knees. Even in the quiet light of my office, sequins winked out from everywhere on the fabric. Instinctively, I knew it would fit, the silk fabric whisper-soft against my skin.

Damn him. Damn Garrett and his "no strings attached" gift. No strings attached my ass.

I slid the dress back into the bag, passing my fingers lightly, lingeringly over it one last time, and zipped it back in. At first, I draped the bag over the back of one of the chairs facing my desk and pulled my laptop from my bag. Firing it up, I went to work on the logistics for the shoot we'd be filming directly following "Dangerous Life."

Not.

The dress mocked me from its spot directly in front of my desk. With a growl, I picked up the dress—chair and all—and set it in the corner beside the window behind me.

I could sense it twinkling, its sequins in the gathering light of the morning, warming my skin with its presence.

"Gah!"

I slammed my laptop shut, pushed away from my desk, and snatched up the dress bag. My feet did not make the satisfying sound I craved as I stomped across the rug to my door and flung it open. "Dana!"

"Your ten o'clock is here, Olivia. Shall I show him in to the conference room?" If you didn't know her well, you might have missed the smirk that ghosted over her face.

Dana and I went back three years to when I took out my first loan and hired an assistant who knew the business. I didn't miss the smirk.

On the other side of her desk, Garrett watched me, a tiny grin tugging the corner of his mouth while I glared at him, the "no strings attached" gift thrust out in front of me, the curve of the hanger dangling from my fingers.

"Please make sure Mr. Phillips grabs this on his way out."

Garrett's grin morphed into a full smile, and I wanted to smack my knees for going wobbly. Instead, I thrust the offending garment bag at my assistant, who snagged it before it could drop to the floor, and stomped back into my office. A second later, I emerged with my laptop, coffee cup, and what I prayed was a serene expression stamped on my face. Without a word, I headed to the conference room.

In my wake, I heard him say, "Miss Dana, that dress is not my style, but it's tailor-made for Olivia. You know where to leave it in her office."

I stopped stock-still in the doorway to the conference room and squeezed my eyes shut. Now was not the time to make a scene, but damn it, he was asking for one. Dragging in a shuddery breath, I willed my feet to keep going until I reached the head of the table where I set my things down and seated myself.

"Garrett, I won't be bribed with an expensive dress." *Even one by my favorite designer.* "Balefire sought me out, and I have what I have to work with. That means your hydraulic stages are out of the shoot," I said as he strolled into the room behind me.

Ignoring my comment, he seated himself in the chair to my left then scooted it to the corner of the conference table, leaving me no room to breathe. Two of us couldn't sit at the head of the table, but I refused to let him intimidate me into taking the seat to my right. Instead, I did my best to push him back with my eyes. His locked with mine, a battle of wills.

Sitting this close, his low voice rumbled through me. "The dress is a gift. No strings."

"Riiight."

For a few more seconds, our eyes tangled. Then Garrett sighed and pushed his chair back a few inches. "Olivia, I was shopping for a new suit and saw that dress in a window. It looked so much like something you'd enjoy, I didn't think. I just walked in and bought it." His head down, he busied himself with unloading his laptop from his messenger bag. "I paid cash and lost the receipt." With a shrug, he added, "It's not my size or style, so—"

My lips thinned as I gritted my teeth over my first response. No, I wasn't some Balefire groupie who could be bought off with an expensive dress. But it wouldn't do for my professional reputation to call his ass out with the door to the conference room wide open to the reception area. Even loyal employees were known to talk. I'd circle back to the dress later—like when I draped it over his arm before he left the studios for the day.

"About the changes you and all the assistants made in the script." I let that sit for a second. "Perhaps your guy moonlights as a script doctor. I'm sure I don't know." Ignoring Garrett's smirk, I sailed on. "My assistant is excellent at what he does. What he does not do is write, direct, or produce videos, which makes me wonder why you were running script ideas past him." Tilting my head, I waited for his answer.

"From what I've gathered since we signed the contracts for this shoot, Jeremy is your right-hand man. When I tried to contact you about the changes we wanted to make, you were unavailable, so I ran them past him. I had no reason to think you would object."

Oh, he was smooth and so sure of himself. So *manipulative*. It was the smile—and that velvety voice that never failed to send shivers through me. Even now when I knew what he was up to, I could sense my body softening, wanting to give in.

"I wouldn't object to major changes to the script, but changes that add more zeros to the price tag, changes you knew from your questions about my studio when we signed the contract that my soundstage can't accommodate? Those changes you ran past an *assistant* and thought I wouldn't object?" I knocked back a deliberate swig of coffee. "What you were truly up to is using my assistant's enthusiasm for working with Balefire as a means to run an end-around on me." In the wake of his wide-eyed innocent expression, I plowed on. "I don't know what your endgame is with this video, but since *you* came to *me* with it, it's my show. And we're doing it my way."

He didn't deny his shenanigans, and I couldn't decide if I admired him more for it or if I wanted to smack him with his script and stomp out of the meeting.

He didn't give me a chance for either option. "The thing is, Olivia, you and your studio are capable of so much more than limiting this production to what you have available with your soundstage, and you know it."

There it was.

It may have been years since we were lovers, but Garrett obviously still remembered my competitive streak. I hid it well behind a façade of competence and hard work, but in the end, I wanted—needed—to stand out. As a woman in a male-dominated industry, that was a given, but I also wanted to stand out as a person, to be more, and to do that on my own. Directing and producing this video would allow me to accomplish that, even if the expanded idea wasn't entirely mine.

"Doesn't matter. The situation is what it is. If this project had come along in five years, I probably would have proposed the revised script using hydraulic stages I could provide, but we're working in the here and now." Opening the script on my screen, I started scrolling through it to an idea I'd had of using Dakota's single hydraulic lift, the one he strapped onto to rise above the stage for his solos in their live shows. It was the only compromise I could make.

He reached over and gently pushed my laptop closed.

"The band's big stage is en route. It'll probably roll onto your lot by the end of today."

I ground out his name through clenched teeth.

"I've also secured the use of the grounds of the Griffith Observatory for Wednesday, Thursday, and Friday of next week—Wednesday to set up and do test shots, Thursday to shoot the video, and Friday to reshoot if we have to and tear down the set." His warm palm and fingers wrapped around my suddenly icy hand. "I'm not running over you, Olivia."

"Oh, really? So what do you call going behind my back to bring in all the band's gear and securing the observatory?" He squeezed my hand when I tried to tug it away. I narrowed my eyes at where he covered my hand and with monumental effort, kept my voice even. "Your ideas are beyond the budget even if we can shoot the script in a day. By itself, the green screen necessary to hang behind the band's stage and the flight simulator at the observatory breaks the budget. Never mind the logistics and people necessary for setting up and tearing down off-site." Leveling my eyes on him at last, I said, "I don't care what you've spent to bring the band's stages here. The answer is no."

His eyes held mine as he smoothed his thumb over the back of my wrist, sending damning goose bumps over my skin. "Like you just said. If we were doing this project in five years, the amended script would be the preferred one." The black velvet tone of his voice worked through me, encouraging me to believe him even when I knew the true state of my resources. Like he read my mind, he added, "We can attach an addendum to the contract that includes the necessary zeros for the changes."

"The band will agree to that?" I hated the breathy pitch of my words, but his thumb creating lazy circles on my skin divided my attention in an irritatingly unprofessional way that I couldn't seem to control.

"I manage them, remember?" His eyes slid away from mine for a fraction of a second. "This will work out well for all of us. I promise."

Once, long ago, Garrett had said those same words to me. A couple of months later, he followed Balefire right out of my life. Now after years of radio silence, he and the band were suddenly front and center in my world. Something about that nanosecond disconnect before he repeated those words plummeted my heart into my stomach. What was Garrett up to? Why did those words make me think my dream, the one that contributed to our breakup, the one I was inches away from realizing, was now on the line?

CHAPTER TEN

Garrett

THE BOYS WERE in a rockin' mood when they arrived at Olivia's studios in the afternoon. Watching them razz each other about how they'd spent their downtime between our last meeting and today alternately buoyed my spirits and soured my stomach. How they'd all gone from the wild-ass bad boys of rock 'n' roll to committed family men in the space of only two bars of their music still stymied me. Then I glanced up at Olivia seated at the head of her conference table.

She'd shrugged off the tan linen jacket from our earlier meeting, revealing a plain white cotton shirt with a sweetheart neckline that hinted at her pretty curves. I'd kept my eyes on her face all morning, but my peripheral vision was an entirely different matter. A thick gold chain resting over her collarbones was meant to draw the eye up to her face, but her jewelry wasn't enough of a distraction from what I remembered was beneath her clothes. She smiled at something outrageous Dakota said, and my breath stuck in my throat. The past ten years melted away as I remembered seeing that smile on the regular. Only then, it was directed at me.

Back in the day, Olivia had gently teased me about liking the sweet stuff as she made my usual hazelnut and chocolate latte. I'd teased back that no amount of sugar could be as sweet as her. No matter how weak sauce my lines were, she always smiled that brilliant smile at me, making me feel like Captain America. Making me feel seen. For once in my life, I was special; I was important to someone I cared about. I was half in love with her weeks before she agreed to our first date.

To my right, Blu snorted out a laugh. "Why Annabelle puts up with you is a mystery for the ages, Dakota."

His comment abruptly dragged me back into the present.

"Hey, she sicced her pain-in-the-ass baby sister on me the night before we left Denver to come out here. I had plans for my lady. Big plans." He lowered his voice. "Private plans." He waggled his brows suggestively. "But when I arrived at her apartment with my goodie bag full of naughty fun, there was Ellie sitting on the couch eating popcorn and scrolling through Netflix. An hour later, Annie came home with a pizza after she'd finished taking her last final early."

Tron kicked back in his chair and folded his arms over his chest. "Your lady was being responsible, Dakota. I've noticed she does that sometimes."

"She does." Dakota's expression turned dreamy, and I ground my back teeth. Then he snapped out of it. "But she didn't need to have Ellie over just because she was home for the weekend and declined their parents' invite to join them for dinner. Ellie's a big girl. She could have taken care of herself."

Jack cracked up at Dakota's pouty face. "Says the guy who didn't grow up with siblings. Trust me, Ellie would have interrupted your evening whether she was invited or not. That wasn't Annabelle's fault. She should lock you out of Parker's place for the whole time we're shooting for scaring the shit out of her with that Jason mask."

Dakota flipped him the bird. "It was a joke. I found it in a closet when I was looking for extra pool towels." He blew out a sigh that sounded remorseful. "Her childhood experience with *Friday the 13th* movies hadn't come up before, so how was I to know she'd react like that?"

"Good thing that woman loves you, dude. But to be safe, you should prolly make sure she gets a spa day while we're out here, something with all the pampering shit women like. Cristy could give you some ideas." Tron glanced down the table. "Or you could ask Olivia. I bet you know some good places," he said.

Inclining her head, she said, "You guys have come a long way since the early days when you competed for how many girls you had swarming around you at any given time."

Tron glanced down at the table, red tinged Blu's cheeks, and Dakota grinned, but I knew better than to think that grin was anything but nostalgia.

"I'll have my assistant set up a spa day for your ladies when your team is setting up your stage at the observatory and we're rehearsing here at the studio." She glanced at Jeremy who dutifully added some notes on his iPad.

The kid had said maybe two words since he'd walked in the door. Guess he was still in Olivia's doghouse. Guess I'd have to find a way to make that up to him. At least he kept his job.

"Make sure that gets charged to Dakota's credit card." Jack's eyes danced with an unholy light. "Since we all had to hear about it from our women."

"Hey—"

"Yep. It's the only way to get back in their good graces," Blu added with a smirk.

The side of Tron's face lifted in half a grin directed at Dakota.

"Fine." Dakota threw himself back in his chair and crossed his arms over his chest. "You set it up, Olivia, and I'll buy our women a spa day." A naughty chuckle escaped him. "Who knows what can happen when they're all nice and relaxed?"

Blu fist-bumped him, and all the guys grinned at each other.

I needed an antacid.

All this anticipation for monogamous hookups with their women left me nauseous. I couldn't understand how that kind of life could be attractive to men in their prime after enjoying ten years of all the first-class pussy the road had to offer. How could any of them give that up for fidelity to a single woman?

Olivia shifted in her chair, and her chin came up, her eyes leveled on mine as if she saw exactly what I was thinking. From somewhere not so deep inside me, my conscience creaked back to life. She would never believe me, but I'd never cheated on her those first six months on the road with Balefire before she called us quits. That damning photo that hurt her so much I wanted to smash the photographer's camera to bits was snapped in the split second between when the woman with nefarious intentions sat on my lap and when I pushed her off.

The guys thought they were helping me when they told me my breakup with Olivia was for the best. Let her have her dream while I followed mine. I wanted to manage them so damn bad, I let myself believe them. Now, here we were. They were all mothered up, and I was alone.

"If you're finished planning your women's calendars for them, maybe we can get to the point of this meeting." Six heads swiveled in my direction, and I cleared my throat to cover the hostility I'd let escape in my tone. Ignoring the wide-eyed stares of Olivia's and my assistants and the narrow-eyed ones of the band, I plowed on. "We've made changes to the script, changes that are going to make this video number one on every platform out there." Turning to Landon, I said, "You brought hard copies, yeah?"

Landon busied himself with extracting the scripts and handing them around to the band while I pulled mine up on my laptop. "Olivia agreed, provided we can film it mostly in one long day. Possibly two if the galleys aren't what we think they'll be."

A brow hiked up over her beautiful hazel eyes, but otherwise, her expression remained impassive.

"We're filming the entire video at the observatory?" Blu asked as he flipped through the script.

"Most, but not all."

"How much does that add to the price tag?" Dakota the serious businessman replaced Dakota the class clown in a blink.

For the most part, the boys being educated about the business side of their rock 'n' roll circus was a good thing. I'd encouraged them when Blu and Dakota decided to pursue online business degrees several years ago. But there were times—like now—when they used that tone and I wished I was the one who had all the answers.

Between my morning meeting with Olivia and this meeting with the band, I'd hastily scrambled together a conference call between Balefire's and the studio's lawyers, drawing up the addendum that added 150 thousand dollars to the price tag for the shoot. The contracts waited in my messenger bag for everyone's signatures—if the band's numbers guy didn't throw a fit. After the way things went down a year ago when Annabelle had been my intern, it was a toss-up as to how Dakota would react—smart or spiteful.

"A hundred fifty K." I put up my hand to stop the tantrum I could see coming. "Which is a bargain for how this thing's going to play once Olivia and her team finish it."

Dakota's jaw worked as he stared daggers at me.

"And I'll cover your ladies' spa day and throw in dinner each night of the shoot."

"*So* generous of you considering Chef Jeff is catering, as usual," Dakota sneered.

"But the food comes out of the band's money. What I'm saying is I'll buy."

"Booze too?" At the wicked gleam in Blu's eyes, my credit card started heating up in my wallet to a point I feared it might burn a hole in my jeans.

"Yeah, yeah, booze too." Over the years, I'd invested my earnings from the band well, so I wasn't hurting for cash. Didn't mean

I wanted to spend it all on a Balefire bash. The boys might have all been coupled up, but they could still party. Didn't help that their women played along with them on certain occasions. No doubt, this would be one of them.

Tron's outburst interrupted the negotiations. Mercifully.

"Fuckin' A! I'm riding that flight simulator right into space." With the hand not marking the script, he high-fived Jack sitting beside him.

From the corner of my eye, I caught Landon's grin. Then my gaze lit on Olivia right in time to see her expel a breath I think she might have been holding for the last ten minutes.

Taking that as my cue, I extracted the contracts from my bag and passed them around. "You'll be playing badass rhythms in space after we take care of business."

The room was quiet as each member of the band and Olivia read through what the lawyers and I had agreed to. The concessions on both sides benefited everyone—if they saw them in the spirit in which I'd written them. That old 70s song by Hot Chocolate, "Everyone's a Winner," played in my head as I watched the five people I cared about most read through the revised contract.

"This adds time to your schedule, but I don't see where you're compensated, Garrett," Blu said.

"Not too worried about it."

"But maybe *we* should be?"

Fuck! Would Dakota never stop suspecting my motives?

"For the last time, everything I've ever done for you guys was with your best interests in mind."

Blu narrowed his eyes. "Uh-huh. Tell that to Ashleigh."

"Or Annabelle or Cristy," Dakota added.

"I don't know how many times I've said I'm sorry." I ran my hand through my hair, landing it on the nape of my neck and giving myself a squeeze. "You have no idea how sorry I am." I stared at each man in turn. "Can't you see I'm trying to make it up to you? I'm trying to keep you and your music front and center on everyone's minds? This video is going to create all kinds of opportunities for you."

"On our dime." Dakota drummed his fingers on his copy of the contract.

"The video was your idea," I countered. "Now I'm doing my job and running with it."

"He has you there, Dakota," Jack said.

Blu pushed away from the table and stood. "Sounds like we need a team meeting."

When he uttered those two words, my heart plummeted into my gut. So much was riding on this video and the way I'd revised the script. The band could afford the additional outlay, and everyone in the room knew it. So balking at the price tag was an excuse for something else. I hadn't interfered in any of their personal lives since the whole debacle on the last US tour, so I couldn't figure out what the problem was.

Not that I could say a damn thing.

"Is there somewhere we can meet in private?" Blu asked Olivia.

Her eyes rounded as she stared down the table at me. "Um, sure," she said then glanced up at Blu. "You can use my office. Dana will direct you." Again, she sent a questioning look my way, and I did my damnedest to remain impassive with my ass glued to my chair.

Team meetings had started happening rather too regularly after I'd made a run at Ashleigh Baker a couple of tours ago. In my defense, none of the guys had ever shown more than a passing interest in a woman in the past, so I had no idea Blu was all in with her until it was too late. When Dakota recommended Annabelle for an internship with the band, it never occurred to me he had ulterior motives. I might have taken my bruised ego out on her after I made a run at her and she flat-out turned me down. By the time I figured out the two of them had a history, the damage was done. The whole thing with Cristy Valor was as much her manager's doing as mine. Plus, she was such a wildcard, I couldn't imagine Tron would stay with her past the end of the tour anyway. But it's always the quiet ones who surprise a person.

Since Jack was the band's second drummer who came in so serious he barely even partied, he'd earned his nickname "the monk." With him being five years younger than the rest of the guys, I thought he held back to keep from making a fool of himself—or to reassure them he wasn't another Dave Brubaker, virtuoso drummer, consummate partier. It never occurred to me there was a woman involved until he announced he was a dad. After that, everything with the band and women went downhill.

As they filed past me and out the door, none of them looked at me, which couldn't be a good sign. Still, I didn't even twitch.

Once they were out of earshot, it was Olivia's turn. "I thought you said the guys were on board with the change in plans. It's mostly why I gave in. That and the band agreeing to pay the added expenses."

Landon's stare heated the side of my face while Jeremy's wide eyes flicked between his boss and me. The assistants' surprise and curiosity were easy to ignore. Olivia's expression of suspicion with a hint of fear? Not so much.

Tapping on my computer to bring up a random screen, I bought myself time. At last, I raised my eyes back to hers. "In the beginning, managing Balefire was easy. We all worked together to map out their goals, and then I implemented the systems and created the opportunities for the boys to hit those goals. That first year when they opened for Nickelback, Slash, and Shinedown among others, they made a name for themselves." I glanced back at my screen, tapped out a couple of commands, and closed my laptop. "With their kick-ass sound and party-band persona, the tabs loved them. In minutes, it seemed, Balefire had rocketed from bar band to arena rockers. We were all having a great time." I blew out a breath. "Then Dave imploded, and for a minute there, I thought Balefire was over. But they auditioned Jack who, it turns out, gives them an edgier sound, and they're bigger than ever."

I stood and paced the width of the room, careful not to let my eyes stray out the door toward Olivia's closed office. "The thing is, they aren't teenagers anymore, and they don't need a big brother watching out for them. I might have forgotten that for a while there." I scrubbed my hands down my face and leveled my eyes on the one person I could never lie to. "Having the contract addendum ready to sign was a calculated risk, one I think is going to work out for them and for you." A self-conscious chuckle escaped me. "The jury is still out for me."

Right then, the door to Olivia's office opened, and the guys headed back to the conference room, cuing me to sit my ass back down.

Dakota stomped through the door first and threw himself back into his chair. Staring fire at me, he growled, "Good thing you didn't fuck things up with Jack. That's all I have to say."

"At some point, you gotta stop holding a grudge, man," Tron said as he passed Dakota and resumed his seat. "Garrett's been doing penance for most of this last year. The work he's put into Cristy's foundation is a damn good example." He nodded at me, but I only marginally relaxed.

Jack and Tron had forgiven me a long time ago.

"What you're truly pissy about is Tron is featured in the flight simulator on the hydraulic lift. You were fine when it was still just Jack and you. But adding that feature to the video is giving you attitude. Get over yourself." Blu's eyes danced over his lifelong best friend who pouted in his chair.

There it was. No matter how hard I'd tried over the years, I could never break into their tight-knit friendship group. Blu and Dakota grew up practically next door to each other. They'd been buddies with Tron since middle school. Though Jack was five years younger, it only took him about ten minutes to fit in with the other three like they'd been together since the cradle. But no matter how often or in what ways I put them and their best interests first, I never quite cracked the code enough to truly be a part of them.

"This mean you need a pen?" I asked, my eyes directed at Blu.

Blu stiffened his gaze at me. "We haven't figured out your angle yet—and we know you have one—but you aren't wrong about this script and the video we're going to make out of it."

His eyes on mine, he reached across the table, grabbed the pen I offered, and signed the contract first. He passed the pen and contract over to Dakota whose eyes tried to set me on fire before he scrawled his signature on the dotted line and passed the contract to Tron. Jack, seated closest to me, signed last and slid everything my way. After I added my name to the page, I walked the contract the length of the table and handed it to Olivia. When my fingers brushed hers in the exchange of the pen, I gritted my back teeth to keep from reacting to the electric spark that leaped from her skin to mine. If I hadn't had my eyes on hers, I might have missed the wide-eyed blink before she quickly glanced down at the contract.

Well, at least something might go right today, I thought.

"Time to get to work. What's first, boss?" I asked.

Taking her time, she handed the signed contracts to Jeremy. "We'll need copies in triplicate. Make sure to file one of ours with our legal department."

The uncharacteristically silent Jeremy gathered up the paperwork and headed out the door.

"When Jeremy returns, he can take you guys over to wardrobe. We have some ideas for costumes we need you to try on."

A slight hitch in his step at hearing his name flicked my attention in Jeremy's direction where a smile ghosted over his face, and he picked up his pace.

Dakota sat up with the most animated expression I'd seen him wear all afternoon. "Costumes?"

Simultaneously, Jack and Tron groaned. Blu grinned at Olivia, and for the first time in months, I allowed myself to sag a bit in my chair.

CHAPTER ELEVEN

Olivia

"I THOUGHT YOU SAID costumes," Dakota whined when Garrett and I joined the band in wardrobe. "Tuxes aren't costumes."

"They are when they're understated James Bondesque tuxes on the members of Balefire." A grin I didn't bother to suppress spread over my face. "I directed the Grammys, remember? That bright red Armani you wore nearly set off the fire alarms."

Dakota shrugged but his eyes danced with mischief. "If only. That would have been righteous."

"For the part of the video we're filming here at the studio, you'll wear the tuxes. When we're out on location, you'll be in flight gear, camo, and your normal concert wear." Preempting what I could see in the naughty glances the guys exchanged, I added, "Nothing obscene. We want this video to play on all the platforms."

Four pairs of shoulders slumped, and I couldn't help but chuckle. It might have been ten years since I saw them last—and they might all have been in long-term committed relationships—but the bad boys of rock 'n' roll were still the rowdy boys I knew a lifetime ago.

Dakota glanced past my shoulder. "Hey, Garrett. You need

to convince your lady here that the shirts we wear in our shows aren't obscene."

Garrett's lady? How much had I given away in that fleeting touch we accidentally exchanged in the conference room?

The fresh citrusy scent I'd quickly come to associate with my former lover wafted over me as he walked up beside me. "Which ones?"

Blu piped up. "Any of them."

"Let me guess. Olivia said to keep it PG, and you want to push a boundary for the hell of it," Garrett said.

As one, the entire band smirked, and I wanted to throw up my hands. We hadn't even started filming yet, and Balefire was causing trouble. I'd expected it, but I thought I might have at least one day of relative calm before the shenanigans began.

"This is as much a promo for you as it is for the film. How 'bout this? How 'bout you wear one of the T-shirts Annabelle was instrumental in creating for the last US tour?" he said, addressing Dakota. "You wear a Be Valorous Foundation shirt, Tron." Turning to Blu, he suggested, "We could have one made for you with the *Rolling Stone* cover featuring Ashleigh's article about Balefire. And you could wear one featuring the *Brothers* album cover, Jack. Slide in an extra little plug for the new disc."

For a long moment, four pairs of eyes riveted on Garrett. Jack broke the silence. "That idea right there. That's why we keep him as our manager."

Wait, *what?* The band was considering jettisoning Garrett? Is that what the "team meeting" had been about? Is that why he'd been so tense around the guys?

"I like it. Our ladies will too," Tron said, a grin splitting his face.

Dakota crossed his arms over his chest and glared at Garrett. "It's one good idea. Don't think you're off the hook yet."

Blu rolled his eyes so hard in Dakota's direction I worried he might injure himself.

"Okay." I dragged the word out. "Costumes are settled. What

we need to do first is lay down several tracks of the song. I hope you guys love 'Dangerous Life' because after today, it's going to play on a loop in your heads for more than a minute." I nodded at the dangerously handsome group of men in their understated tuxes. "I'll meet you in the recording studio in thirty."

Garrett fell into step beside me. "You know what's sexy? Assertiveness," he said, his words more believable for the quiet way he delivered them. "You were always sexy, but now even more so."

A snort escaped me. "Ha! I was wearing an apron and a doofy hat when you met me. Nothing sexy about that at all."

"After you figured out I was spending time in that coffee shop for you, your eyes would dance a little whenever I walked in the door. Believe me, babe, there is nothing sexier than a woman's interest."

Though I tried to control myself, his words sent a shiver through me.

"That long, thick braid you wore back then begged me to unravel it." From the corner of my eye, I caught him giving my hair a once-over. "But I'm lovin' this sophisticated layers thing you have going on now too."

"Are you flirting with me?" I asked as we entered the lobby of the small recording studio situated next to the massive building housing the soundstage.

He shrugged.

"I'm not a Balefire groupie, Garrett. I'm a thirty-three-year-old businesswoman. Whatever it is you want from me, it's best to state it straight up." With a smile I wasn't feeling, I waved to the production assistant handling the desk and walked with a purpose into the control room.

Waiting until he caught my eyes again, he nodded at my words, the banked fires in his gray eyes changing them to steel, and a swarm of bees started buzzing in my belly. Whatever he was up to, I needed to stay on my guard.

"How serious are you with this studio exec you're dating?"

What the hell? Then I remembered that little charade with Jeremy a few days ago in my office. "None of your business."

"Not that serious, then. Good to know."

Before I could sputter a rebuttal, he turned to the sound engineer and another man I didn't recognize and extended his hand. "Nick, my man, thanks a bunch for helping us out on this gig." Turning to Rudy Guptil, my sound engineer, he added, "Thanks for allowing us to bring in someone we're used to working with," as he shook Rudy's hand.

"No problem, Mr. Phillips. It's an honor to work with a legend," Rudy said, grinning in Nick's direction.

"Olivia, this is Nick Parker, the genius behind the records. Nick, this is Olivia Carter, the genius behind the video we're making. The flight simulator was her idea."

Nick and I smiled at each other as we shook hands. "I'm looking forward to working with you," he said. "Garrett started singing your praises from the minute he suggested this gig to me."

My gaze slid to Garrett whose Cheshire Cat grin made me nervous. He was up to something—again. After that tense little meeting in my office earlier, I would have thought he'd back off the surprises, especially with his job apparently on the line.

"You've heard the 'Dangerous Life' demo, yeah?" he asked Nick.

"Yeah." Nick's face lit up. "They've written another winner for sure. Are we working from the same script you showed me?"

"Not quite." Garrett pulled out his phone and tapped out a quick text. "We added a few things, but as far as how to record the song, it's mostly the same as the script you already have."

"Rudy's an ace at overdubbing, so if you're close on the timings, everything will line up in editing," I reassured them.

Garrett smiled at Nick. "What did I tell you? Olivia's a total pro."

I wanted to bask in praise that sounded sincere, except I knew Garrett. That comment about my love life had already put me on my guard. Never mind he would not be moving in on someone I was dating. The idea that he thought he could disrupt my (non-existent) relationship worked on me because I'd caught him a few times looking at me the way he did back when we were together. What did it say of me that I was not sure I could resist him? Yet for the sake of the people who relied on me for a paycheck, I had to resist him. That "boyfriend" Jeremy alluded to probably needed to become real in some way.

Yet I sensed something else going on with Garrett too. Somehow, I'd landed smack in the middle of a game of cat-and-mouse with my former lover and the band—if that standoff in my conference room was an indicator—and I had no choice but to play along. Everything I had was riding on this project.

Landon interrupted my morose thoughts. "Here are the scripts you asked for, s—Mr. Phillips."

Garrett's raised brow and Landon's unapologetic half smirk added another undercurrent to the turbulence buffeting us. With a nod to his assistant, he grabbed the scripts, flipped to page two, and handed them to Rudy and Nick. "The changes are here," he indicated with his finger. "And here." He pointed to a spot farther down the page. "As you can see, the first one happens at the end of the second chorus, and the second one happens during the bridge."

Rudy glanced up at me and grinned. "I'd heard a rumor you were taking this show on the road." He read a bit more and looked my way again. "We can work with this. Easy."

I inclined my head his way. "Never doubted it."

At that moment, Jeremy and the band entered the sound room. No one needed hot mics to know they were teasing the hell out of my assistant. The pink tops of his ears gave him away every time. *Perhaps I should encourage him to grow his hair*, I thought idly, a grin tugging the corner of my lip.

Touching his finger to a button on the sound board, Garrett said, "Right on time."

Five pairs of eyes glanced through the window separating the engineer's room from the studio. Then Dakota stepped over to a mic and flipped the switch. "Hey, Olivia. Jeremy here couldn't find my cool spacesuit in wardrobe. He said something about there being only one, and it's Tron's. Are you sure we can't have both me and Tron wearing the cool spacesuit? After all, I fly in this video too."

As he climbed behind his drums, we could hear Jack say, "What are you, Dakota? Six? You get the badass camo tux, so what are you whining about?"

"Aw, man. But it's not a spacesuit. Everyone wanted to be an astronaut when they grew up, right? This is my chance."

I couldn't suppress a laugh at the puppy dog stare Dakota gifted me through the glass. Garrett moved half a step when I walked over to the mic. "Dakota, you've read the script. It doesn't work with two spacemen. But the band can keep the suit as a souvenir of the shoot. You can use it in your shows."

"Damn it, Olivia. Now you've done it," Blu said into his mic as he slipped his guitar strap over his chest. "There's going to be a fight over that suit before every show on the next tour." Though he sounded put out, his eyes danced.

"I imagine you'll find a way to work that out," I said drily.

"Doing shots, most likely," Garrett said in my ear.

I hated what I gave away with a shiver as his warm breath blew over my skin with his words.

Oblivious to the little drama happening between Garrett and me, Nick slipped up on my other side and took over the mic. "Good to see you boys again. This song you've written for the movie is one of your best yet. Thanks for inviting me to work on it with you."

"No offense to Olivia's guy there"—Blu pointed at Rudy—"but having you at the controls will make all the difference, for sure." Returning his gaze to my sound engineer, he added, "No offense, man."

Rudy joining us at the mic allowed me to move back, away from Garrett and his maddeningly delicious smell and velvet voice washing over my skin.

"None taken. I'm damn lucky to have the chance to work with all of you, and I know it."

When he stepped away from the mic to let Nick give the band some directions for the first run-through of the song, I smiled and whispered to him, "Thanks for being cool about this. Balefire stipulated it in the contract before I could even talk you up and share some of your work."

"No worries, Olivia. I know you always have our backs." Rudy grinned. "I truly am excited to work with a legend in the industry. Over the next week or so, I'm soaking up every second of the master class Nick's going to give me just by doing his job."

Garrett said something low to Nick who glanced back at us, a smile in his eyes. Then he pulled a pen from his pocket and started making notes on the script Landon had given him while the band warmed up.

As they each did their own thing, Balefire sounded like a band rather than a cacophony of musicians. Stunning. Back in the day when they were still too young to drink legally in the bars where they played, they showed the incredible musicianship of masters of their art. After ten years of honing their skills and their sound, they were tight even when none of them was playing the same song.

On some silent cue, they snapped into the opening bars of "Dangerous Life" and blew me completely away. The demo I'd listened to as I came up with ideas for the shoot was as professional as any polished piece I'd ever worked with. But the band live, even in the studio, was something else entirely. No wonder they routinely sold out arenas and stadiums wherever they played on tour.

As the song ended, Garrett whispered in my ear, "You're glad you've joined us, aren't you, babe?"

Listening between the lines, I closed my eyes against the years melting away in his voice. In all this time, nothing had changed. Managing Balefire would always be his dream, his life. Whatever was going on between him and the band, it would always come down to this. Good thing I had that "boyfriend."

Ignoring his innuendo—and what it did to my insides—I said, "Balefire deserves every platinum record, every Grammy, every accolade they've ever received. That's one super-talented group of musicians."

If I disappointed him with my response, he didn't show it.

Rudy glanced back at me. "That was the warm-up? Holy shit!"

About to address the band, Nick had depressed the button for the mic when Rudy made his observation, which met with chuckles from the guys on the other side of the glass.

"Thanks, man." Blu's grin said that wasn't the first time they'd heard the sentiment.

Nick smiled at Rudy then leaned over the mic. "I have some ideas for extending the first chorus where you're going to lift off on your stage, Dakota."

I joined Nick at the mic. "I was wondering if you could add some instrumentation after the bridge, extend the sound while Tron rockets into space."

Dakota waggled his brows in my direction even as he ad-libbed a stunning riff that I hoped wasn't a one-off.

"If only you'd caught that on tape." I sighed to Nick.

"Oh, we did, boss," Rudy chimed in. I blinked at him. "Nick warned me to keep the tape rolling no matter what was going on in that sound booth."

Turning my attention to the band's preferred producer, I caught his wink at Rudy before he shot me a tiny grin.

"When you sing 'Savor this life,' Blu, I need to hear you savor that word more. Hold the vowels for a touch longer. Jack, I don't know what that riff was between the last two lines of the chorus, but damn, that works."

Jack saluted him with his sticks, and they launched into the song again.

CHAPTER TWELVE

Olivia

NO DOUBT, EVERY night for the next six months when I closed my eyes to sleep, "Dangerous Life" would be my soundtrack. Whatever drove these guys, including Garrett and their producer, perfection had to top the list. The entire session was the most professional recording experience I'd ever had. No one bitched. No one pulled the diva card. No one slammed anyone else's ideas. When at last they called it a day, we had so much incredible material, I knew I'd be pulling all-nighters through the weekend in order to choose the version of the song that would best convey the script, song, and movie. Each version brought something slightly different to the table, a subtlety with the power to change the entire theme. I'd have to choose carefully.

The band did that to me on purpose, no question.

Landon gathered the fourth—or maybe fifth?—round of empty coffee cups from around the control room while Jeremy busied himself setting out pizzas in the lobby. Gourmet, from the smell of them. Handmade by the band's chef who, Garrett informed me, always traveled with them.

A couple of bottles of Jameson and a row of shot glasses held pride of place in the middle of the pizza spread, telling me we'd completed our recording session for the day. I grabbed a seat in the corner of the couch in the lobby and busied myself with my notes. The guys had worked their asses off, so I figured they should be first in line for dinner. Besides, their virtuoso instrumentation had given me some ideas I didn't want to lose once the alcohol started flowing.

Within seconds, I was so absorbed in my ideas, the video already playing in my mind, that I lost all contact with the space around me. Something about the extra guitar riff Dakota added to the bridge worked on my imagination, and I sketched a crude cartoon in the margin of my script. Morphing his costume from a formal to a camouflage-patterned tux as that riff rippled through a viewer's ears would create a surreal, almost out-of-body experience. If we could fade it through from him playing atop his platform to standing on a mountaintop with the overhead drone shot from the film spinning around him as he played, we could extend the theme. When he nailed the screaming vibrato about two-thirds of the way in, we could jump-cut to Tron in the flight simulator.

In my almost feverish need to commit my ideas to paper, my hand cramped. Only when I stopped writing to massage it did I notice the depression of weight of another person sitting so close beside me, he nearly sat on my lap.

With a gasp, I reared back. "Garrett! You startled me."

He whisked his plate of pizza away in the nick of time. Otherwise I might have upended it onto his jeans when my hand flew to my chest.

"Easy to do with how wrapped up in your notes you were." A smile danced in his eyes. "You hungry? 'Cause if you are, now would be a good time to belly up to the buffet before the rest of the team devours it." He glanced at the table in the middle of the lobby where half the pizza Jeremy had set out was already gone.

Raucous laughter and the clinking of glasses penetrated my

consciousness seconds after my eyes surveyed the scene. It wasn't uncommon for me to lose myself in the planning of a project. But never before had I disappeared so far into my head that I tuned out a room full of rowdy men doing shots.

I blamed it on Garrett's steady presence. All day, he'd remained close to me. At first, I'd managed to keep my guard firmly up, but as the day wore on and more ideas flew around the studio and the control room, I relaxed into the work and forgot. Without having to confirm with him, I knew he'd seated himself right where he was minutes after I'd started writing notes. He didn't intrude to offer suggestions or even to touch me. Instead, he maintained that steady presence and waited for me to pay attention. Exactly how he'd watched out for me in another time and place a lifetime ago.

Abruptly, I flipped my script closed and shoved it into my over-sized purse resting on the floor at my feet. "Sorry I disappeared on you there for a minute." I glanced at the slice of pizza on his plate. "That smells delicious. What kind is it?"

"Seafood. One of Chef Jeff's specialties. Want a taste?" He picked up his slice and offered it to me.

The gesture was too damn intimate, especially when, from the corner of my eye, I caught Blu openly watching us.

"Thanks, but I'm going to want a whole slice." As I'd worked, I'd melted so far back into the corner of the plush leather couch that I couldn't slide off it with any grace. Giving up on being lady-like, I pushed myself up and walked over to the table. "Is there any seafood pizza left?" I asked in general, keeping my eyes averted from the too-observant lead singer's.

Tron pushed a quarter-full pizza pan in my direction. "Probably better take both slices, O," he said.

I slid him a side-eye at the use of Garrett's old nickname for me and slid the pizza onto a plate in the middle of the table. The move necessitated me leaning forward, and I appreciated how Dakota kept his eyes on my face. Though I'd buttoned my shirt up beyond my cleavage before I'd left home for work, the old Dakota probably would have levered himself up a bit in his chair to see down the front of me anyway. As if he knew what I was thinking, he winked and saluted me with his shot before tossing it back.

"Have a seat, Olivia," Jack said, indicating the chair to his right between Jeremy and him. "We haven't heard your thoughts on this afternoon's little practice session." His eyes glittered over the top of a generous slice of some kind of pizza loaded with peppers as he bit off half of it. No wonder there wasn't much left on the table.

"Practice session?" I said with a laugh as I reached for the pitcher of water between Jack and me. After taking a long drink of cool water, I lifted my glass to the guys. "Glad to see you've become smart. I remember a time when the only drinks on the table were eighty proof."

"They still are after a show," Dakota said, directing a dare at Jack across the table.

"Dakota's messing with you, O," Tron chimed in. "We also make sure to travel with a stock of Denver's finest microbrews. We have refined tastes these days."

The entire band found Tron's comment hilarious. It even twitched a grin out of Landon, who'd sat quietly beside Dakota throughout the meal, from what I could gather. As did Jeremy beside me. A half-full glass of water waited beside an empty shot glass in front of my assistant's plate. He grabbed and downed it when he caught me looking at it. Hastily, he refilled his water glass, and I wondered how many shots the boys had had after I'd dropped into my own little world. One glance at the nearly empty fifth of Jameson in the middle of the table told me all I needed to know.

"Don't worry, Jeremy. I'll pay for the Uber to drive you home and return you to work tomorrow," I whispered for his ears only. The pink tinge along the tops of his ears was his only acknowledgment of my words.

Returning my attention to the band, I said, "You guys were

impressive from the first time I heard you." My gaze slipped back to Garrett who remained seated on the couch. Only then did I notice we were one chair short at the table. I glanced around at the space and back to him. He inclined his head, a knowing smile tugging the corner of his mouth. Exactly which of us was the odd one out? Either one didn't sit well with me.

Blu tipped his chair back, balancing on the back legs. "Which begs the question—why did we have to wait this long to work with you?"

I was still stuck on the seating arrangements. "Why are we short a chair at the table?"

"Don't worry about it, Olivia," Garrett said at the same time Jeremy scrambled out of his seat. "Shit! Sorry, boss."

He hotfooted it into the control room and emerged a few seconds later with another chair, sliding it up to the table at the end nearest the couch.

For a second, Garrett hesitated before he stood and joined the rest of us. "Thanks, man," he said to Jeremy.

"I've made a few changes to the script, ones I think you especially will like, Dakota," I said around another mouthful of succulent shellfish bathed in tangy cheese and seasoned tomato sauce. "Where in the hell did you find this guy? I could gorge on this stuff," I said and savored another bite.

"Don't bother entertaining thoughts of poaching our chef. He's been one of the guys since before Garrett came along," Blu said with a smirk aimed at my old flame.

The undercurrents between the band and their manager swirled around me. This was another complication I didn't need, not when I could taste the potential for success even more than Chef Jeff's out-of-this-world cooking. This video was only the appetizer for the dream I'd harbored in my heart for ten years.

The dream I'd given up love to follow.

The dream I couldn't let the band steal from me the way I'd let them steal away that love.

I had to play along until I figured out the game going on between Balefire and Garrett, a game in which I could end up the biggest loser.

"His food is incredible. If I toured with you, I'd have to buy a whole new wardrobe."

"What's your new idea, Olivia?" Dakota asked, bless him. How they ever finished anything when no one could stay on one topic for more than a minute was a mystery for another day.

"It involves you and more hydraulics. I gather you have a thing for flying, so I think you'll love it." At my cursory description, Dakota sat a little straighter in his chair, and I let a grin tug up the corner of my mouth. Having finished my second slice of seafood pizza, I pointed to the pie in front of Jack. "What flavor is this one?" Though I never ate more than two slices of pizza, the gourmet fare the band's chef provided was more than I could resist.

"Jeff calls it 'Jack's favorite.' All the roasted peppers you can handle," Jack said, a dare in his eyes.

"Bring it."

He tugged a piece free and slid it onto my plate while the rest of the band watched in avid fascination. Only then did I catch on that none of the rest of them appeared to have eaten any of it. Gamely, I sank my teeth into my slice and gave myself a second to test it on my tongue. Serrano, jalapeño, poblano, red chilis, and something hotter—a hint of ghost pepper, maybe? The combination of peppers with the soft tang of Mexican cheese, oregano, and black pepper fired my taste buds. I swallowed the bite and took another, chewed, closed my eyes to find even more flavors, and swallowed. When I blinked my eyes open, the whole table stared back at me.

"That seafood pizza is to die for, but this?" I indicated the two pieces left on the pizza pan with the one in my hand. "This is quite possibly the most intense pizza ever created." Narrowing my gaze in Blu's direction, I asked, "Are you certain I can't poach your chef?"

A laugh burst from Jack. "None of you pussies can get past the first bite, and Olivia wants to steal Jeff to make more for her." He slipped his arm around my shoulder for a one-armed squeeze. "This bunch told me a bit about you before we met, but they left out the best part."

I shot him a question from beneath my brows. "Which is?"

"You're tough enough to hang with us."

"Yeah, until we get serious with the Jameson, right Olivia?" Dakota challenged.

"Not apologizing for that either," I said, smiling at him over my slice of lip-numbing deliciousness before I took another bite.

"Damn. She honestly likes that shit," Blu said, awe in his voice as he watched me eat the rest of my slice.

"Impressive, O. My mama raised us on spicy food, but I can't do more than a bite or two of that particular pizza," Tron said.

Jack abruptly dropped his arm from my shoulder. "Shit. From now on, I suppose I'll have to share."

It was my turn to laugh. "Damn straight. Mind if I wrap a piece up to take home for later?"

Then his words sank in. The only way I'd have to share anything with Balefire was if our working relationship extended beyond this video. In no universe could I see that happening, but for some reason, the band did.

I must have given myself away in my expression because Jack took one look at my face and sobered right up. "Hey, I was messing with you. Jeff makes this for me any time I ask for it. I'm glad there's someone else who enjoys it as much as I do. Help yourself to the rest of it." For emphasis, he slid the last two pieces onto my plate.

A mischievous gleam lit Dakota's eyes as he opened the second bottle of whiskey and poured a shot into the lone glass left in the middle of the table. He reached across the table with it, holding it directly over my plate. Injecting as much long-suffering drama as possible into my sigh, I took the shot from his hand and set it down in front of me.

The man was undeterred. With the precision of long practice, he poured shots of Jameson around the table, slamming the bottle down in the middle after he poured his own shot last. "The song is called 'Dangerous Life.' Time for us to live a little dangerously." Lifting his glass in the air, he added, "Right, Olivia?"

Back when they started, Dave Brubaker, their former drummer, was always the one starting things. Yet when I thought about it, Dakota was never far behind. These days, he was the instigator. Something in his steady stare told me this was more than a dare, though. So I lifted my glass as I stood and reached across the table to clink it with his. He unleashed a genuine smile, and I blinked.

"Thatta girl."

We tossed back our shots, and he refilled our glasses almost before the whiskey could finish its fiery journey down my throat. He called a toast to the video, and the rest of the men joined us. Afterward when he attempted to refill my glass, I was ready, flipping it upside down and slamming it onto the tabletop. "Time to go back to work."

"You're joking, yeah?" Blu said with a chuckle.

"'Fraid not." For a minute, I let myself enjoy the horrified expressions on the band members' faces before I relented. "*I'm* going back to work. You lot will be on set tomorrow at nine a.m. on the dot." I stepped around Jeremy and Garrett and gathered up my oversized purse. "As I understand it, all your ladies are in town with you. I imagine they want to spend some of today with you and vice versa." I glanced down at my lovely pizza then up to my assistant. "Jeremy, would you do me a favor and see if the coffee kiosk has any to-go boxes, please?"

He was headed to the door almost before I finished speaking. "Sure. Should I grab a coffee for you while I'm there?"

"That'd be great. Thanks."

Inwardly, I chastised myself for even hinting to him that his job was on the line when he brainstormed ideas with Garrett behind my back. In hindsight, I should have seen something like that coming, knowing both of them the way I did. I wanted my cocky Wonder Kid back, not this meek creature who jumped before I even said how high.

"Landon—"

Garrett's assistant glanced up from his phone. "Just ordered the town car, sir."

If I hadn't been standing near him, I might have missed Garrett saying, "Fuck sir," under his breath.

Dakota smirked in Garrett's direction, but he only said, "Sweet. I wonder if I can coax Annabelle into skinny-dipping in Parker's pool with me," as he tossed his napkin and paper plate into a nearby trash can.

Watching him, the absurdity of gourmet pizzas served on paper plates hit me, and I frowned. We'd have to be better prepared on set in the future. Yet the band seemed unfazed. Each of them followed Dakota's lead as they cleaned up the detritus of dinner and tossed it in the trash. These guys were superstars, rock legends, and not a one of them played the diva card.

In the studio, they'd blown me away with their precision musicianship and professional approach to recording. Then they reminded me they were still a bunch of boys, flipping each other— and anyone else in the vicinity—as much shit as they could get away with. Now they showed me that no matter how big-time they were, they were still decent men with humility and manners. No wonder they sold out every show they ever played.

Landon consolidated the few slices of leftover pizza onto one pan, stacking it on top of the empty ones in the middle of the table. But the band's shot glasses and the half-full bottle of Jameson went with them as they headed out the door.

"Don't work too late, Boss Lady," Blu said as he brushed past me.

"We need you fresh in the morning," Dakota teased as he traipsed after Blu.

"Looking forward to the shoot tomorrow, O," Tron said, a wicked grin playing over his mouth.

"If you're burning the midnight oil, that pizza warms up real nice," Jack suggested with a nod toward the two slices on the lone plate left on the table.

Landon hung back, waiting for Garrett who said, "Go on and join them. Make the best of a free evening." He glanced over at me. "I have a feeling it's the only one you're getting until the end of the shoot."

His assistant tilted his head, confusion playing over his features, and Garrett nodded emphatically toward the door. With a shrug, Landon followed the band out, meeting Jeremy as he reentered the studio lobby with a couple of to-go boxes and a venti Americano.

"Thanks, Jeremy." I glanced inside one of the boxes to find a handful of cream cups and smiled at him. "You're the best, Wonder Kid."

He blinked at me, and once again, I cringed inwardly. Damn it, it was like kicking a puppy—not that I'd know how kicking a puppy felt firsthand—but my imagination could fill in the blanks as I watched my assistant's expression.

"I'm going to work on an idea I have, but you're good to go. Enjoy your evening."

Surreptitiously, his eyes slid between Garrett and me. "Are you sure you don't need me anymore?"

"Don't worry. You'll have a long to-do list in the morning." I did my best to put a smile in my tone as well as on my face, but Jeremy's shoulders still slumped as he gathered his messenger bag and headed out the door.

Turning to Garrett, I said, "Truly, I'm only going to listen to the tracks the guys laid down to see if my idea is going to work. You don't have to stay."

"What if I want to?"

CHAPTER THIRTEEN

Garrett

FROM THE FIRST day we started working on this project, I'd been trying to find a way to have time alone with Olivia. At first, I'd thought working with her on the script would give us days of time together, but she preempted that with the damn Zoom calls. We did work alone together, but it wasn't what I'd had in mind at all.

After I arrived in LA, she'd made sure to have her assistant with her every time we'd met. As shields went, Jeremy was pretty malleable, but I only took advantage in terms of softening Olivia up about the changes in the script. It never occurred to me she might fire the poor kid over that, but judging from his subdued demeanor the last couple of days, he certainly was in Olivia's doghouse.

After today's recording session with the band, and after filling her belly with Chef Jeff's incredible food, it seemed she might have let her guard down. Sending everyone home—including Jeremy—after dinner gave me the perfect opportunity to have her to myself—at last. I didn't actually have an agenda. I only wanted a little time with her, a chance to discover more about who she was now beyond a kick-ass music director and producer. In ten years, my band manager dreams had never wavered, but this studio Olivia was working so hard to build these days looked a whole bunch different from the dreams she'd had that took her away from me.

"Seriously. You don't have to stay. I'm only going to be listening to some riffs and parts of the song to figure out some timings is all. Probably, it'll bore the hell out of you, Garrett."

I couldn't figure out the puzzled expression on her face. Did she think I wouldn't be interested in her ideas?

"I might have sneaked a few peeks at your doodles in the margins of the script while I ate my first pizza slice," I said.

Her narrow-eyed glare did not bode well for my plan to stick around for the evening.

Before she could call me out, I put my hands up in a slow-down gesture. "I asked if you minded if I sat next to you, and you grunted a sound I took to mean yes." I shoved my hands in my pockets. "But maybe I misunderstood. Maybe that sound had more to do with your singular focus on your work than with tuning in to me sitting beside you." Admitting that she hadn't even noticed me beside her didn't sit well, but I had to swallow that disappointment. One shoulder went up along with the corner of my mouth. "But I saw enough to pique my curiosity." Staring straight into her eyes, equal to equal, I asked, "May I stay?"

She stared back at me, her lips compressed in a thoughtful line. No doubt, she was trying to decipher my angle. Since I wasn't too sure what it was myself, good luck to her figuring it out. Tilting her head to one side, she studied me for a couple seconds and finally said, "Suit yourself." Turning on her heel, she headed to the control room.

Without a word, she seated herself at the main controls and slid a pair of headphones over her ears. I raised my brow then sat on the stool beside her. After consulting her notes, she cued up Jack's drum riff and listened to it four or five times, her eyes closed in concentration. I lost track of the sound in my headphones as I cataloged her features. Time had stripped away the baby fat softness of her cheeks, leaving behind a classic angular beauty. The contours of her cheeks didn't even need the barest hint of the makeup she wore to highlight them. Though square and strong, her jaw had a feminine quality that always drew my eyes to her mouth. Her lips were so plush and rosy they begged for a kiss. I remembered a time when I didn't even have to ask if I could kiss them.

Long lashes rested on the tops of her cheeks, her real ones, not the trendy Hollywood fakes. My fingers tingled with the need to brush the pads of them over her skin to discover if it was as satiny as it looked. She blinked her eyes open and caught me staring at her.

For a long second, our eyes locked, and memories swirled in my head, taking me back to her tiny student apartment at Denver University.

In my mind's eye, the two of us were naked in Olivia's narrow bed, our eyes locked as I took my time moving inside her, long, languid strokes as she tightened herself around me. My fingers entwined with hers as I held her hands down on either side of her head on the pillow, her hair fanned out in a silky halo. She planted her feet on the mattress on either side of me so she could lift her hips to move with me. Skin to skin, our bodies did all the talking as we made easy, slow love. All around us, the sunset bathed the walls of her bedroom in golden light. Never before—or since—had I experienced a sense of such profound belonging to anyone. She was mine. And I was hers.

The golden green of her eyes in this moment took me back. There had been a time when her changeable eyes had only ever looked at me with that golden light in them. How had I let that go?

With a blink and a slight shake of her head, she ended the memory, as if she too had experienced it with me.

"If Jack extends that riff for two more bars, we can build the scene behind him with the urban jungle clip from the film, the one where Parker Malone is moving in the shadows. It'll add an element of suspense right before Blu drops back in with the 'Wanted out, but she's there' lyric. What do you think?"

Shifting on my stool, I bought a second to shut my libido down and give her idea the consideration it deserved. I nodded to her to play the track again, and this time I listened as I let her sketch play out in my mind. Setting my headphones aside, I said, "May I see your script?"

Wordlessly, she passed it to me, careful to make sure our fingers didn't touch. I let that go—for now. A pen appeared in her hand as if by magic, and she passed that to me as well. An involuntary grin slid over my lips. The long gap in our time together hadn't interrupted our rhythms in the least.

"What about using the scene right after that one where he's playing cat-and-mouse with Jennifer's character in the warehouse? It fits the riff without extending the song."

At her raised brow, I added, "Radio still likes the shorter songs. They give them more airplay. If we can make your point, add the suspense with the riff, and still keep the song to four minutes or less, we all win." I touched the pen to the script, waiting for her decision.

"I see your point." A drawn-out sigh escaped her. "It's just that— Jennifer Hartwell irritates the hell out of me, to be honest." Dipping her head, she slid me a frown. "I kind of only want to use the clips of Parker on his own and the chase scenes."

A chuckle slipped out. "If the band could hear you now."

The furrow in her brow deepened. "Why?"

"They aren't Jennifer Hartwell fans either."

She reared back a bit on her stool. "But I thought Dakota was staying at Parker's house during the shoot."

"He is. *Parker's* place."

With a tilt of her head, she asked, "Doesn't Jennifer live with him?"

I snorted. "She wishes. She also wishes she'd hooked up with one or more members of Balefire."

Olivia's eyes rounded. "*What?*"

"She's a piece of work, that one."

"But—"

Shrugging, I said, "She's still kind of old-school. All publicity is good publicity. Except that's not so true in this day and age." A niggle of guilt had me repositioning myself on the metal stool, its padding suddenly inadequate.

"So she and Parker aren't a thing?"

"Nope."

"But they were while they filmed the movie, right?"

"Not according to Dakota. But Parker didn't put up much of a fuss when she attached herself to him like Velcro the few times they hung out with us on the last US tour. They're actors, so who even knows?"

"Maybe I can bleed the clip a bit, cross-fade it into the part where we focus on Blu and Dakota in their camouflage tuxes without adding any extra bars to Jack's drum solo." Absently, she tugged the script from me and produced a pen seemingly out of midair. Her tongue slipped out of the corner of her mouth as she crossed off some scribbles and added others.

How many times had I caught her focusing this exact same way and sneaked a taste of that tongue?

Shaking my head to clear my wayward thoughts, I said, "What about shortening the urban jungle clip a touch and editing in a two-second shot of Jennifer watching from the shadows right before that cross-fade?"

"A minute ago, I thought we established how none of us likes the woman. If I could keep her out of the video entirely, I would." A black cloud drifted over Olivia's face for a second before she glanced back down to the script.

"The thing is, O, she's the reason the band even wrote the song. During her tag-alongs on the last tour, she wore the guys down until they finally agreed to write and perform the song on the movie."

Clearing my throat, I added, "We kind of need to include at least one clip of her by herself in the video."

Olivia narrowed her eyes. "What are you up to, Garrett?"

Fuck. How was it that when no one else could ever read me, Olivia could see inside me like staring through glass, even after all these years?

Pushing my hands in front of me in a simmer-down gesture, I deflected. "Hey, now."

"Don't you 'simmer-down' to me, Garrett Phillips." She glared at my hands. "A lot is riding on this video for so many people. Now tell me what side hustle you've got going."

"None."

Her brows went up.

"I swear. No side hustle at all. Only, this is Jennifer's movie. To stop the rumors before they can start, we might want to include her in the video, if only for one short clip. That's all."

The gold in her eyes turned almost to brown as they glittered at me, her tell that she wasn't buying my bullshit at all, and I held my breath. Then she shrugged and added more scribbles to the script. "I need the focus to stay on the music and the quality of the video. We'll add one and a half seconds of Jennifer in shadow cross-fading into the band playing the next verse in the song." She glanced up from her notes. "This is for the band and my studio. Whatever game you're playing behind the sets, it better not come back to bite me in the ass."

"Trust me, O. I'd never do anything—ever—to hurt you."

A long beat ticked between us, before she gave me a pass. She slipped her headphones back over her ears, consulted her notes, and slid the controls to another section of the song. This time, Dakota's improvised guitar riff right past the bridge soared through my headphones. The man truly was a sorcerer when he picked up his axe. No matter how long I managed Balefire—and due to Dakota, the jury was still out on how long that would be—I'd never figure out where the notes came from. He could conjure the most impossible sounds from a guitar, from hauntingly sweet melodies to heart-pounding, head-banging riffs you couldn't help but move to. That musicianship came from some deep place in the marrow of his bones and had drawn me to the band—and away from Olivia. Even after everything that had gone down in the last couple of years, it still tethered me to the band.

The "Dangerous Life" solo Dakota had dreamed up on the fly resonated with breath-catching suspense as he ran up to a note and held it, like teetering on the edge of a cliff. A second later, his fingers raced up and down his fretboard, the notes flying at supersonic speed. Every time I'd watched him perform this solo, I wondered how the neck of his guitar didn't catch fire.

"I want to focus on Dakota's hands as he plays the solo, overlaying it with him rising into space with a flash of flames projected on the green screen as we hold the shot for a second. Then we'll jump-cut to Tron in the flight simulator as Blu sings the 'Dance along the edge of a knife/Ain't no justice in this dangerous life' lyric. Thoughts?" she asked.

For a second, I pretended to consider her idea. A brief contraction of her brow prompted me that this wasn't a game. "I love it." Reaching for the controls, I reset the sound to Dakota's solo. At the penultimate point, I stopped the music. "What about shooting the scene from a track setup so the camera rises and stops with Dakota 'playing' from the top of the observatory. That way, it appears if he takes a step in any direction, he'll tumble to his death. Stop his hydraulics at that point, but let the camera continue to rise as the flames engulf him?"

Tapping her pen against her lips, she thought about my idea. "We'll have to change his costume, which necessitates additional shots…" She scribbled something on the script then her eyes locked with mine. "I've been trying to come up with the best way to convey the idea of dangerous life specific to the band and the song, and I think your idea nails it. Dakota 'falls'"—she air quoted—"and Tron rises like a phoenix from the flames. Blu drops in with the lyrics—this time from behind Jack and without his guitar, both of them in the camouflage tuxes as the chase scene plays behind them."

Her pen flew across the script.

"Do you think Blu would be up for a bit of choreography? Or would that be too off-brand?"

"Depends on what you have in mind."

"I was thinking Jack could do some of those fancy moves with tossing and twirling his sticks and we could cross-fade into Blu dancing with a woman in a red dress, something at half speed and seductive as he sings 'Salvation wears a red dress/If we can escape this.'"

This woman. Her ideas for the video blew me away when we were working on the script, but clearly, she'd held back a few.

"Blu will be all over that." A thought struck me. "What if instead of using a union dancer, we ask Cristy?"

"Cristy Valor?" She shot me a what-the-fuck-is-wrong-with-you glare from beneath her brows. "The video is going to stand on its own merit, not on rumor and innuendo. Didn't we already establish that?"

"Sorry. I was just thinking about how well the woman dances and the illusions she creates on stage."

"The dancer needs to be someone anonymous." She pulled out her phone and started scrolling.

Seeing another chance, I said, "What about Blu's fiancée? She's the right build, Blu would definitely dance seductively with her, and she's anonymous."

Olivia's brow went up. "Why are you so determined the dancer has to be someone associated with the band?"

"We came up with the idea a minute ago, but we film next week. On such short notice…" I shrugged. "Just trying to save time and money. The ladies are here in town with the band, so I thought—"

"It would be good to stay in-house, so to speak."

"Exactly."

"You're the one who knows her. Do you think she'd want to do it?"

A picture of Ashleigh Baker and her pen and notebook flashed through my head. No, she'd probably want to do about anything else than to be seen in a video. But the offer could go a long ways toward repairing relationships I'd fucked up in one way or another. All the memories assaulting me as I'd watched Olivia in action had me thinking I needed to step up and make amends. It might be too little too late, but it was worth a shot.

"All we can do is ask. If she's not interested, we use whoever you were looking for a minute ago." I pointed to the phone in her hand.

With a nod, she slid her headphones over her ears again. Since the annotations I'd read over her shoulder had only pertained to these two parts of the song, I was curious about where she was going next. So I followed her lead and watched in fascination as her eyes closed and her shoulders relaxed on the opening riffs of "Dangerous Life." We must have listened to the song a bare minimum of thirty times during the recording session alone. But the expression on her face said this time she was listening purely to enjoy it. I sneaked a peek at the track she'd chosen, and surprise flowed through me. It was Nick's third or fourth choice, but as I closed my eyes and keyed in on the sound, I started to hear nuances that weren't there in the other versions.

By the time Jack emphatically ended the song on a rolling down-beat, I knew Olivia was going with that version. Further, she wasn't going to be persuaded by the band's producer—or by the band them-selves—to use a different track. I also knew I was going to support her. A subtlety in the way Dakota's guitar blended with Blu's vocals on her chosen version reached even farther into the gut than any of the others. This was the hit version, the one that was going to win the band the Oscar I promised when I talked them into giving Jen-nifer Hartwell what she wanted.

Olivia's expression as she blinked at me banished all thoughts of the band, the movie, and the song. So much rode on the success of this video, but in this moment, all I could think about was the way golden rings surrounded her pupils, the hitch in her breathing, and the soft parting of her lips.

Chapter Fourteen

Olivia

THE ENTIRE VIDEO played through my mind as I listened to "Dangerous Life" for at least the thousandth time or maybe the thirtieth since the first recording session after lunch. Suspense and seduction played out in front of a soundtrack of Blu Connolly's panty-melting vocals, Dakota Perri's soul-stealing guitar riffs, Adam Tron's virtuoso bass rhythms, and Jack Whitehorse's heart-pounding drumming. When Jack's sticks ended the song on a downbeat, it was all I could do to keep from crossing my legs and giving away the orgasm threatening to wash over me.

Especially since the scene playing in my head substituted Garrett for the tuxedo-clad spy and me as the woman in the red dress, dancing him away to safety. I blinked my eyes open and fell into two pools of molten steel as Garrett stared back at me. For a brief second, his gaze dropped to my lips, and I couldn't control the hitch in my breath. Our eyes locked and I squeezed my thighs together until my bones almost touched. My clit throbbed. My pussy pulsed in anticipation of enjoying his hard length inside me.

The rational side of my brain clamored for me to pay attention, to focus on the *former* part of former lover. But it was too late for that. He sat so close that if I turned slightly, he'd have to spread his knees to avoid knocking mine. The citrusy musk of his cologne, though faint after a long day in the studio, reached my nose, and I wanted to bury my face in his neck and breathe in as much of that scent as I could.

Garrett's nostrils flared, and he shifted on his stool. His eyes remained locked to mine as he slid his headphones from his head and set them aside. Cursing the tiny tremor in my hands, I removed my headphones and set them somewhere on the control board beside me.

"Olivia."

My name on his lips rasped over me like calloused hands over my skin. Involuntary shivers rippled through me, and I clamped my thighs even tighter together.

I stopped whatever he wanted to say next with my finger pressed to his full lips. For a long moment, neither of us moved. Then he reached up and smoothed his fingers up my palm and higher along the length of my fingers. His eyes dipped to our hands. Though we barely touched, sensations like electric currents sparked every nerve, beginning in my hand and arcing up my arm to trip my heart nearly into arrhythmia. My breath caught as he slid his fingers through mine, up and down, up and down, before he twined our hands together with a gentle squeeze. I closed my eyes and worked to find some air.

He let me go only enough to draw light circles over my palm with his fingertips. The electricity flashing through my body from his touch threatened to set me on fire, and to my everlasting mortification, a whimper escaped me. My eyes flew to his, and I clamped my teeth down hard on my bottom lip. The gray of his eyes deepened to shimmering steel, mirroring the molten desire coursing through me. I couldn't have torn my gaze from his if a thousand screaming Balefire fans suddenly raced through the room.

Though he focused his fingers' exquisite torture only on my palm, I felt them inside my soaked panties. This time when a moan escaped my throat, a tiny smile tugged at the corner of his mouth. The pads of his fingers slid down to the inside of my wrist where my heart pulsed hard and insistent against his touch. His smile stretched across his full lips while his eyes remained locked on mine.

I couldn't help but to squirm on my stool, and Garrett took advantage, gliding his fingers between mine again. Up and down. Up and down. Slow and easy. In and out. Up and down. Beads of sweat broke out on my forehead, and my breath stuttered in my chest. When he leaned forward only enough to leave a lingering kiss in the middle of my palm, I cried out.

"Garrett!"

Laughter rumbled deep in his chest even as his tongue slipped out to tickle my skin. His eyes held me captive as he plied his tongue over my hand the way I remembered he liked to use it on my clit. His dark laughter greeted the sigh that gusted from me as if he knew exactly where his touch had sent my thoughts. Then he brushed his lips over my skin once more and gently lowered my hand to my lap.

"You haven't forgotten how good we were together either, have you, O?" Though the tone of his words was playful, something deeper, darker, more insistent flashed in the steel-gray depths of his eyes.

That flash of desire scared me back into the present and what was riding on the absolute success of this venture. I couldn't let a momentary longing for a different outcome to our past derail the importance of keeping my professional distance in the moment. Garrett was dangerous.

"We're different people now." I hated the breathy way I uttered the truth. "We can't go back to those two starry-eyes kids with unreasonable expectations."

He hiked a brow. "Those two kids didn't have enough experience to figure out their dreams weren't mutually exclusive."

"Don't even think about trying to start something," I warned him.

A smirk twitched his lips. "Because you're seeing someone else right now?"

"No—I mean, yes." I cleared my throat and busied myself with gathering my notes and stuffing them into my purse. "We have an important job to do here. You and the band are clients, and I have a strict policy about never getting involved with clients."

He ran a hand over his mouth and down his gorgeously perfect square jaw. "I see." His tone said he didn't believe me for a second.

Damn it.

The soaked state of my panties combined with the echoes of "Dangerous Life" playing in my head after our little interlude a moment ago said he was right not to believe me. This was exactly why I had to leave the studio right this minute, put some distance between the past and the present. Not only couldn't I trust myself, I also clearly couldn't trust Garrett not to push whatever had just happened between us to a different conclusion.

Holding the door open to the lobby, I said, "That's it for tonight. Time to lock up."

"So I need to leave, is that it?"

Deliberately, he walked past me as close as possible without touching me. Yet the air around us vibrated with unfulfilled desire, and my body shivered from my scalp to my soles. Forcing myself to ignore what he did to me physically, and denying any emotional response whatsoever, I switched off the lights in the control room and studio and locked up. While we'd worked on my ideas for the video, the night staff had made a pass through the lobby, stowing the table and chairs we'd used for dinner and emptying the trash. Garrett chuckled when I retrieved the box of Chef Jeff's delectable pizza from the reception desk. With a shrug, I shot him a did-you-think-I'd-leave-this stare and headed for the outer door.

"Want me to hold that for you?" he asked with a grin as I struggled to locate the keys in my purse while holding on to my prize.

Having nowhere to set the box down, I huffed out a "Fine" and let him hold it for the five seconds it took me to find my keys and lock up. Playfully, he pretended to tug the box from my grip when he handed it back to me, and I might have growled at him. While he enjoyed Jeff Scott's food on the regular, this was a treat for me, one I did not intend to share.

He slipped his hands into the back pockets of his jeans and slid me a side-eye. "You're not sharing, I take it."

How did he *do* that? It had been far too many years for him to still be able to read me so well.

"Nope."

Falling into step beside me, he coaxed, "Even if I pick up a bottle of red?"

After what had happened in the control room, I had no doubt what would follow if I split a pizza and a bottle of wine with him. We had that in our history too.

"Especially not then."

"Olivia." A warning warred with a plea in his voice.

"Like I said, Garrett, I don't get involved with clients. There's too much at stake."

"So your studio head isn't a client?"

"Stop fishing."

We'd reached the front door of the building housing my entire professional world. A night guard greeted us. "Hello, Miss Carter. Another late night at the office for you." He saluted Garrett with a hand to his head. "Sir."

I smiled. The guy was a human mountain and, as one of my first hires when I signed the lease on the studio, someone I trusted implicitly. "As usual, Seth. Thanks for locking up behind us."

Seth nodded and grabbed the door. I sailed past him with my pizza prize gripped in two hands while Garrett followed me out into the parking lot. A heavy metallic thud signaled the security of my space as Seth turned his key in the lock behind us.

My car waited about ten steps away, and I wasted no time reaching it. After setting the pizza box on the roof, I went on another treasure hunt in my purse for my car keys. Someday, I needed to take the time to organize myself so I could find my keys without so much fanfare. Probably would be safer too. I slid the box onto the passenger seat, closed the door, and headed around the front of my car. All the time, I could sense Garrett's eyes on me like laser heat on my shoulder blades and then on the side of my face.

"You're really not inviting me to share that pizza, huh?" he asked as he leaned against the door of my car, his arms stacked on the roof. "You could offer me a ride to my hotel, at least."

"I did."

Consternation pinched his features. "When?"

"I hit my ride app and ordered you a car." On cue, lights flashed through the parking lot, the low rumble of a BMW growing louder as the car approached. I shrugged at his narrowed eyes. "Your hotel is in the opposite direction from my apartment. Ordering you a car made sense."

"Did it, now?"

His ride pulled up beside us, the class of the sleek black BMW 850 overwhelming my humble used sedan whose silver paint looked more gray than expensive.

"I'll see you tomorrow, then." He slapped the roof of my car twice and stepped over to the hired car. Aiming one last dazzling smile my way, he disappeared inside, clicking the door shut behind him.

The taillights of the car lit up the night as I let out the breath I'd practically held since we walked out of the studios. After that play he made in the control room, I had no idea how he'd react to my obvious attempt to put distance—so much distance—between us. Though he didn't put up an argument, that parting smile told me the games had only begun. The thought terrified and thrilled me in equal measure.

Oh, boy, was I in trouble.

♪

It was midnight when I unlocked the door and entered my studio apartment. My stomach rumbled, and I remembered that I hadn't eaten since I told the band and crew we were done for the night. That had been hours ago, and the heavenly scent of peppers and cheese had tormented me the whole drive home.

Normally, when I returned home hungry after a late night at work, I'd have ignored my stomach, downed a glass of water, and gone to bed. Tonight, I popped the smallest leftover slice of Chef Jeff's pizza into the microwave and tucked the rest of the temptation into the fridge. Sitting at my two-person-size island, I nibbled my treat and rehashed the day in my head.

No matter how hard I focused on the video shoot and the song, pictures of Garrett insisted on interrupting. Shifting on my barstool drew my attention to the state of my panties, and I growled at myself. I'd had other men's hands on me—with the added incentive of their mouths on mine and both of us consenting to what was going to happen next—and I hadn't been as turned on as when Garrett brushed his fingertips over my palm. It had been ten freaking *years*. How could he still affect me this much?

More importantly, why did he even bother with his little seduction? I'd given in on the script changes. We'd added the addendum to the contract. He'd had his way, so he had no incentive for that charade this evening. With the clarity of a bit of time and distance and being in my own space, it occurred to me he was up to something. Back when we were in love, he was always scheming, always working an angle. It was how he managed to go from ground zero to catapulting Balefire to the top of the charts in less than half the time it took for nearly every other big-name group in the history of rock. I admired his skill, his tenacity, his ability to play his cards close to his chest and lay down a winning hand at the exact perfect moment. But this time, he was scheming *me*, and I worried about his angle. I couldn't afford even a whiff of scandal associated with my studio, not in these crucial early days.

My pizza gone, my mouth pleasantly on fire, and my thoughts in turmoil, I set my dirty plate in the sink and headed to bed. Beginning with my offending panties, I peeled off my clothes and tossed them in the laundry basket at the foot of my bed. After scrubbing my face and slipping into my favorite night shirt, the one that read, "There is no sunrise so beautiful it's worth waking me up to see it," I grabbed the romance novel I'd been reading and tucked myself into bed.

A too short time later, my alarm forced me awake in time to see the sunrise as visions of Garrett Phillips doing all sorts of dirty lovely things to me swirled through my head. I picked up the book that had fallen to the bed beside me and threw it across the room then threw myself back against my pillows. It wasn't my reading choice that had put those dreams in my head. Staring at the ceiling, I repeated my new mantra over and over until my snooze alarm went off: "I will resist Garrett Phillips. I will resist Garrett Phillips. I will resist Garrett Phillips."

Chapter Fifteen

Garrett

M
Y DAY STARTED with a phone call from Jennifer Hartwell.

In other words, it began in the shitter. It could only go up from there.

Nope.

Jack and Blu joined me in the lobby of our hotel. Both of them were sipping our head road engineer's special green-smoothie hangover cure from go-cups, which told me exactly what happened when they left Olivia's studio with that bottle of Jameson the night before. They grunted a greeting, slid into the back of the town car, and tipped their heads back on the cushions. We rode in silence on our way to pick up Tron from Cristy Valor's place. As if by magic, Blu produced another go-cup of hangover cure, handing it to Tron when he slid onto the back seat of the town car with a groan. At least we were all going to be on time.

Not.

Dakota rolled in forty-five minutes after the rest of us. The bags under his eyes reminded me of a basset hound, but his nasty demeanor was more of a cornered grizzly. The rest of the band was almost finished in makeup and wardrobe, not that it mattered. The shoot couldn't start without him, and it was going to take makeup more than a minute to fix whatever he'd done to himself the night before. Worst of all, I couldn't call him out on it, at least not without serious repercussions. The thin ice beneath my feet where the band was concerned didn't leave me much support for managing them the way I'd successfully done in the past.

"Landon," I said to my assistant who stood beside me reading over something on his iPad.

"On it, sir."

Before I could remind him about that damned "sir," he was already out of earshot. Minutes later, I watched him walk into the makeup room carrying a go-cup filled with the special hangover cure. Hopefully, it wouldn't only improve Dakota's attitude but also his looks. The guy looked like death warmed over.

"I hope this isn't going to be a daily occurrence during the shoot," Olivia said as she strolled up to me.

Feigning a nonchalance I was far from feeling, I asked, "Are you saying you've never seen this with a rock band before?"

"The all-night parties might work when you're touring, but that's not how a film unit functions. We're on a tight deadline for your purposes, Garrett. If you want us to meet it, the band needs to be on time and ready to shoot. Perhaps you will convey that to them?"

A prickly boss lady had replaced the soft-eyed woman I'd accompanied out of the control room the previous evening. I wanted my Olivia back, the one who looked at me like she could eat me whole rather than this suspicious woman bristling at me about deadlines.

"Hey, hey, it's me, remember?"

The glare she shot me was like a knife to my solar plexus. Still, I took a chance, reaching a hand to her arm. My caress met vibrating cement instead of soft woman, but she didn't flinch away. "What happened since last night? I thought we were on the same page."

"I don't know what this is"—her eyes dipped to where my hand remained on her arm—"but you and I"—for a tiny second she softened then drew in a breath and tensed again—"are ten years beyond being on the 'same page' as you're implying."

Her words stung like a slap across the face, which I must have given away if the flash of pain in her eyes was any indicator. That tiny slip shouldn't have given me any hope with her, but life had taught me the only way forward was to believe I could make things happen.

Yet pushing her at this particular moment would be a monumentally bad move.

Shoving a hand through my hair, I said, "Yeah, yeah. I'll talk to the band about being on time." Like that would do any good.

She glanced over to the stage where her team waited with the three band members who'd arrived with me. After a short perusal of her notes, she headed over to the crew. With my hands on my hips, I blew a breath at the ground and followed her.

"Hey, you saw the way they worked yesterday. They're pros."

Her brow nearly disappeared into her hairline.

"It won't happen again. I'll see to it."

As though we hadn't spoken at all, she focused her attention on her crew. "Let's dial in the cameras for the opening scene with the band walking into the bar," she said as she walked over to the stage.

"Don't we need Dakota for that?" Blu asked.

"To shoot it, yes. To set it up, you three are fine. When you walk in, be suave, understated. Play it as though everyone knows you own the world, so you don't need to advertise."

She donned her headset and hoisted herself up onto her stool, which only emphasized the perfect tightness of her jeans across her lovely round ass. Rather than downplaying her assets, the sleeveless turtleneck she wore showed off her gorgeous, mouthwatering curves. I shouldn't have paid so much attention to how enticing she looked when she was so obviously put out with the band—and apparently with me—but Olivia Carter had blown me away with her effortless beauty from the first time I'd laid eyes on her. Even though we'd been apart for years, that hadn't changed.

A tap against my bicep alerted me to Jeremy standing beside me with another headset in his hands. With a "Thanks, man," I settled it on my head and sat on a stool a couple of feet away from Olivia. The guys awaited their cue right outside the door to the "bar," a *Casino Royale*-style affair. When she called action, they sauntered in one by one and took their marks. Pride swelled in my chest at how professional Jack, Blu, and Tron acted even when they were still working through the side effects of their we're-back-in-LA celebration.

Taking her time, she perused the lighting and angle of the scene. With a nod to the cinematographer, she said, "It's a start. When we begin filming, I'll need something more atmospheric. The mood we're going for in this opening shot is suspenseful, kinda brooding, you know?"

The cinematographer, an older woman with an iron-gray ponytail and a squinty-eyed stare, tilted her head at the screen, made an adjustment to the main camera, and nodded. About that time, Dakota sauntered out to the stage and immediately threw a tantrum.

"What the fuck? You're filming the scene without me?"

Blu stepped to the edge of the area. "Light and sound checks only, man."

"With the way you looked when you walked in, we all thought it might be an hour in makeup for you." Jack smirked.

Dakota flipped him the bird. "You partied as hard as I did, asshole." He mugged in front of the nearest camera, turning his face this way and that, straightening his bow tie, and flicking his cuffs. "I look damn fine this morning." Shooting a pointed stare at Olivia, he added, "I'd look even better if you moved the start time back to eleven, or maybe noon."

She leveled him with a steely-eyed stare. "You liked the changes we made in the script, right? The ones that added to your solo and featured you in the bridge?"

"Fuckin' A! Those are Bad. Ass." He stood a little taller.

"In order to film those with any sort of quality in the time frame we have for the observatory and the loan of the flight simulator, we need to start work in the morning." Her gaze dropped to her watch and back up to him. "Last night, you said you understood that."

"Jesus, Olivia, when did you turn into such a hard-ass?" He joined the rest of the band on the stage. "Next time, let's make sure to invite the director to the party, guys. Keep her loose, maybe even fun." His conspiratorial stage whisper added insult.

If I hadn't been so tuned into her, I might have missed the tiny flinch at Dakota's words. Generally, he was the class clown, the fun guy everyone wanted to have around. But ever since our last tour, his cynicism held a nasty edge, one I probably deserved, but Olivia damn sure didn't.

"Knock it off, Dakota. You don't get to take out your fuckup on everyone else."

"That's rich, coming from you," he shot back. If looks could kill, I'd have been ashes on the floor.

Ever the peacekeeper, Tron stepped in. "Not the way we want to start this off, boys." His attention drifted to Olivia. "You'll have to excuse us, O. We maybe had a little too much LA last night. We'll save the next one till the end of the shoot." Glancing around at the rest of the band, his eyes coming to rest on Dakota, he added, "Right?"

After waiting a beat, Dakota strolled back over to Olivia. "Tron's right. We have a plan, and it doesn't include taking out a hangover on you. I'll be on time tomorrow." He stuck out his hand. With a bemused expression, she reached out and they shook. "But you have to promise to join us at the after-party—and you don't get to stop at two shots."

The unholy light in his eyes didn't bode well for my gorgeous ex-girlfriend, and something inside me shifted. Before I could call him out for having his own lady, the one in question took care of herself.

"I'll attend the after-party, but how much I imbibe is up to me."

"Oooh, 'imbibe.' I love it when someone uses twenty-dollar words." Running his index finger beneath his collar, he said, "Makes me hot."

Olivia laughed. "Knock it off, Dakota."

"Looks like she still has your number, dude," Tron called from the stage.

"The smart ones usually do." With a smirk, Dakota turned on his heel and joined the others on the stage.

Olivia directed them to reenter the bar, the cinematographer adjusted the lighting, the sound tech played the opening bars of "Dangerous Life" over the sound system, and the shoot was underway. Time flew as I watched a consummate professional draw emotion and depth from a group of twenty-somethings whose entire lives were all about the party, playing music, and having a good time. Though playing and recording music was serious business, and every member of Balefire took the music seriously, they were still boys at heart. Everything they did was about fun. In ten years of touring and working with them, I couldn't recall a time when they played a video straight.

Olivia wasn't a taskmaster, but her quiet, focused steadiness lent a gravitas to the work that rubbed off on the guys. Either that, or the green smoothies hadn't worked as fast as usual. When at last she called a break for lunch, it was obvious to anyone on the set that she'd created an opening scene that rivaled anything Hartwell Studios had produced in the ten years since they won their Academy Award.

"You're pretty incredible, you know that?" I said for her ears only when I stepped up behind her in the lunch buffet line. In a move that didn't surprise me at all, she'd insisted the band and the rest of the crew precede her, which made it easy for me to find a minute mostly alone with her.

A tiny shiver stole over her, one she tried to pass off as something it wasn't. "You startled me. Did you already eat?"

"Was waiting for you."

"You didn't need to do that. You're the client, so you should be first."

"You've ignored me all morning, so—"

An exasperated sigh fluttered from her full, rosy lips. "I was *working*, doing the job you and the band hired me to do."

"And working hard to ignore me sitting right beside you."

She grabbed a plate and ignored me again as she perused the spread her team had laid out along a narrow table on the lot right outside the studio where we'd worked all morning. It must have been Greek day on the menu as authentic Greek gyros and an artful array of kebabs were arranged first. Platters of tomato and zucchini fritters had been fairly well raided by the diners ahead of us, but a few were still left with a dab of tzatziki sauce to dress them. A couple of massive bowls of Greek salad and trays of crudités followed the entrées with a mouthwatering assortment of desserts including baklava waiting at the end of the long table. We made our choices, and I followed her to a table where the ever-present Jeremy already sat.

I didn't need special powers to know she was avoiding me, but I didn't give her the chance to push me away. Taking the seat opposite her assistant, I left her no choice but to sit between us at the table for four. With a smile, I moved the Americano with extra cream in front of her plate.

"Greek food is one of my favorites. Did you remember that, O?" I asked, deliberately using the nickname I'd given her back when we were still us. Smoothing my napkin over my lap, I cut into a tomato fritter, dipped it in sauce, and took a bite, my eyes on hers as I chewed and swallowed. "Mmm, these are delicious."

A rosy glow tinged her high cheekbones, but she gave her attention to her assistant. "Thanks for the coffee, Wonder Kid. I needed it." Savoring a sip with her eyes closed didn't fool me for a second.

After swallowing another bite of fritter in tzatziki, I directed my conversation across the table. "Did you know that Olivia and I were dating when I discovered Balefire?"

She choked on the second sip of coffee, and I reached over to pat her back. "You okay there, O?" I asked at the same time Jeremy said, "You two dated?"

Composing herself with a glare in my direction, she said, "It was a long time ago."

"Doesn't feel like it though, does it?" My eyes strayed to her pillowy lips, and I wanted nothing more than to taste her coffee on them.

"Is everything ready for the next scene? We're shooting it as the band plays, so we need all the track cameras and gimbals in place."

It had started to dawn on me she intended to ignore me even when we sat at lunch together. *Fuck that.*

Jeremy's eyes ping-ponged between his boss and me, his questions right there, but self-preservation won the day. "Yeah, the concert scene is all ready to go on the other stage."

"Super. Thanks." She tucked into her kebabs, dunking succulent lamb into tzatziki and closing her mouth around her fork, slowly dragging it from her mouth as though to torture me.

Leaning over the table, my shoulder a breath from hers, I whispered, "We know each other too well for whatever it is you think you're doing."

"I'm not the one who's up to something, Garrett," she shot back under her breath.

My phone buzzed in the back pocket of my jeans. When I fished it out, Jennifer Hartwell's name flashed on the screen. I clicked the off button and shoved it back into my pocket.

"Who are *you* ignoring?" she asked.

"No one important.

"That begs an entirely different question."

"I'm not involved with anyone," I said quietly, locking my eyes on hers. "In fact, there's been no one special for a very long time."

"Then what's that all about?" she asked, pointing her fork in the direction of where I'd returned my phone to my pocket.

"Work related, and not something I need to deal with right now."

Landon chose that moment to interrupt. "Jennifer Hartwell is on the phone. I told her you were busy, but"—he shrugged—"she's Jennifer Hartwell," like that explained everything.

Which it did, damn it.

Chapter Sixteen

Olivia

GARRETT LEFT HIS lunch half-eaten when he stepped away to take the call from Jennifer Hartwell. As small mercies went, I'd take it. He goaded me as though he saw inside me and determined to make me recant my new mantra concerning him, which turned my lovely lunch to dust in my mouth. Staring down at my plate, I gave myself a mental slap. I hadn't thought about Greek being one of his favorite foods when I'd ordered it from the caterers for our first lunch on set. No wonder he pushed me. I stabbed a cucumber slice and stuffed it in my mouth.

"What?" I barked when I caught Jeremy's open-mouthed stare.

He clamped his lips together and shook his head. "Nothing." He stood from the table. "I'll head over to the other set and, uh, check on things."

Poking through my salad for another slice of cucumber, I thought, *You're batting zero for two, Olivia. Get your head back in the game.*

I finished lunch by myself and wondered what to do with Garrett's half-eaten plate of food. With a shrug, I decided he was a big boy who could figure out his priorities himself. Stacking our plates on top of each other, I carried them over to the table where a group of people loaded them in containers to return to their kitchen for washing. Hitching my bag higher up on my shoulder, I settled myself for a moment before striding over to the second soundstage for the afternoon shoot.

♪

With their instruments in their hands, the guys were on a completely different plane. Either that or having a good meal and a few hours to metabolize their party improved their energy levels. Whatever it was, they were on fire. After a single walk-through, we shot the band scene in one long take. Experience with other videos taught me not to trust it would be enough, though, so we shot the scene again.

The second take was even better, the sound tighter, their stage antics more dangerous. Dakota literally ran up the side of an amp and flipped backward while not missing a note. At one point in his solo, Jack didn't miss a beat when he stood and performed a spin while his sticks pirouetted in the air above him. Blu and Tron staged an unscripted miniscene where they were two spies backing up to each other. When they met, they pushed their backs against each other and slowly lowered to the floor and back up then turned and faced each other with a nod. Blu's voice never wavered. Tron's bass beats powered the band's sound, and he never dropped a single note.

Throughout the song, I called directions into my headset. "Roll camera one back along the track. Spin camera two around Dakota. Grab that overhead shot above Jack. Zoom in on Tron and Blu." By the time Jack's final downbeat evanesced into air, my heart pounded like I'd sprinted flat out for two miles. Into my mic, I said to Sarah, my cinematographer, "I hope we got all that."

Her smoker's voice rasped drily in my ear. "Of course we did." More quietly, she added, "Jesus. These boys are something else."

The light citrusy scent I was coming to associate with Garrett wafted over my left shoulder, my only warning. Gently, he tugged my headset aside and set his lips close to my ear. "They had that in them the first time I saw them play. It's what I wanted you to see back then."

I couldn't decide if he was calling me out or trying to make me wish I'd made different choices or what.

Sliding my headset down around my neck, I turned to him. "You're right. Balefire was legit from the get-go. Doesn't change the trajectories of our separate dreams." Though I aimed to keep my voice even, a tiny wobble slipped in anyway. Pulling in a breath, I injected more professionalism into my tone. "And here we are, all working together after all."

Something I couldn't read flashed in the gray steel of Garrett's eyes, but I didn't have a chance to pursue it. The four members of Balefire stood on the edge of the stage, grinning their heads off and demanding my attention.

"You like that, O?" Tron asked.

"Fuckin' A, she did," Dakota answered for me. "How could she not?"

"Exactly," Blu added.

Jack only contributed a nod, but his wicked smile said it all.

No wonder women threw their bras and panties at these guys at every one of their shows. For a minute there after that second take, I wondered if maybe cynical Sarah might even toss her bra at them.

"I never doubted for a second that you guys are the real deal. Now I have to decide how to splice some of those antics in with what we've scripted out at the observatory."

"You'll figure it out," Blu said with a wink.

That sort of unshakable confidence in my skills should have buoyed me. Instead, it dropped a worry stone the size of a basket-ball in the pit of my stomach. After only two sessions of working with the band, I already had enough excellent material to make two or three kick-ass videos. We hadn't even set up the shoot at the observatory yet or included the background scenes from the movie. It wasn't smart to get ahead of myself, but already I worried about editing it all into one four-and-a-half-minute video without it looking like a mashup.

Beside me, Garrett whispered, "I can help you, Olivia."

I blinked at him.

"If you'll let me."

How did he *do* that? After all this time, how could he still read me so well?

Sounds of jostling on the stage returned my attention to the band. When I glanced at them, four pairs of eyes avidly focused on Garrett and me. From the glints flashing in the original three band members' eyes, I knew something was up, something I'd need to figure out before we set up the next shoot.

Blu broke first. "You want another take, O?"

Directing my attention to my cinematographer, I raised a brow. She shrugged. "Couldn't hurt."

It already hurt, but I had to let that go. "All right. Take your marks and we'll shoot this one more time." Privately, I hoped they played it straight so I wouldn't have so much material to sort through in post, but a sound outside the set put a stop to that little wish.

As the band took their places, a score of screaming fans poured into the studio and raced up to the front of the stage. I shot a glare at Jeremy who followed them in. His hands went up in a defensive gesture and his head tilted toward the band. The breath I pulled in through gritted teeth did not cleanse or calm me down.

"What. The. Fuck."

Blu had the audacity to laugh into his mic. "It's not a Balefire show without the fans."

Then I noticed Dakota making eyes at one of the women near the stage on his side and recognized her as his fiancée Annabelle Stewart. My clenched jaw loosened a fraction as my eyes wandered through the small crowd. When they landed on Ashleigh Baker,

Blu's fiancée, I began to figure out what the guys were up to. Beside Ashleigh, Clio Whitehorse, Jack's wife, blew him a kiss while Cristy Valor did one better and climbed up on the stage to land a smooch on her fiancé Tron's mouth, because of course she did. A big pop star like her would always draw attention to herself. When I perused the crowd again, I discovered Jennifer Hartwell among them, and my shoulders sagged. The woman had found a way into the video as more than a shadow thrown up on a screen.

The mystery phone calls and the enigmatic stares of the band earlier all made sense now. They could have just said they wanted their ladies in the video. Hell, Ashleigh Baker had even been a suggestion for the lady in red at the observatory. For a second, I considered playing the diva director card and storming off the set at the way the band hijacked the script. But their professionalism to this point in the shoot meant we were ahead of schedule, and it was their show, after all. If they wanted to play a private concert for their ladies in front of the cameras, who was I to say no?

Cristy dropped down off the stage to join the others, and with smirks all around, the guys awaited my cue. With a massive eye roll, I conveyed my thoughts to them and said into my mic, "Make sure you focus on Annabelle, Ashleigh, Clio, Cristy," I paused. "And grab about one second of Jennifer Hartwell. Pan over the rest of the ladies. We only need one shot."

I cued the band and called, "Action."

Of course, I should have known the surprise wouldn't stop with the women showing up to scream and swoon as the band played. Oh, no. By the second verse, lingerie started raining down on the stage like a monsoon. Where it all came from was anyone's guess. The band put on a show of enjoying certain women's offerings: Dakota slipped a lacy thong over his left hand to hang off his wrist as his fingers blistered the fretboard. Blu tied a red bra to his mic stand. Tron draped a white bra around his neck. Jack caught a pair of silky champagne boy-shorts panties with one of his sticks and draped it off the front of his bass drum.

"I hope you caught who threw what because I don't plan to reshoot this impromptu little scene," I said into my mic.

The storm of lingerie and the band's antics with it drew my focus to the crowd, but somehow I'd forgotten about Jennifer Hartwell until she appeared on the stage behind Tron in a slinky red dress during the second chorus, and involuntarily, I groaned into my mic.

Sarah's voice sounded in my headset. "What do you want us to do here?"

"Follow her with A, avoid her completely—or as much as you can—with the track cams and the gimbals. Focus those on whichever player she's not flirting with and move on when she does."

The way Jennifer moved between the members of the band was eerily reminiscent of a video of a Balefire live show I'd watched. Only in that show, Cristy Valor was singing with them, and her moves were sexy and flirty in a way that drew everyone's enthusiasm. She brought fun to the stage. Jennifer's attempt at a sort of dancing femme fatale fell flat. Perhaps if we'd rehearsed it, she and the band wouldn't be so stiff with each other.

As the song played out, I had the sense the boys had talked Jeremy into helping them with their "crowd" scene involving their special ladies. But the addition of Jennifer Hartwell inserting herself into the performance hadn't been part of the plan. The side-eyes between the guys when she moved from one of them to another told me they were as surprised at her appearance as I.

Beside me, Garrett trained his focus on the stage even when I tried to catch his eye. Wasn't that rich? All morning he'd worked for attention I'd refused to give him, but now with Jennifer's arrival, he ignored me. But he'd ignored her when she called during lunch.

I didn't have time to try to wrap my head around the situation. The song ended, and I called out, "Thanks everyone. That's a wrap for today."

Only when the last echoes of the women's screams joined the final reverberations of Jack's drums did I scan the crowd of women in front of me. Most of their faces were unfamiliar, but a couple of A-list actresses were sprinkled throughout. I recognized Sylvie Ortega from a recent Marvel film and Jackie Simone from *A Paris Adventure*, the rom-com nominated for an Oscar last year. The others were apparently extras the band hired or something.

I clamped my arms to my sides as sweat broke out in my armpits. I hadn't budgeted for extras. *Shit.*

Even if we didn't use any of the footage from the pop-up concert, we'd still have to pay these women—and have them sign NDAs and contracts and—Jeremy might lose his job after all. How could he have been talked into more nonsense after the dressing-down I'd given him over colluding with Garrett on the changes to the script?

"Have those galleys ready in the projection room before you leave for the day, please," I said to Sarah who nodded to me with a smirk. I flipped her a sneaky bird, and she flat-out grinned. Normally, I relished this silent communication born from working super-closely together. Though she'd only been with me a year, we already knew each other's tells. From her response, I'd used all of mine. Damn it.

As if by magic, a cocktail bar materialized in the usual spot for the coffee cart. I glanced around in a panic. If I was going to make it through the galleys tonight, I *needed* coffee. Gallons of it after the way the band performed during the shoot.

Off to my right, Jeremy fidgeted, clearly wanting my attention but also clearly wishing he didn't need it. I hung my headset over the back of my chair and beckoned him over.

Before I could even ask, he said, "The band wanted to surprise you. They said you'd enjoy it, something about for old time's sake. I should have said something anyway." Scuffing a toe at the cement floor, he reminded me he was only twenty-four with so much to learn.

He made me feel every second of my thirty-three years. Closing my eyes, I aimed an eye roll at my pathetic self. When I opened them again, I said, "You'll figure it out. Trial by fire usually has that effect. But out of curiosity, what happened to the coffee cart?"

"Garrett paid them to knock off early so the band and their friends could have an impromptu after-party." He stuffed his hands in his pockets. "I got the idea they knew how the shoot would go, and they wanted to celebrate."

"I see." Though attitude dripped from my voice, I truly did see. I saw how Garrett had found yet another way to manipulate me. Glancing over my shoulder, I discovered the man in exceptionally close conversation with a particular video-crashing movie star. His hand rested lightly at the base of her spine while he leaned in to hear something Jennifer whispered in his ear. While the band involved their fiancées—and wife—in the shoot, their manager found a way to include his love interest.

So that was the way of it. Play the video director "for old time's sake" while waiting for the movie star to show up. Green acid roiled my stomach, and I growled at myself in frustration. I'd done my homework on the band—and their manager—for crying out loud. Over the years, Garrett had earned a reputation for spending his free time with groupies and B-list actresses and hangers-on. Jennifer Hartwell had a reputation, too, for using whoever she could as the next rung on the ladder to the top of the A-list. It didn't hurt that her dad owned a production company and made her a producer on the film for which Balefire had written the music. No wonder she and Garrett were so cozy.

I had no business experiencing singed feelings. Hadn't I spent most of last night in bed and all of this morning as I dressed for work repeating my new mantra: I will resist Garrett Phillips? The two of them together should have made that even easier for me. So what the hell was the deal with the green-eyed monster rising up like a phantom from deep inside me?

Jeremy cleared his throat, reminding me he was waiting for something from me.

"Wonder Kid, before you join that party, make sure I have coffee and plenty of it in the projection room. And no matter what the band says, be on time in the morning."

A smile broke over his face. "On it. Thanks, Olivia."

Jeremy headed in the opposite direction of the party where Dakota held center stage lining up shots of tequila along the makeshift bar they'd erected. Behind him, two guys were doing their best imitation of acrobatic bartenders like in that old Tom Cruise movie that regularly showed up in my Netflix queue. The rest of the band and all the ladies they'd invited to the shoot egged him on with screams and laughter. But in the few minutes it took for me to give Jeremy his marching orders, Garrett and Jennifer had disappeared.

An unwelcome stone dropped into the acid still roiling my stomach, and I gritted my teeth against the jealously sickening me. After giving up my claim on Garrett when he chose to follow Balefire, I had zero reason to be jealous. He'd begged me not to let him go, not to give up on us, and I'd done it anyway. One of us had to be realistic. I had no business second-guessing that decision now.

After Dakota's morning pronouncement about me joining their end-of-the-shoot after-party, I had no doubt he'd try to include me in this little surprise as well. I had zero intention of letting the band sidetrack me into doing shots when I needed to work. They were the big time I had yet to reach. Shooting tequila instead of studying today's galleys would not help me push my studio to the next level.

Choosing not to expose myself to the melee, I slipped out a back door behind Jack's drums on the stage. After a pit stop at my office to grab a light sweater, I entered the projection room to discover an avocado-chicken wrap waiting on a plate next to a venti Americano on the table beside my chair. Further inspection revealed a thermos of coffee, a small pitcher of cream, and a blond brownie with a note on top penciled in Jeremy's quick scrawl. "This is for later to soak up the dregs of all that coffee."

Gah! Not him too.

I cued up the day's film and settled back to watch with my notes and my dinner. The morning's takes were decent. The guys' energy levels were a bit off, but that could work with the right lighting techniques in post. We could emphasize they were up to something sinister with their subdued demeanors. Juxtaposed with the afternoon's shoot on the stage today or sandwiched in with what I hoped we'd record at the observatory, these scenes could create an effective counterbalance to the rest of the video. Pausing the footage, I made a note and froze as the hair on my arms stood at attention. Someone else was in the projection room with me.

Slowly, I lowered my iPad to the table beside my half-eaten wrap and surreptitiously glanced around for a weapon. Then a faint citrusy scent floated in the air around me, and I marginally relaxed.

"Hey, you. What are you doing in here by yourself?" Garrett asked as he sidled up beside my chair.

"My job." My words came out more waspish than the situation called for, but then again, I wasn't the one playing games. "What are you doing here? Shouldn't you be out at the party making sure your charges don't overdo and show up to the shoot late and hungover again tomorrow?"

"Whoa! Whoa!" He slid into the chair beside me and swiveled it to face me. "What's with the attitude? We're on the same team here." The concern in his gray eyes might have leveled me if I'd believed it.

A picture of his hand possessively resting on the small of Jennifer Hartwell's back flashed unbidden in my head, and I lifted my chin. "Exactly, which is why you should be out on the set making sure your boys are maintaining. We knocked off pretty early for them to start doing lines of tequila shots."

"We don't shoot tomorrow, remember? Your crew is setting up

for the big show at the observatory day after tomorrow," he patiently reminded me.

"Well, then, by all means, party your asses off tonight."

He whistled his response, his eyes wide.

I picked up my wrap sandwich, tore a huge bite from it, and chewed. It wasn't mannerly in the least, but it kept my mouth too busy to say anything else I might wish I hadn't. Reaching for my coffee, I gulped a chaser for my too-big bite of avocado-chicken goodness. My food had forfeited all its flavor the second I met Garrett's stare. "What?"

"Did something happen since we wrapped for the day?" His tone, his whole demeanor, showed genuine confusion.

Even though he believed I was seeing someone else, he'd come on to me like a tsunami, overwhelming my senses and sending me spiraling back to graduate school days. Back then, with one touch, one charged look, he could have me begging to give in to whatever naughtiness he had in mind. In the control room last night, he'd done that to me again. But after that sneaky scene this afternoon with the band's significant others—and apparently Garrett's as well—I knew better. He'd become a player, and the last thing I needed was to be played.

"How's Jennifer? When we were scripting the video, I had the distinct impression she wasn't too popular with the band—or you. Impressions can be deceiving though, can't they? I wasn't quite to that part of the shoot yet, but I can fast forward through the galleys if that's what you're here for." I twisted around in my chair, looking for the woman in question. "Did you ditch your date?"

"Olivia, what the hell?"

"What the hell, indeed." I swigged down steaming coffee and choked. Of course, he rushed to my rescue, but I put a hand up, swallowed once, twice, and rubbed my fingertips beneath my watering eyes, totally wrecking the effect I'd been going for.

Once I had myself back under some semblance of control, I

asked, "Are you going to tell me about the surprises I can expect at the observatory shoot, or do I have to guess?"

He shoved a hand through his hair, and that lock he could never quite tame dropped onto his forehead. My hand itched to smooth it back, so I shoved my hands between my knees and squeezed my thighs tight around them.

"Look, now that every member of Balefire is all engaged or married or whatever, they want to include their women in everything." Distaste dripped from that last word, and I had the distinct idea all was not well in paradise. "With the way they looked in the car this morning when they ran that fan scene idea past me, I admit, I felt a little sorry for them. They caught me in a weak moment, all right? But it didn't hurt anything. We'll put it in the outtakes, okay?"

"I doubt your girlfriend wants to find herself on the cutting room floor." I flipped the lid off my coffee cup, blew on the hot brew and took a careful sip. "To be honest, I don't have to watch the galleys of that version of the song to know we won't use much of it. Once Jennifer showed up onstage, the entire band went stiff."

His brows went up.

"They're pros, so their sound didn't falter, but the way they played stopped looking natural. It was as though each of them tensed for the moment of contact when Jennifer danced"—I used air quotes for that word—"near them and put her hands on them. Plus, she wasn't dressed for the scene at all." Sipping more coffee, I gathered myself. "Were we auditioning her for the femme fatale scene at the observatory? Because if we were, she didn't pass the screen test with the leading men."

"You truly don't think she could play that part?" His expression remained flat, so I couldn't tell if he wanted a yes or a no.

Jennifer's impromptu performance made my answer easy. "No. She thinks too much to be a fluid dancer, and none of the guys are comfortable with her." I pulled up the last take of the day and played it for him. "See? She's too practiced, too rehearsed. Honestly, she plays her role in the movie in much the same way. Parker Malone makes her look better than she is."

"Can you let her have two seconds when she makes her appearance behind Jack?

"It seems you and the band want some favors 'for old time's sake,' but I don't recall owing you any." Turning the sound off, I stared at the screen, cataloging all the ways I disliked Jennifer Hartwell. Petty for sure, but I couldn't bring myself to care, not with that green-eyed phantasm hovering over my shoulder.

"Please, Olivia? I need this."

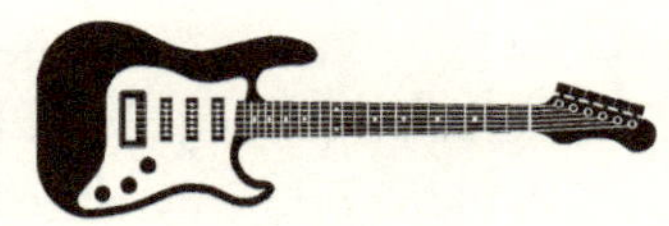

CHAPTER SEVENTEEN

Garrett

I HATED ASKING OLIVIA for a favor, especially this one. Especially after the way she'd responded to my touch when I finally had her alone in the control room. How Jennifer caught wind of the band's silly idea with their girls for today's shoot I didn't have a clue—but I needed to find out. I'd held up my end of the deal when I talked the band into writing the song and making the video to promote her movie. But the woman couldn't be satisfied, something I should have figured out after that one disastrous night I spent with her when she tagged along on our last tour.

Yeah. That night I'd drunk far too much tequila during a sexual dry spell Jennifer was only too happy to slake. Somewhere during the middle of what I now referred to as "the nightmare," I'd let my plans slip for inviting Mali Tatum along on the last tour to shake up Tron's relationship with Cristy Valor. In the end, it hadn't been worth it, not even a little bit. In front of the cameras or in the bedroom, the woman was always "on." I don't think she had a clue how to loosen up, have some real fun. But she'd mastered the art of zeroing in on a person's weaknesses and manipulating them for her own ends.

Now here I was with the one woman in the world I wanted to impress, in total honesty, the one woman I'd never moved on from, and she thought I was tangled up with that blackmailing bitch. Trouble was, I couldn't come clean about all the moving parts in this drama without looking like the world's biggest jerk—and maybe losing my job with the band. What a cluster.

Olivia pulled her iPad onto her lap and tapped in some notes. "One and a half seconds when she makes her entrance. I'm cutting it a frame before Jack clocks her standing behind him."

I shrugged. "Fine." Clasping my hands in front of my knees, I hazarded another favor. "About the woman in red scene at the observatory."

"Did you not hear what I said a minute ago? As auditions went, she tanked that one. I need someone Blu can be comfortable with fast. After watching his fiancée dance in this crowd, I think she'd be perfect."

Pulling my lips between my teeth, I drew a breath in through my nose and let it out slowly. "There was a snafu with a video a couple of years ago. It broke the two of them up for a while." *And almost cost me my job*, but Olivia didn't need those details. "I seriously doubt she'll be interested."

"Doesn't hurt to ask."

A puff of air fluttered my lips, but Olivia ignored me, her eyes glued to the screen as she forwarded through the video, stopping it several times and watching and rewatching segments. Sneaking a peek at her iPad, I saw where she kept track of time stamps and descriptions. From her list, I had a sense each of the guys' girls would make an appearance in the video, something that would lend credibility to including Ashleigh as the femme fatale in the red dress—if she agreed to it.

Olivia checked the time on her wrist. "I imagine the party in the studio is still going strong?"

"Probably. Why?"

"Maybe you could grab Ashleigh and Blu and bring them up here. If I run the idea past Ashleigh myself, perhaps she'd be willing to play along with it."

"What happened to hiring someone from an agency if we're not using Jennifer?"

From the arch of her brow, I hadn't managed to keep the worry from my voice.

"I'm watching the galleys."

"So?"

"So check this out." She backed up the tape to where Ashleigh danced in the crowd, while wearing, of all things, a red dress.

In about a nanosecond, I saw what Olivia saw, and I had to admit Ash was the perfect person to play the mysterious femme fatale.

"We can shadow her face when Blu dips her, keeping her identity from the general public. But you have to admit the way her body calls to his is too damn sexy not to use in the scene." She put a finger to her lips in thought. "Plus, it adds a layer of mystery since you insist we include a touch of Jennifer in this section of the video. It leaves the viewer wondering exactly who the woman in red is."

"It could open a can of rumors that Jennifer is having a thing with Blu."

"Which is a good thing for movie publicity, correct?"

"Maybe, but that could backfire on the band. The fans loved how Blu proposed to Ashleigh at the end of a concert in Florida. They might not be very nice about Blu even appearing to dump her for Jennifer."

"It's a music video, Garrett. A fantasy to sell a song and a movie."

"Fans are what they are, Olivia. You know that. They'll draw their own conclusions, so we need to make sure they draw the right ones."

"By casting Jennifer as the woman in red? You're making zero sense." She sat back in her chair. "In fact, you're making a strong case for not including even a second of Jennifer's scene crashing in the video."

It was a damned inconvenient time for Olivia's training as a lawyer to surface. Of course nothing I said made any sense unless I made her aware of all the subplots playing out with this production, something I couldn't do without jeopardizing any chance at what I was starting to figure out I truly wanted.

Pinching the bridge of my nose, I said, "How 'bout this? If Ashleigh agrees to do the shoot, we shadow Jennifer's face behind the drum set and leave the woman's identity completely up to the viewer." I leveled my eyes on Olivia's. "But if Ashleigh doesn't want to do the shoot, we let the viewer see Jennifer's face when she appears onstage and use Jennifer at the observatory."

Olivia tilted her head in thought. "Or, I find someone last minute for the observatory shot." She shrugged. "This town is full of dancers looking for credits wherever they can find them."

I stuck out my hand. "Deal."

For a second, she stared at my outstretched palm before she slowly raised her hand and clasped mine. Like in the old days when she was still mine, fiery tingles sizzled up my arm, and my cock perked up behind the fly of my jeans from that innocuous point of contact. Holding her eyes with mine, I brought her hand to my lips, turned it over, and placed a lingering kiss in the center of her palm. She rewarded me with a tiny gasp, and I smiled against her skin before I let her go.

"There is no producer-director boyfriend, is there, O? And nothing between you and Jason Stahl either."

"I-I." She swallowed hard and threw her shoulders back. "My private life is none of your business."

"What if I want to make it my business?"

"What will your girlfriend think of that?"

My brows pinched together. "Girlfriend? What girlfriend?"

The sarcasm in her wide-eyed stare could have burned a hole in the projection screen. "Jennifer Hartwell? The woman you had your hands all over after the shoot today? The woman you disappeared with after the boys opened the bar? The woman you so desperately want in this video?"

I scooted to the edge of my chair and took her hand again. When she tugged on it to take it back, I rubbed the pad of my thumb over her silky smooth skin, and she stilled for the second I needed. "She's a colleague, not a girlfriend. When the boys ignored her at the end of the take—and you didn't ask to film another one— she wanted to throw a tantrum. I prevented her from making an unpleasant scene."

"By promising her you'd sweet talk me into letting her into the video."

"By promising I'd *talk* to you about it. But this is your show, Olivia." Damn, her hands were so soft. I wanted them all over me. *Head in the game, buddy*, I admonished myself. "If you don't want to use a single second of Jennifer Hartwell, you're well within your rights. Contractually and as an artist, you're making the art you want to make."

She glanced down at our joined hands. "So this isn't you sweet talking me?" A tiny smirk tugged the corner of her mouth.

"Not even a little bit." I twined our fingers together, our palms flush to each other. "This is me being happy for the chance to spend time with you again." Giving her fingers a whisper of a squeeze, I added, "This is me wanting you."

"Garrett—"

The warning in her tone played at odds with her squeezing my fingers back.

"Never once since the day we met have I not wanted you, Olivia Carter. Do you have the faintest clue what a sexy woman you are?" Taking a chance, I clasped her other hand in mine. "You were incredible when we were kids, and now, you're—Jesus." Our knees touched. "The way you run the show is so fucking hot." I slid my fingers through hers, up and down. "If anything, you're more gorgeous than you were a decade ago. Then you were a beautiful girl. Now, you're a breathtaking woman."

"I told you already. I don't get involved with clients." The raspy tone of her voice told me how hard she was fighting the attraction between us.

"I'm not a client, though, am I?" The pad of my index finger found the pulse point of her wrist. "The band is your client, yes. You're working with me for them." Dropping my voice, I whispered, "Which means your rules don't apply to us."

She held her breath, and so did I. I'm not sure which of us moved first, but when my lips met hers, all the years and time apart faded away. The pillow softness of her mouth beneath mine, the tiny puff of a sigh, the way she melted into the kiss—into me— was my homecoming. All my life, I'd wanted to belong, and for a while, I thought I belonged with the band. But this? Right here in this moment with Olivia? This was where I belonged, where I'd always belonged.

I slid my hand up her arm until I cupped the back of her neck beneath the silky strands of her hair. Pushing my fingers up into those strands, I held her still as I deepened the kiss. When she opened for me and let me sweep my tongue into her mouth, sensation shivered through me, arrowing directly to my solar plexus. My heartbeat pounded through me, hard and insistent, as blood rushed south. The glide of her tongue over mine tore a groan from deep in my throat. When her arms came around my neck, I gave in and dragged her into my lap.

My hands roamed the supple length of her spine, down to cup and squeeze her perfect ass then back up to tangle in her hair. She wasn't idle either. Cool fingers slid along my jaw and up into my hair and back down my neck to knead and scratch at my shoulders. She tasted of creamy coffee and something primally feminine, and I wanted inside her so bad I couldn't stand it.

As though she read my thoughts, she shifted to straddle my lap, drawing her heated center exactly where I needed her. With a whimper, she rubbed the fly of her jeans along the fly of mine. The friction lit me up, and I moved beneath her in a rhythm we both loved. Slipping my hands beneath the knit of her turtleneck and the lace of her bra, I cupped her breasts, my skin remembering hers, every cell seeking her.

With a gasp, she tore her mouth from mine and held my eyes with her wild ones. The flickering light of the screen behind me revealed only a thin golden ring around her black pupils. In my hands, her chest heaved, filling my palms with her firm perfect curves. A tiny smile met mine, and then she stopped time with more drugging kisses.

A lifetime later, she pulled back again to smile against my lips. "This is nuts. You know that, don't you?"

"This is perfect. You're perfect." My lips found the corner of her mouth. "I've missed you."

She sat up to look into my eyes, and I didn't like the troubled expression I saw in hers. "Garrett."

"Olivia."

"Nothing has changed."

I squeezed her hips. "Except us."

"What do you mean? We're both still chasing different dreams."

"We're grown-ups now. We've learned things." I traced a fingertip along her hairline down the side of her cheek and cupped her jaw. "Things that have changed us, allowed us to see the world differently." Holding her eyes, I whispered, "We have options now."

The worry in her expression didn't waver, telling me I had work to do. "Let's just finish the job." She slid back on my lap. "Maybe not complicate it."

"It's already complicated, O. It has been from the minute the boys decided you were the only director they'd trust with this video."

Hurt flashed in her eyes. "I thought it was your idea to work with me," she said in a small voice that jerked at my guts.

"You were *my* first choice from the second you started this studio. But when it comes to who the band wants to work with, I'm limited to making suggestions, not final decisions." Giving her hips another gentle squeeze, I added, "After the way you ran the Grammys, you were the only director they wanted." I cupped her cheek, drawing her eyes to mine. "Even if we didn't have a history, I would have wanted them to work with you. But honestly, I wondered if they'd go along with the idea because we do have a history." My eyes followed the pad of my thumb as I stroked along her jawline. "I haven't exactly been number one on Balefire's hit parade the last couple of years."

"I picked up on that in our meetings. What's going on?"

"This last decade with the band has been one hell of a ride. I didn't want it to stop. I mean, since I gave you up to follow them, I wanted that to count." Keeping my eyes on my hand, I smoothed my fingers along her hairline, tucking silky strands behind her ear and enjoying the shiver that went through her when I ghosted them over the shell of her ear. "When they each started to show more interest in certain women than one-night stands or the occasional short-term fling, I interfered."

Her eyes grew wide. "Why would you do that?"

With a shrug, I said, "I was afraid if one or two of them landed in a serious relationship with a woman, it would break up the band. If the band broke up, where would that leave me?" At last, I let my eyes return to hers.

A troubled hazel stare met mine. "You're the reason Balefire hit the big time and stayed there. Your business acumen. Your management skills. You're the reason they weren't playing bars anymore before the end of the first year you started with them. Surely, they appreciate that." She tilted her head. "But even if the band broke up, you wouldn't be out of a job for long. Some other band seeing what you've done for Balefire would scoop you up in a blink."

If she knew everything I'd done, I doubt she'd have the same opinion of me. But for this little minute, I wanted to bask in the warm sunshine of her belief in me.

"If I've learned anything from working with you and seeing you in action directing the video, it's that I made a terrible mistake in not fighting harder for us back when there was an us."

"Garrett, we can't go back and change the past."

A ruckus outside the door to the projection room alerted us to the crazy seconds before it spilled through the door to interrupt us. Olivia leaped off my lap, tugging at her top and stuffing it back into her jeans. Then she was moving toward the loud commotion, meeting the band as they burst through the door.

"Blu! You're right on time." She sounded breathless, which I had to admit, I liked. "Garrett and I were discussing a proposal we want to run past you and Ashleigh."

Chapter Eighteen

Olivia

IF THE BOYS noticed the high pitch of my voice, none of them let on as they spilled into the room. Surreptitiously, I patted at my hair, hoping it wasn't sticking up in all directions from the tour Garrett's hands took through it.

Dakota tipped up a bottle of Patrón, took a long pull, and handed it to Blu. Blu grinned and tugged at Ashleigh's hand, encouraging her to stand beside him. More of the band and their ladies trooped in behind them as Blu swallowed some tequila and said, "What's up, Boss Lady?" He wasn't quite slurring, but I noticed most of the party had the glassy-eyed look of people who'd been enjoying copious amounts of alcohol.

Maybe I needed to order dinner.

As though he'd read my mind, Garrett whispered in my ear, "You run the idea by them while I order some food."

"If you're up for it, I'd like to show you something from today's shoot," I said to the crowd in front of me.

"What we're up for is a party, and you need to join us," Dakota pronounced as though he came from on high. Admittedly, Balefire was rock 'n' roll royalty, but they were in my house.

"I'll say this slowly since you seemed to have missed it last time, Dakota." I enunciated each word. "I. Will. Party. With. You. At. The. End. Of. The. Shoot." I crossed my arms over my chest and stared him down. "We're not done with the shoot."

"Are you always such a killjoy?" Turning to Jeremy who trailed in behind the rest of the band, Dakota repeated his question. "Is she always this unfun?"

"No. Olivia's"—he attempted to cover a hiccup with his hand—"great."

"What's your big idea, Olivia?" Blu asked, taking another swig from the bottle before he handed it to Jack.

Apparently, the women weren't drinking? As if by magic, a second bottle of tequila appeared in Ashleigh's free hand. Tossing a wicked smirk in her fiancé's direction, she tipped it back, swallowed a couple of times, and ran the back of her hand over her mouth before she handed the bottle to Jack's wife, Clio.

So that was the game, and not my scene at all, Jeremy's endorsement to the contrary.

"After watching the way you and Ashleigh interacted when the 'groupies' crashed the shoot," I said with air quotes, "I thought she would be perfect for the scene with the woman in red at the observatory. We'd keep her face in shadow, but your chemistry is exactly what that scene calls for."

It took me a second to catch on that all the raucous laughter and general messing around had abruptly stopped. Like flipping a switch, the band and their significant others had gone utterly sober. Every pair of eyes was laser-focused on me. I glanced around for Garrett, hoping he could tell me what I'd said wrong, but he'd mysteriously disappeared.

Blu narrowed his eyes. "Whose idea was it to include Ashleigh in the video?"

Smoothing the frown between my brows with my fingertips, I said, "Mine. Is that a problem?" I dropped my hand and met his gaze. "If you'd watch today's galleys, you'd see why I want to use your fiancée as our lady in red." Turning to my computer, I cued up the part I wanted them to watch and hit Play.

The groupie scene played across the projection screen, but Blu paid no attention. "This wasn't Garrett's idea?" The hostility in his tone made no sense. Hadn't the band invited the women to the shoot specifically to include them in the video?

Facing him, I said, "Actually, Garrett suggested Jennifer Hartwell. But she has zero chemistry with any of you. In fact, she turns all of you sort of mechanical, which is not the effect we're going for with this video at all."

"Garrett wants to put Jennifer in the video?" Dakota asked. Something suspicious in his expression sent up red flags in my heart.

Garrett said there was nothing between them. "Work colleagues," nothing else, he'd said. So why did Dakota have that look on his face at Garrett's suggestion of adding Jennifer to the cast?

"No fuckin' way am I dancing with Jennifer," Blu chimed in. "Come on, Ash, let's see what Olivia wants to show us."

Whatever the weird undercurrents swirling around us meant, at least my idea hadn't been summarily trashed. Yet.

I reset the cue and hit Play again. The band and their screaming "fans" lit up the projection screen. When the camera found Ashleigh, I manually zoomed in on her and Blu as he sang "Salvation wears a red dress/If we can escape this/Dangerous, dangerous life" and watched their reaction. Ashleigh's hand flew to her mouth while Blu let go of her other hand to wrap his arm around her and tug her into his side. His eyes remained on the screen even as he laid a kiss on his fiancée's temple.

"You see what I see, too, don't you? I don't care how great an actor you are, you're not going to manufacture that kind of heat on screen." Tilting my head, I studied them. "So what do you say, Ashleigh? Want to be in a music video?"

"And this was all your idea." Blu's eyes bored into mine.

"Yes. Why is that so important?"

Dakota answered with a sneer. "Ask Garrett."

The other two guys and their ladies remained silent, but their solidarity behind Blu and Ashleigh and whatever they decided was as palpable as the energy of a coming storm. Holding my breath, I waited them out. Blu whispered something to Ashleigh who nodded and whispered back to him.

"You said you'd shadow her face?"

I nodded.

"How will our chemistry come through, then?"

"Like it does in this scene, most of which only shows Ashleigh's back."

Blu's brows went up. "But what if we want to show Ashleigh's face?"

"Garrett didn't think she'd do it if we showed her face, but if you want the audience to see her, I'm all over that." I grinned. "The two of you will burn up the screen in that scene."

"Of course Garrett didn't think she'd do it," Dakota chimed in again. "Bet he wishes she won't do it." He smiled at Ashleigh. "But you're going to, aren't you?"

She grinned back at him. "Since I'm already in the video, it would be silly to say no, wouldn't it?"

"Thatta girl."

I planted my hands on my hips. "I *really* wish someone would tell me what the hell the subtext is here. I don't like directing in the dark."

"Like we said, ask Garrett," Blu replied.

"Ask me what?" Garrett said from somewhere behind Jeremy near the door. "But maybe ask over dinner. Food's waiting in the lobby of the sound studio."

♪

The group passed the tequila bottles around the table during dinner, one for the guys and one for the women. Jeremy, I noticed, helped the band with their bottle, which meant the women were down a player. Unfortunately for them, I had hours of work to do with the galleys and last minute checks on logistics for setting up the next shoot. I slugged back another gulp of the Americano that miraculously appeared with my dinner and marveled at the interplay with the band.

"If you weren't such a pussy, Blu, you'd show up at Parker's place tomorrow and surf with us. Even Jackie-boy is gonna be there," Dakota goaded from across the table.

Since I was sitting beside her, I could hear when Ashleigh whispered to Blu, "You should go surfing with the guys if that's what you want to do."

Not bothering with subtlety, Blu replied, "Nah. I'd rather look at pretty flowers with my pretty girl." Playfully, he bopped her on the nose, and she laughed.

"Whatever flower bed she wants you to see will still be there after we finish the video," Dakota said, a challenging gleam in his eyes.

"The flower bed is called South Coast Botanic Garden. Ash says it has a Garden of the Senses where we can touch and smell the orchids and passion flowers up close." Sliding his arm around his fiancée, he dragged her in and smacked a kiss on her mouth. Waggling his brows at her gasp of mock outrage, he said, "Who knows what else we can touch and smell while we're there." He returned his attention to Dakota. "But it's damn fact I have a better chance of getting up to something fun at the botanical garden than I have chasing waves off Parker's beach."

Dakota's voice rose half a step. "You think the botanical gardens are more private than a private beach?"

"Long lenses have a harder time penetrating thick foliage than open sand. Just sayin'," Blu shot back.

Annabelle folded her arms over her chest and slammed back in her chair. Singeing Dakota with her glare, her lips thinned. "I told you that when we stayed at Parker's before. But you keep insisting we're too far away for the paps to take any clear shots."

"Aw, Anna-baby. That beach is too far away for them to shoot anything they can post or print. Even if they enhance the shit out of it." Dakota's voice wheedled, and I had the distinct impression he wanted something naughty from Annabelle—like skinny-dipping in the ocean—and she wasn't having it.

I grinned down at my plate and speared another bite of delectable chicken enchilada and swirled it around to pick up as much green chili sauce as possible.

"What's that for?" Garrett said into my ear.

Why, oh why, did my entire body react to his breath on my skin? Clamping my legs together, I sat up straighter and turned my attention to him. "The boys flip each other even more shit than I remember is all. It's fun to listen to them."

He was too close, his gray eyes dialed up to molten silver, and I could swear he knew the state of my panties after his lips ghosted over my skin with his question.

After a minutes-long stare down, he shrugged, letting me off the hook. "They do like to hard-time each other. It's part of what keeps them sharp."

Before someone opened the boxes of flan and sopaipillas Garrett ordered for dessert, the bottles of tequila were empty, replaced with a round of Dos Equis. Not my idea of a dessert drink, but fortunately, I still had a swallow or two of my Americano left. Garrett, I noticed, limited himself to water. I guess someone needed to stay sober to make sure everyone made it back to their various residences in one piece. When dinner ended, Landon glanced up from his phone to say the town cars were waiting outside the studio whenever they were ready.

As they left the sound studio, Dakota said, "Don't worry, Olivia. We'll all be on time—and straight—when we arrive on set. Promise." With a wink for me, he tossed his arm over Annabelle's shoulders and led the others out of the lobby.

Blu stopped beside me, his tone low. "Ask him, Olivia. Ask Garrett about Ashleigh and a video the band made in Texas." Beside him, Ashleigh nodded, their serious expressions utterly at odds with the joking fun of the last hour.

Landon stepped up to Garrett who'd held back from the others. "What time should I send a car for you, sir?"

"Don't worry about me. I'll figure something out," Garrett said. "And for the love of God, stop calling me 'sir.'"

With a tiny smirk, Landon gave him a half salute and trailed after the band.

"You're not going with them?" I asked.

He stuffed his hands in his pockets, an expression of pure innocence on his face. "Thought I'd help you with the galleys. Take notes for you or whatever."

"I'm good, Garrett. You can go with your boys."

"I know you're good, Olivia." A smirk ghosted his lips. "But I want to help."

In my peripheral vision, Jeremy shifted from foot to foot. "Hey, Wonder Kid. Don't worry about cleaning up. The night staff will take care of it. See you tomorrow."

A loopy grin broke over his lips. "Thanks, Olivia. I"—his hand flew to his mouth as a belch escaped him.

The tips of his ears brightened, and the muscles in my jaw hurt with the effort it took to hold back a smirk.

"I'll see you tomorrow."

As he headed out the door, I noticed his gait wasn't quite steady. "Hey, do you have a ride home?" I called after him.

"Riding with Landon and a couple of the boys." Pure joy danced across his face before he hiccupped again. Turning on his heel, he staggered, righted himself, and set off at not quite a jog to catch up with the band.

With a sigh, I said, "I've warned him about being starstruck over the band, but he's a massive fan. Working with them on this video might be the highlight of his life."

Garrett smiled. "Can't blame him. Hanging with the band is a good time—mostly."

The smile dropped off his face, and Blu's words echoed in my head. *"Ask him, Olivia."*

After we settled ourselves in the projection room, I cued up the "groupie" scene when Blu sang to Ashleigh.

He'd just settled himself into the butter-soft leather chair beside mine, when I said, "Tell me about Ashleigh."

Blowing out a breath, he sat forward, dropped his head to his hand, and pinched the bridge of his nose, gathering himself. Using a trick I'd learned in law school, I waited him out with a slow count to fifteen in my head. I'd reached eleven when he clasped his hands between his knees, his eyes finding mine.

"When Ashleigh showed up at the band's home studios, I thought she was an opportunistic journalist looking to expose the band somehow. Initially, I put a run on her."

Crossing my arms over my chest, I held in the pain his words stabbed into me. I had no claim on him, so the fact that he'd pursued something with Blu's woman shouldn't have mattered in the least.

But it did.

"She's beautiful and intelligent." His eyes bored into me as though he could see the wounds he gave me. "She reminded me of someone I thought I'd never know again."

His quiet words only drove the pain in deeper.

"I wanted to see what she was truly after. But it turned out, Blu was behind it all. He'd messed up one of her gigs for a blog or something, so he invited her to join the band on tour and set up a freelance job with *Rolling Stone*." He glanced down at his clasped hands. "He was already sleeping with her. From the territorial way he acted with her around the band, I figured out she was more than a casual thing. Then, Jack announced that he was a dad, and I panicked."

My brow shot up, but I remained silent, my heart beating a slow, ponderous rhythm.

"Like I said before, if the guys fell into serious relationships with women—relationships that could dictate how they want to live, where they want to live, how often or even if they want to tour. Relationships like those could break up a band."

I opened my mouth, but he put up a hand. "Your confidence in me landing another management gig with another band flatters me. I love you for it, but I don't know if I could recreate the success of Balefire with anyone else. Their talent made my job too damn easy and made me look good."

Uncapping the bottle of water he'd brought with him from dinner, he swigged about half of it and recapped it.

"There are lots of things you could manage, Garrett. It doesn't have to be a band."

"Olivia, do you remember how obsessed I was with music, with following local bands?"

I nodded.

"Guess I haven't grown up much because that hasn't changed. I love everything about managing Balefire. Watching them hit the stage every night on tour is a rush that never gets old. When their songs zoom to the top of the charts, I'm not sure who is more excited, the guys or me." His voice dropped to a whisper. "I gave up everything to be a part of them, and when I made the mistake with Ashleigh, I didn't see how close I came to losing the band."

"What did you do?"

He slumped back in his chair and blew a breath at the ceiling.

"Something I'm not proud of. Something I've apologized for a million times over the last couple of years. Something including her in this shoot might erase finally." Turning his head on the cushion, he leveled his eyes on mine. "I set up a video shoot for 'Helluva Ride' as part of the halftime show the band played in Dallas during the Thanksgiving football game. I made up a weak excuse for why Ashleigh needed to go back to the hotel ahead of the band rather than with them. At the hotel, I had the director film the scene with Blu crashing into his room with two scantily dressed actresses falling in with him."

Garrett looked away for a moment then turned back to me. "The whole thing should have been filmed in an empty room, but I convinced the director it would be more authentic or some shit to use Blu's room."

I shook my head. "Let me guess. Ashleigh had no idea, but she was in the room when he burst through the door with two women."

"Got it in one. But instead of coming to me for an explanation or something—"

I could guess the "or something" as well, and I tightened my arms around my chest.

"She packed up and left. It took Blu months to find her and reconnect, months he was an absolute asshole to work with—for everyone." A pleading expression overtook his features. "I was trying to keep the band together, but I seriously underestimated Blu's feelings for Ash—and hers for him. It was a dick move, one I truly regret, but I did it to keep Balefire together."

The sincerity of the palms-up don't-you-see gesture he gave me showed me his remorse, but I had questions. "You don't still have a thing for Ashleigh, do you?"

"I never had a thing for Ashleigh. Attractive and intelligent as she is, if she'd said yes to me, it would have been one and done."

My dinner was in danger of making a nasty reappearance.

A derisive laugh huffed out of him at my expression. "It would have proved what I thought of her when I first met her—that she was an opportunist and someone I needed to separate from Blu and the band." He sat forward again. "But she's the real deal, and as much as I struggle sometimes with it, she's good for Blu. The music he's written since the two of them got together is the best of all he's done. 'My Beauty,' his love poem to her, stayed at the top of the charts for months." His lips thinned into a grim line. "I fucked up, O. I fucked up big-time. So I get why the two of them were skeptical about Ash being in the video. It makes it easier that it was your idea."

"So why do you struggle with them being together?" I hated how small my voice sounded, what it revealed about my feelings, ones I should have buried long ago.

He shrugged. "Envious, I guess."

"But—"

"Look, Olivia, I'm not proud of some of the things I've done with the band over the last ten years. But I can't take any of it back. I can only move forward." Reaching out, he pried my hand from my body, tugging it toward him. It was only as he massaged it that I noticed how cramped I was. "Making this video with you is a gift."

My brows furrowed even as the tension ebbed from my hand at his gentle touch.

"It gives us a chance to remember what we had." His attention strayed to our joined hands. "We have a chance to reconnect, maybe think about what we could have now."

CHAPTER NINETEEN

Olivia

WITH GARRETT'S FINGERS doing mesmerizingly erotic things to mine, it was easy to let myself fall into his fantasy for a minute. The timer on the computer timed out, and the screen went dark, reminding me I hadn't done one second of work since arriving in the projection room.

Tugging my hand from his, I leaned forward and rebooted the computer. Blu Connolly filled the screen, and I pulled my iPad into my lap.

"Olivia."

"Garrett." I blew out a breath. "I admit, our chemistry is as off the charts now as when we first met. The thing is, like our chemistry, our dreams haven't changed either. You still want to manage the band. I still want to build this studio."

"Those dreams aren't mutually exclusive, and you know it."

My attention returned to the screen. "I thought you said you were going to help me with this."

The side of my face heated under his intense scrutiny. For a long moment, I stared at the screen in front of me and pretended to be absorbed in the scene while I waited for Garrett's next move. At last, he leaned forward and tapped the cursor, moving the frames ahead to where the camera shifted from Ashleigh to key on Annabelle.

We worked in silence for a bit before we found our rhythm. Soon, we were riffing off each other, one seeing something the other missed, or both of us keying on the same expression or nuance we wanted to make sure survived final edits. As usual when I worked with galleys, time disappeared as I wrote notes, consulted the script, and adjusted the plan. The addition of Garrett to the process added a sense of adventure, a sense of fun, and before I knew it, midnight chimed on the alarm on my watch.

"No shit?" Garrett ran his hand over his flat abs. "No wonder my stomach's been growling for the last hour. What do you say we give this a rest for the night and find somewhere that serves greasy breakfast?"

Visions of the two of us sharing breakfast in the middle of the night when I was studying for the bar flashed through my head. From the look on his face, he remembered those nights too—and how they inevitably had ended. The thought heated my core. Involuntarily, I squeezed my thighs together and willed my mind to focus somewhere not on my clit.

The wicked grin on Garrett's handsome face said I hadn't hidden my response to his suggestion at all.

Busying myself with shutting off my equipment, I said over my shoulder, "Food only."

"Did I say anything about anything else?" Knowing laughter tickled his voice.

I clamped down on my lips to stop myself from digging my hole deeper and headed for the door.

He stuffed his hands in his pockets as he sauntered along beside me through the lot to my car. From the corner of my eye, I caught him sliding me sideways glances, his brows waggling when he caught me looking. I kept a determined pace until he playfully bumped my shoulder with his, knocking me off my stride. Taking his dare, I bumped my shoulder to his and took off at a dead run. Since mine was the only car left on the lot, he had no trouble racing me to it. We arrived at the passenger side at almost the same second, both of us laughing through our labored breathing.

"There's an all-night diner not far from your hotel. Guess we can try it since it looks like I'm your ride anyway." I flicked the button on my key fob to unlock the doors as I walked around the front of my utilitarian compact car.

He folded himself into the passenger side and winked at me over the console. "It would be hard to get up to shenanigans in this."

I shot him a side-eye.

"But not impossible."

My eyes took a tour of their sockets then I shoved my key in the ignition and turned over the engine. Even though it was a little after midnight, traffic still flowed like a river through the LA streets. Yet my concentration strayed from my driving to the man sitting next to me. The lights of the city set his profile in chiseled relief except for that unruly lock of hair that insisted on hanging out on his forehead. He drummed his long fingers on the console to the rhythm of the Black Keys tune playing on the radio, his demeanor totally relaxed.

All I could think about was how close those fingers were to my thigh and how much I'd loved it when he'd used them to play rhythms over my bare skin. With my attention not where it belonged, no doubt I would have driven right past the diner if not for the timely placement of a red light.

The diner was quiet with only a few occupied tables. We found one beside the windows looking out onto the street and perused our menus.

"What are you gonna have?" we said simultaneously.

"Waffles." Again at the same time.

Our eyes met and held and smiles broke over our faces.

When we ordered, I admonished myself to show some restraint. But when our meals arrived, mine covered in strawberries, his covered in chocolate sauce and whipped cream, I couldn't seem to contain my covetous glances at his plate. The wicked grin on his face as he forked a mouthful of creamy, chocolaty, carboliciousness told me I'd broadcast my thoughts like the ten o'clock news.

His eyes danced with naughtiness as he chewed and swallowed. Pointing at my plate with his fork, he said, "Trade you a bite."

There it was, the slippery slope I desperately needed to avoid.

"It's fine. I'm off chocolate these days," I said airily.

He chuckled. "Afraid I'm going to have to call bullshit. You've hardly taken your eyes off my plate since it arrived."

I pulled my lips between my teeth then said, "Well, maybe a tiny taste."

He started to cut off a bite but I stopped him.

"Maybe we could just trade plates."

"That doesn't sound like a tiny bite, O." His grin was a dare as he leaned across the table with his fork full of food in one hand, his other hand beneath it in case of drips.

I sensed the ground beneath my feet shifting. Careful to close my teeth but not my lips over his fork, I took the bite he offered. His fingers slipped beneath my chin as he held the fork to my mouth until I had no choice but to close my lips over it. Only then did he tug it away. The molten silver of his eyes on my lips had me clamping my thighs together beneath the table, and it took several long seconds before my brain returned to the flavors invading my mouth. Decadent hot fudge, rich thick cream, and buttery, spongy waffle reminded me of another late-night diner in another city when the two of us would taste each other's meals from forks first and kisses second.

"Good, huh?" he asked, a knowing smile on his handsome features.

"Delicious."

Indicating the food in front of me, he said, "You gonna share too?"

I cut a piece of waffle, speared a fresh strawberry, swirled the whole works in a dollop of cream, and reached across the table to share. His eyes never leaving mine, he covered my hand with his, guiding the fork to his mouth where he took his slow sweet time with my offering. His warm touch on my skin as his thumb caressed the inside of my wrist arrowed sensation directly to my core. My breath backed up in my throat at the naked desire in his expression as he savored the bite.

From the second I heard his voice on the phone the day we set this project in motion, Garrett Phillips was dangerous. This moment proved exactly how dangerous. Another forkful of stupidly good chocolate waffle appeared in front of my mouth, and helpless to deny him, I accepted it, sealing my fate.

"You know what this is, Olivia." His voice was low, commanding.

"It's never going to work," I countered.

"You don't know that. And you can't find out if you don't take a chance." His gaze flicked to my lips and back to my eyes.

Alongside the desire, something soft, a scrap of vulnerability stared at me from the depths of those eyes that had haunted my dreams throughout my twenties. Even when I was with someone else, I longed for his eyes looking at me exactly this way. Until he sat right in front of me, I'd let myself forget how much I'd missed him. How much I wanted him.

"Give me a chance, O. Give us another chance." His warm hand covered mine. "Please."

The server stepped over to our table, but Garrett's eyes never left mine as he silently signaled for her to bring the check. His hand found mine again as we walked out to my car. The warm pressure of his skin on mine sent fiery sizzles up my arm. After I slid into the driver's seat, I remained careful to keep both hands on the wheel. Not that my ploy stopped him. It was all I could do to maintain a steady pressure on the accelerator with his hand sliding up and down my thigh.

For most of the ride, he kept it PG, moving between the top of my knee and the middle of my thigh. But as we neared the hotel, each trip up from my knee brought his fingers closer, ever closer to my now throbbing center. When his pinky found the sensitive crease at the top of my thigh, I slid a sideways glance his way. Though his gaze focused on the street in front of us, a wicked grin deepened the lone dimple on the left side of his face. He knew exactly what his touch was doing to me and was enjoying himself immensely.

Bastard.

I drove up to the valet drop-off at the front entrance, and for a fleeting second, I toyed with the idea of dropping him off and driving away. Then he squeezed the top of my thigh, leaned across the console, and kissed the corner of my jaw. "Come inside with me, Olivia," he whispered, his breath on my ear sending shivers through me, tightening my nipples and leaving my core heavy and pulsing with need. "Take a chance."

A valet stood outside my driver's side window, waiting for me to exit the car. Gripping the steering wheel tight, I closed my eyes, my body and mind in a tug-o-war over my next move.

Garrett kissed my jaw again and let his pinky ghost over my center, and that was it. I unbuckled my seatbelt and when he sat up to unbuckle his, I reached into the back seat for my bag. Once again, he clasped my hand in his as he led me into the hotel—and back to the past—or possibly the future.

♪

The elevator stopped on the penthouse floor. Garrett walked me down the hall to his suite and keyed us in. Once the door closed behind us, the enormity of my choice to follow him home settled over me like a weighted cape.

"Hey, hey, O. Nothing to be scared of here," he said as he gently rubbed my arms. "It's just us. We can do—or not do—whatever we want. No pressure."

I couldn't help relaxing slightly beneath his touch. "This could make a big mess."

"It could," he acknowledged. "It could also lead us back to where we were always meant to be."

For a long moment, we held each other's stare. In the subdued light of the sconces on the walls, I could see the desire—and the vulnerability—I'd glimpsed in his eyes back at the studio. No doubt he saw something similar in mine. By some psychic agreement, we moved together, stopping a breath from our lips touching.

"Your call, Olivia," he whispered and waited.

A whimper escaped the back of my throat as I brushed my lips over his beautifully sculpted mouth. That was all it took for him to crush me to him, my breasts flattened against the hard wall of his chest. He coaxed my lips open with his insistent tongue and devoured me when I let him inside. Ten years of separation, ten years of longing poured into that kiss. My heart pounded as I wrapped my arms around his neck. I met his tongue thrust for thrust, both of us trying to touch and taste every corner and crevice of the other's mouth—tongues, teeth, the insides of lips, everywhere at once.

When at last we both needed to come up for air, he grinned. "God, I've missed swappin' spit with you."

"Garrett Foster Phillips! You are not twenty-five anymore."

The naughty gleam in his eyes belied his amused chuckle. "I feel twenty-five with you in my arms like this."

That was all the warning he gave me before he scooped me up high in his arms and carried me through the bedroom door of his suite. I bounced up a bit after my back hit the mattress where he tossed me, his laughter following me down to the bed as he lay on top of me. "I've missed you so fucking much."

This time, the kiss started slow as he nibbled at the corner of my mouth, nipped at my lower lip, and soothed it with a couple of pecks. He traced his tongue over the contours of my mouth then slid along the seam, asking permission. Opening for him, I chased his kiss, stoking the flames of need with each caress of lips and tongue. He rolled to my side, allowing him access to my body. Chilled air ghosted over me as he tugged my shirt from my jeans, then his warm hand was on my skin, and I shivered for an entirely different reason.

He found his way around my back, and with a flick of his hand, the elastic of my bra relaxed beneath my breasts while my nipples puckered in anticipation. I tried to chase after him when he lifted his lips from mine to trail them along my jaw and down the column of my neck. The turtleneck of my shirt stymied his intent, and he pushed up on his knees to stare down at my clothes. His expression of pure frustration was so adorable I had to smile.

"You think this is funny? This top is hot to look at, but it's like Fort Knox to access."

I smiled wider, not bothering to hide my amusement at his consternation.

"Sit up."

My brow went up at his tone.

"Sit up, *please*."

Using more effort than the situation called for, I did as he asked, deliberately setting one hand on his thigh to leverage myself up. Then my fingers took a little tour up to the spot where his thigh met his groin, and he sucked in air.

"You've grown quite naughty in your advanced age, haven't you, O?" His eyes glittered in the low light coming from the living room of the suite. In one quick move, he swept his hands up my sides, taking my bra along for the ride as he divested me of my turtleneck. "Jesus, babe. You're incredible."

Leaning into me, he gently pushed me back down on the bed, his hand gliding up my side. He traced the pad of his thumb along the outside of my curves and he finished the tour of my neck that he'd started with his lips earlier. Open-mouthed kisses along my collarbone had me arching into him, seeking more contact with his body. In the back of his throat, he chuckled darkly, his palm at last coming around to cup and plump my breast. When his mouth finally meandered its way to my turgid nipple, I was writhing and squirming beneath him like a woman possessed, my moans loud in my ears.

Closing his lips over the tip, he sucked me deep into his mouth, his tongue doing an erotic dance over my skin that left my core heavy and aching. I plowed my fingers into his hair, alternately tugging and pushing his head. I wanted his hands and his talented mouth everywhere all at once, and I wanted him to stay right where he was, pleasuring my nipple with long sucks and quick nips and teasing flicks while he pinched and rolled and tugged the other one with his calloused fingers.

He kissed his way from one breast to the other, switching the attentions of his hands and mouth. At the juncture of my thighs, my clit throbbed and my core pulsed in rhythm with my heartbeat. Without my permission, a long moan tore from my throat followed by Garrett's name on a breathy sigh.

"Mmm, that good huh?" His dark laughter vibrated over my skin.

Incoherent mumblings were the only response I could manage, which he took as agreement. He kissed and licked his way down the center of my belly until the waistband of my jeans interrupted his progress. With a long-suffering sigh, he went to work on the button and zipper. In seconds, cool air fanned my overheated body as my jeans tangled around my ankles. Rolling off the bed, Garrett stood and grabbed one foot, unclasping the buckle of my wedge sandal and tossing it on the floor somewhere behind him. A second later, the other one joined it, followed by jeans and panties he'd pushed off me at the same time.

I lay there in front of him, utterly naked while he remained fully clothed. In another time, the perceived imbalance of power would have had me covering my vulnerability with my hands. But I was older now, and I reveled in the power of my body. My eyes on his,

I stretched my hands over my head and arched my back, offering myself up to him.

"Aw, fuck, Olivia." His tone was reverent. "You're glorious."

In two breaths, Garrett's clothes had joined mine on the floor, and it was my turn to stare. Heavy shoulders and thick pecs arrowed down to a flat stomach. Obviously he'd spent time in the gym sculpting the contours of his biceps and triceps, and my mouth watered at his masculine beauty. It had been a bit too easy to overlook his toned physique with my attention on the strange fashion choices he made these days. Or because I was trying hard not to notice his broad shoulders and tight ass. But here in this moment, I could look my fill and appreciate every delectable inch of him, especially the thick, hard length jutting out proudly between his powerful thighs.

The corner of his mouth tipped up. "Like what you see?"

"Very much."

"Yeah?" He toured my body with his eyes. "Me too." He flicked on the bedside lamp. "And I want to see it all."

The bed sagged as he kneeled on it with one knee. Starting at the tops of my feet, he skimmed his fingertips the length of my leg and smiled when my skin rippled beneath his touch. He stopped a breath shy of the crease where my thigh joined my hip, and I might have growled in frustration. I needed his touch exactly there. His dark laughter told me he knew that too as he started again on my other leg.

This time when he glided his fingers along the top of my thigh, he said, "Open for me, O."

With desire pulsing through my body like the relentless rhythms of a thundering waterfall, I was helpless not to do as he demanded. When my thighs fell open, Garrett's eyes darkened almost to black as he zeroed in on my soaked center. He dragged one thick finger through my folds, and his name tore from my throat on a raspy moan.

"Jesus, Olivia. You're so incredibly wet." His gaze flicked up to mine. "And all for me."

Snatching his pants from the floor, he extracted his wallet, pulled a condom from it, and flipped it onto the table. He passed the foil packet to me and climbed over me, inserting himself between my legs. "You do the honors."

I peeked up at him through my lashes and gifted him a coy smile. Then I tore the packet open with my teeth and took my time enjoying his length as I smoothed the condom over him.

Slowly, he leaned down until his lips were a breath from mine. "You have no idea how much I've missed you."

His mouth covered mine, his tongue sweetly coaxing mine to play, our lips and tongues doing what I longed for our bodies to do. I wrapped my arms around him and arched up into him, silently asking for what I wanted, what I needed.

With a groan, he broke the kiss and pushed up onto his knees. "Watch, Olivia. Watch us come together again."

Something deep and permanent lurked in his words, but my body needed him too much to let my mind dwell on them. I leaned up on my elbows and watched as he slowly, deliberately kissed the head of his cock to my folds. I lifted my hips to draw him in and he pulled away.

"If you want this, you have to be patient and watch."

A whimper escaped me. "You're a cruel, naughty man." I panted.

"Good things come to those who wait, Olivia." His tone teased as much as the head of his cock barely pushing in before sliding back out over and over until I thought I'd lose my mind.

When at last he pushed all the way inside me, filling me as only he ever could, my eyes flew to his. "Garrett. Oh, oh, oh Garrett." I sighed. "I need you so much."

Then there were no more words, only our bodies moving together, our hands rediscovering the sensitive places that heightened our pleasure, our breaths coming faster. When he slipped a hand between us with the perfect pressure on my clit, I closed my eyes tight as millions of golden stars exploded behind them. He shouted my name as he pounded into me then his body tensed, the veins in his neck in sharp relief in the lamplight as he came.

Afterward when he collapsed on top of me, flattening me into the mattress in the most delicious way, my body continued to pulse around his, prolonging our pleasure.

"Fuck, Olivia," he said into the pillow beside my head. "How did we ever let this go?"

CHAPTER TWENTY

Garrett

THE SECOND THE words left my mouth, I wanted them back. Beneath me, her body tensed—and not with pleasure. Resting on my forearms, I stared into her eyes. "Don't start. Not now while we're still enjoying the aftershocks."

"This was a mistake."

I wasn't quick enough to shield my heart against those words—or something similar—I sensed were coming. Three quick jabs and one twist of the knife on "mistake" and my breath wouldn't come. Closing my eyes, I held on through the initial piercing pain then rolled off her onto my back. Remembering the condom, I knotted it and dropped it into the trash beside the bed and flopped back onto the pillows.

"That was too glorious to ever be a mistake, Olivia, and you know it." I rolled onto my side and propped my head on my hand. "You're just scared." Smoothing my knuckles along the silky skin covering her jaw, I gentled my tone. "Our mistake was not trying to figure out a way to make it work in the first place. We're older now." I smiled. "Wiser."

"Our dreams are still worlds apart."

A little chuckle escaped. "Which totally explains why and how we're working together now."

She turned her head on the pillow to face me. "This is a one-off, and you know it."

"Do I?"

"What's that supposed to mean? My studio is only contracted with Balefire for this one video."

My hand strayed to her hair, pushing a sweaty strand behind her ear and letting my fingers linger there. "But I've seen your notes—and the galleys. Once the guys see the finished video, they're not going to want to work with anyone else."

Abruptly, she sat up. "My dreams are bigger than being on Balefire's payroll as their videographer." She swung her legs over the side of the bed, paused for a long breath, and slipped off to gather her clothes. Her bra and shirt already covered her before I woke up from the dream I'd tried to draw her into. In the seconds it took me to roll off the bed, she'd shimmied into her panties and was hopping around on one foot as she hastily dragged on her jeans.

"Olivia, you don't have to leave. Spend the night. Here." I covered her forearm with my hand, stopping her progress. "With me. Please."

Pain flashed in her eyes in the second before she lowered her lashes, her gaze on my hand. "I can't." She finished hiking up her jeans and went in search of her sandals, one of which had mysteriously found its way under the bed. With her ass in the air as she felt around for her shoe, my mind went places it absolutely had no business going, especially under the current circumstances.

She jammed her shoes on her feet and sailed through the suite in search of her bag, locating it on the floor by the door. At last she faced me. "I can't do this with you. Not now. Too much is riding on this project."

"I thought we established that we, you and me, are separate from work. What's going on between us, what happened back there just now"—I gestured with my thumb to the bedroom with the messed up bed visible through the open door—"is so much bigger than this video or your studio or my situation with the band." I took a step toward her. "You know I'm right."

"Garrett. I have to go."

Probably half my life passed as I stood in the middle of the room bare-ass naked and staring at the back of the door to my suite. How could she walk away like that after we'd shared something so profound, something so beautiful? How could we be so connected one minute and oceans apart the next? How did I let her walk away again?

♪

"What's this I hear about someone catching Olivia doing the walk of shame out of your hotel room in the wee hours this morning, Garrett?" Dakota asked as he slid into the booth across from me at brunch.

Refusing to look at him, I tossed back a long drink of coffee. "No idea what you're talking about."

"Not gonna kiss and tell, huh? Classy," he added with a smirk.

"Fuck off, Dakota. Olivia and I are none of your business." I stared morosely down at my half-empty coffee cup and wondered if I'd just signed my walking papers. Of the entire band, Dakota held the biggest grudge.

"You hear that?" He glanced around at the others seated in the booth with us at the back of the hotel restaurant. "Garrett's love life is none of our business." Returning his attention to me, he said, "That's funny considering how you thought you had a say in all of ours."

From the hard look on his face, it was fifty-fifty that this was my last gig with the band. After what went down in my suite last night, I struggled to find it in me to care.

"Let me get this straight," Jack said. "You and Olivia used to have a thing back when Balefire was starting out."

"A pretty damn intense thing from what I remember," Blu said.

"I've noticed you haven't been spending time with groupies, not even at that charity event we did following the Grammys when they were hanging off you like barnacles," Tron added.

Over the years, I'd heard the other three flip Tron shit for needing more to do so he didn't have so much time to observe everyone else. I'd thought it funny when his observations were about them. Now that he'd set his sights on me? Not so much.

"Your point?"

"After you saw hot Olivia at the after-party, you went all quiet on the groupie front. Guess I was connecting the dots." He hid his smirk behind his tall glass of magic green hangover smoothie.

"Yeah, that's what I saw too." Though awkward since they were sitting beside each other, Jack fist-bumped Tron.

"Are we taking care of business today or what? Thought you guys wanted to get this meeting over so you could spend your day off with your women." I pushed my plate of half-eaten omelet toward the middle of the table and signaled the server for more coffee. After not sleeping last night, I felt more hungover than if I'd spent the night doing tequila shots with the boys.

"What's the deal with Jennifer? Why the hell did you invite her to the surprise scene yesterday?" Blu's change in topic did nothing for my roiling guts.

I appreciated the server's perfectly timed interruption with more coffee for me and a question about the band's brunch orders. Since I'd had nothing else to do with myself all morning, I'd come down early, but I was only toying with my meal when Blu and Jack joined me from their suites. With Tron staying at Cristy's place and Dakota and Annabelle taking advantage of Parker Malone's hospitality, the two of them arrived several minutes after the agreed-upon time. Anticipating their hangovers after Dakota lined up the tequila shots early yesterday evening following the shoot, I'd had their smoothies waiting for them. Guess it wasn't enough to put off their surly inquisition.

"You gonna answer the question?" Blu asked again after the server walked away to put in their orders.

"On the last tour, how could you miss what a big fan of yours she is, what with how many dates she hit?" I hedged.

"We didn't invite her then, and we sure as hell didn't invite her yesterday," Dakota snarled. He'd barely touched his hangover cure, rolling the glass between his hands instead. His restlessness did not bode well for me.

"Look, we all know she's a diva, but she's also the reason you all have a shot at an Oscar for 'Dangerous Life.' I didn't think tossing her a little bone was out of line." Though I glanced around the table, I didn't make direct eye contact with any of them.

"'Tossing her a little bone' meant letting her take over the scene?" Blu asked, his attitude ominously mirroring Dakota's.

"I didn't give her permission to sashay over the stage. She was supposed to remain in front with the rest of the groupies. But you know Jennifer—" With a shrug, I added cream to my coffee, more for something to occupy my eyes and hands than that I wanted it. After I took the first sip, I could have kicked myself as I caught Tron's knowing stare. What the hell was I thinking trying to find one second of comfort in copying Olivia's coffee preference?

"Make sure Olivia doesn't use a single frame of Jennifer in the video," Dakota said.

"What he said," Blu added. "Especially after Ashleigh agreed to do the shoot tomorrow."

"You hired Olivia because you trusted her to make you all look good." Now I did look them each in the eye. "Guess you'll have to trust her professional judgment."

Blu leaned forward, resting his forearms on the table. "You pissed her off, didn't you, dumbass?"

My eyes took a round-the-world tour of their sockets. "No, I did not piss Olivia off. And I don't plan to by second-guessing her artistry or her choices. It was her idea to put Ashleigh in the video in the first place, remember?" Sipping my coffee again did nothing for my attitude.

Blu turned to the rest of his bandmates. "Did you all notice how Garrett deflected there?" His attention landed back on me. "You're not going to give away one second with her from last night, are you?"

Before I could *not* dignify his question with an answer, Dakota jumped in with his nasty observations.

"On more than one occasion, I've watched Garrett stroll out of an after-party with a groupie or two already half-naked, their lips locked, his hands inside their clothes. But when it comes to Olivia"—his singsong delivery of her name reminded me of a fifth grader—"he's as buttoned up as my guitar racks before we head out on the road." With his elbow cupped in one hand, he stroked his chin with the other, training his eyes on me like I was some sort of lab experiment. "Interesting." He sounded the word out like a bad imitation of Gene Wilder in *Young Frankenstein,* which I'd seen once on late-night TV.

"I learned my lesson, all right?" I snapped. "I don't pry into your personal lives, and I expect the same courtesy from you concerning mine."

The four of them exchanged knowing glances among themselves, and my balls drew up. Whatever was going on here was not good for me. From the way they were acting, my job remained safe, but I had the vibe that they didn't have quite the full pound of my flesh they wanted.

Attempting to steer them into the conversation that was the reason for our meeting, I asked, "Where do you want to tour the new album first? East Coast? West Coast? Start at home and swing through the Midwest? Also, I need to know if you want to do a European tour for this one. Since the events of the movie take place mostly in Balkan countries, it might be good to tour a few cities over there."

"Do you think Olivia will go out on tour with us? Maybe film a documentary or something?" Blu's innocent tone didn't ring true, especially with that wicked look in his eyes.

"Olivia's studio and business are right here in LA. I doubt she'd be game to ride your tour bus even as far as San Diego."

"You could ask her." The smirk in his tone drew my balls up tighter.

"If you want her to go out on tour with you, ask her yourself." Blu could take a chance with his own balls. I was partial to keeping mine.

"So that's the way of it," Blu said with a sage nod like he had Olivia and me all figured out.

"You like cold breakfast?"

The server had dropped off the guys' orders several fishy comments ago, yet Blu and Dakota had yet to tuck in. Jack and Tron watched our exchange with half interest while they focused on their eggs and pancakes and a shared plate of breakfast meat.

"Okay, Dad." Dakota grinned and picked up his fork.

This time Blu was the one who couldn't let things go. "We've been on the road for ten years. Isn't it time someone did a documentary on Balefire? With how well she works with us, Olivia is the perfect choice."

"Make sure to mention that when you ask her," I said. "So about touring the new album."

"It's been a couple of years since we treated the folks at home to a show at Red Rocks. Maybe we should start there," Jack said around bites of sausage.

"Because Clio's morning sickness is killer?" Tron asked.

"Exactly. I'd like to be closer to home so I can help with Angel when Clio is having especially tough mornings."

A year ago, the others never would have let him up about being so whipped. Now they were all there, commiserating with him rather than flipping him shit. I waited for my stomach to sour at the thought as usual. Instead, a picture of Olivia Carter staring up at me, her luminous eyes more gold than green or brown as I drove into her, flashed through my head.

What the fuck?

I pulled out my iPad and started typing. "So we start the tour in Denver, head south to Phoenix, Houston, and Dallas then back up to Salt Lake and Vegas. We can stop over for a couple of days in Denver to check in then head back out to Chicago, Omaha, Minneapolis, Cincinnati, and St. Louis. That's ten dates. Do you want more or do you want to take another break?"

Four pairs of eyes stared at me with equal curiosity.

"What?" I tried to keep the irritation out of my voice, but it was there all the same.

In sync, they turned to each other. "Whipped. Totally whipped," Blu said.

"Was bound to happen," Dakota added like he was a philosophy professor or some damn thing.

"Happened to us, so I guess it stands to reason," Tron said, a smirk playing at the corner of his mouth.

"Good timing," Jack said with a nod. "His plan will make my wife very happy. Anything that makes Clio happy makes me happy."

"What the fuck, you guys?"

"Exactly, Garrett." Dakota smirked. "Before we started working with Olivia, if Jack had suggested Denver to start our next tour, you would have had all kinds of reasons for why that was a bad idea."

Blu chimed in. "But this time, you started plugging in dates that let us come home in the middle to 'check in' and asked if we wanted a break after ten shows, which is less than a month on the road. Makes a guy wonder what's gotten into you."

"Or who you've gotten into." Dakota choked on his laughter at his bad joke while Blu almost snorted green smoothie, Tron smiled down into his lap and Jack surreptitiously wiped a tear from the corner of his eye as he stared out the window.

"You're fuckin' hilarious, you are, Dakota," I sneered. "But hey, if you want six months on the road, I can arrange that, no problem. Of course, we'll have to be careful to have an opening in the schedule for when the movie premiers since you'll want to walk the red carpet for that."

I'd typed in Kansas City and Louisville when Blu covered my keyboard with his hand. "It's not so funny when it's you, is it?"

Chapter Twenty-One

Olivia

"IT'S LATE, JEREMY, and you've been a champ with all the bizarre logistical snafus we've had today. If you want to head home, be my guest," I said as I flopped back in my chair in my office. "I'll finish what needs to be done tonight."

"I owed you after my hangover-induced slow start." His sheepish expression combined with the flaming tips of his ears was adorable. "Learning the hard way that I don't have the stomach to party like a rock star was painful enough. Thanks for not rubbing salt into my tequila wounds." He smirked at his bad metaphor and I smiled back.

"Those of us on this side of the camera all have to learn that lesson sooner or later." Rolling the kinks out of my neck, I added, "I learned it when I was about your age and with the same rock stars. Well, except for Jack." Placing my right hand over my head to flatten it against the left side, I executed a stretch that alleviated the worst of the kinks threatening to bind up my spine. "The original drummer, Dave Brubaker, made the other three look like amateurs when they were all still in their teens." Switching sides, I stretched again.

His mouth rounded into an *O* that cracked me up. "No wonder they had to replace him."

"From what I gather, Garrett put him in rehab to save his life. When he finished, Dave admitted he couldn't be a rock star and stay sober, so he chose to stay sober."

Saying Garrett's name aloud cracked the dam around emotions I'd determined to keep sealed up. I stood and stared out the window at the red snake of taillights endlessly gliding along LA's streets to their late-night destinations and wondered what he was doing right now.

"I can't imagine anyone on the planet who can keep up with those boys let alone out-drink them. From what I heard, the party yesterday moved to Parker Malone's place and ended a little before dawn. I was weaving and slurring by dinner," Jeremy mused as he stood up from his chair too.

Facing him, I smirked. "I noticed."

Again, his ears brightened, and his neck joined the party. "Sorry if I embarrassed you, Olivia."

"You didn't."

At the door, he turned and said, "I'll be on my game from the second I step on set tomorrow. Promise. G'night." With that, he was gone.

Turning back to the nighttime view from my tenth-story window, my thoughts strayed to what Garrett and I had been doing twenty-four hours ago while the band and their buddies partied. I'd have been far better off if I'd taken Dakota up on his offer of tequila shots. At least then I would have had an excuse for what happened between my ex and me.

Even thinking of him as my ex left a bad taste in my mouth. Last night didn't feel like a walk down memory lane or scratching an itch after a while of doing without or taking advantage of a convenient opportunity. No. Last night set off an earthquake of emotions that decimated my resolve to leave the past in the past. What happened between us was more than off-the-charts sex. But I had no intention of exploring it further. Having already traveled that road once, I knew it was a dead end.

So why was my stupid heart revving up its engine for another trip?

A ping on my open computer alerted me to an incoming text. As though I'd conjured him with my thoughts, Garrett's name flashed across the screen of my phone when I picked it up.

Garrett: Are you still at the studio?

Me: Yes. Why?

Garrett: I'm in the neighborhood and thought I'd drop by.

Me: Probably not a good idea.

Garrett: Probably the best idea I've had in ten years. See you in a few.

Me: Seriously. I'm almost done, and tomorrow is a long day.

Aaand, crickets. No response meant he wasn't taking the hint. Damn it.

Since I hadn't been able to fall asleep after arriving home from Garrett's hotel at dark-thirty a.m., I'd rolled out of bed, showered, and driven to the observatory, arriving a few minutes after seven. My timing was fortuitous since the truck carrying the flight simulator showed up around half an hour early, officially starting my day before eight. Overseeing the setup of the flight simulator, green screens, cameras and tracks, lights, and sound exhilarated me and focused all my energy and thought on the shoot. It was only after Jeremy and I drove back to the studio to go over the script one more time, marking all the equipment and people we'd need and where, that exhaustion crept in. When my reserves dropped below fumes, I couldn't block thoughts of Garrett and the hours we'd spent together.

With my defenses so depleted, now was *not* a good time for him to show up.

A light tap on my door was all the warning I had before the man himself stood across my desk from me.

His expression was so serious. "You left last night before we were finished."

"We'd finished. Both of us." My expression was equally serious.

He came around my desk, cornering me between the window and a side table where my Keurig and a couple of dirty cups told a story of my assistant and me burning the midnight oil. His hand rested on the wall beside my head, the heat from his nearness warming all the cold places inside me.

"You can do your lawyer semantics thing with me all you want. Doesn't change the facts. The two of us have unfinished business, and you know it." His steel-gray eyes dipped to my lips for a split second. When they flicked back to mine, they shone quicksilver, so hot and sexy I had to clamp my thighs together to stop myself from wrapping around him like a vine.

"You're a super-smart man, so it shouldn't take so much repetition to make a point with you. Nothing about our dreams has changed. You still want to manage the band. I still want to run my own studio. Both of those visions require ridiculous hours of work, plus, you're on the road for at least half the year." A whiff of fresh citrus and clean male hit my nose, momentarily making me forget what I wanted to say.

"Still waiting for the point."

I blew out a sigh. "We don't have any business to finish. We finished it a lifetime ago when we wished each other well and walked away to chase separate dreams."

"You know, when you're riding for weeks at a time on a tour bus, you have loads of downtime to think," he said in a conversational tone. "What I've thought about long and hard, especially these past two years, is that we had something truly special, something worth saving." His focus shifted to his forefinger trailing lightly along my hairline, over the contours of the side of my face, and down the column of my neck, stopping at the collar of my button-down shirt. His action left a trail of goosebumps behind. "From the first email we exchanged for this project, I had a feeling this was fate bringing us back together."

"You always were a romantic."

"Trying to blow this off"—he gestured between us—"isn't going to work, O. The two of us have always had a connection." He slid his fingers into my hair, and I closed my eyes against the shivery sensations zinging over my scalp and down the back of my neck, arrowing straight down my spine. Though he barely touched me, my entire body buzzed in anticipation of his hands on me. "We belong to each other."

My gaze flew to his. Dark, powerful emotions swirled in the depths of his gray eyes, turning them silver. Though I desperately wanted to shield my own emotions from his stare, I couldn't look away. His chin tipped up, a barely there nod telling me I'd outed myself, and he lowered his head.

Like the night before, his unhurried movements left me more raw and open than if he would have dived right in and ravaged me. That kind of out-of-control passion after all the time apart I could have understood and dismissed afterward. But the deliberate way he took my lips, like we had all of eternity plus a day, left me utterly powerless to do anything but respond to him.

He brushed his mouth over mine once, twice, and nibbled and sipped at my lips until I chased him, needing more pressure. At last, he gave me what I craved, but when I opened for him, he shook his head and concentrated his attention on the corner of my mouth before he trailed his lips to my jaw, nibbling his way to my ear. After he nosed my hair over the shell of my ear and kissed the sweet spot behind it, I became aware of his fingers working on the top button of my shirt.

"Ooh," I moaned. My hands found purchase on his waist, fisting his T-shirt as his lips took a leisurely tour of the column of my neck.

Involuntarily, I arched into his mouth, seeking more of his touch, his warm breath on my skin. With my head against the wall, the only way I could move was to offer my throat and chest to him. He popped open two more buttons over my bra, but the cool air of my office did nothing for my overheated skin. I wanted his tongue tasting me, but he withheld it as he kissed along my collarbone to the hollow of my throat. Another button below my breasts came undone. The backs of his fingers grazed the skin beneath the band of my bra, and he laughed deep in his throat as I trembled. Yet he made no other move to touch me, his other hand remaining flat on the wall beside my head.

"Garrett."

He laughed at my breathy whine. "Patience, O. We'll get there."

His clever fingers slid open another button as his mouth toured the other side of my neck up to the shell of my ear. At last, he let his tongue join in, tracing my ear and sending hot shivers through me.

I turned my head and captured his mouth with mine. My tongue slid along the seam of his lips, demanding entrance. When he opened and let me in, all the teasing stopped. He grasped my shirt with both hands and yanked it from the waistband of my slim, knee-length skirt. In two moves, he finished unbuttoning it. Then his hands were inside, roaming the bare skin of my back as he dragged me into his body while he deepened the kiss.

My arms wrapped around his neck, anchoring me to him as our tongues twined and danced with each other. Heat pooled low in my belly where my pussy pulsed in time with my heavy heartbeat. Garrett's kisses drove me wild, and I couldn't help but push my hips into his, rubbing my lower belly and pubic bone along the hard length filling the front of his dress pants.

He unclasped my bra, and then his hands were where I most wanted them. Calloused palms cupped and kneaded me, teasing the hard peaks of my breasts before he made them even harder when he plucked and rolled them between his thumbs and forefingers.

I tore my mouth from his and stared into the blazing infernos of his molten steel eyes. "I want you. God, I want you so much," I panted.

The corner of his mouth tipped up. "You have me."

Then he turned me and backed me around my desk and over to the couch beside the door of my office. The backs of my calves hit the edge of the couch, but before I could lose my balance, he turned us and sat down, pulling me with him to straddle his lap.

Digging my nails into his shoulders, I cried out as he set his perfect sculpted lips on my breast and drew me deep into his mouth. I clamped my knees to his hips and arched my back, seeking as much of his touch as I could. While he sucked my breast, he palmed his hands along my thighs to the hem of my skirt, slipped his fingers beneath it, and pushed the fabric up over my ass to bunch at my waist. One hand smoothed over the globe of my ass, his fingers toying with my thong. His other hand got busy plumping and tweaking the nipple his mouth wasn't pleasuring.

I writhed and moaned on his lap, desperate to be closer to him. "Please," I begged. "I need you."

Slowly, he pulled off me and grinned. "I'm right here."

An exasperated sigh puffed out of me. "You know what I mean." For emphasis, I ground my center over the fly of his pants.

His eyes held a wicked sparkle. "I think I need a bit more explanation."

Meeting his dare, I slid back on his lap enough for access to the front of his pants and got busy unbuttoning and unzipping them. Matching my own wicked smile to his eyes, I slipped a hand inside his pants and boxers, finding my prize and giving his hard length a squeeze and a tug. "Did you need more explanation?"

"Unnhhh," he groaned. "I love it when you touch me like that."

"It would be easier if all these clothes weren't in the way."

"Stand up, then."

I pushed myself off his lap, but my feet had barely touched the floor when his trousers and boxers were already off his hips and down by his knees.

"You too," he said.

When I didn't immediately respond, he leaned forward and jerked at the waistband of my thong. A ripping sound told me I wouldn't be wearing this particular pair again.

"Those were Agent Provocateur."

The smirk on Garrett's face said he didn't care. "I'll buy you two new pairs." He tugged at my hips. "Now come back here and take what you want."

Somewhere in all the divesting of clothing, he'd managed to snag a condom from his pocket. Dangling it in front of my face, he said, "Whenever you're ready." The impish expression in his eyes told me he knew exactly how impatient he'd made me for what only he could give.

I tore the foil packet open and smoothed the condom down his length. A groan escaped my throat when I centered myself over him and sat down. My body pulsed around his for the first few seconds as I acclimated to him filling me. Then I started to move, and I wasn't in the mood for slow. He clamped his hands on my hips, stilling me, and I might have growled at him.

"What are you doing?"

"Savoring this. Savoring you." He leaned forward and caught a nipple in his mouth, sucking and nipping, licking and kissing me like I was the tastiest dessert he'd ever enjoyed.

I squirmed on his lap, and he pushed up higher into me, but he still wouldn't let me move. Pulsing my inner muscles around him and grinding down on him, I silently demanded he give in, but all he did was kiss his way to my other breast, giving it the same attention as the first.

At last, he loosened his grip on my hips and started moving.

"Take your time, Olivia. We have all night."

He smoothed his hands over my ass, his fingers finding their way to the crease, the move stealing my breath. I dug my nails into his shoulders as I ratcheted up the pace only to have him clamp down on my hips again.

"Easy, babe." He held me where he wanted me and slowly pistoned his hips, pushing into me in long languorous strokes that drove me straight out of my head.

"Garrett." Did that mewling sound come from me?

"That's it, babe. Take it all."

His eyes glittered up at me, and a devilish smile curved his lips. Still, he kept his maddeningly deliberate pace that held me on a razor's edge of coming. Sweat beaded my brow and slid down the center of my back. My breaths came shallower and shallower.

"Please. Please let me come."

"Hmm, I'm not sure I heard you correctly. Why don't you come a little closer and tell my lips what you want." Emphasizing his directive, he puckered his lips then grinned.

I crashed my mouth to his, kissing him like the out-of-control wild thing he'd made me. Only then did he let go of my hips, and we smashed together in a rhythm guaranteed to rocket me into space. The pad of his finger on the hard nub of my clit lit the fuse, and I shot into the stratosphere.

When I finally came down, my forehead rested on his as my breath sawed in and out. It took several long minutes for me to quiet enough to register how hard he remained inside me as the aftershocks pulsed deep in my core. He pushed a sweaty lock from my face, a smile in his eyes. "The ride's not over yet, but hop off."

My brow creased, but I did as he said, standing on wobbly legs. He nudged me back and stood. "Now I'll give you what you really want."

His hands on my hips, he turned me to face my desk. I glanced over my shoulder at him. "Are you serious?"

"Very. Probably better close your computer and move it to the side."

I'd barely finished following his suggestion when he had me bent over my desk. He guided himself to my entrance and pushed inside. "You're gonna want to hold on for this."

I gripped the edge of my desk and he gripped my hips as he pounded into me. Here I'd thought the first orgasm he gave me had sent me to space, but this wild, savage coupling truly took me to a place I'd never been before.

"Come, Olivia. You need to come now!" he ground out.

His thumb found my clit, and every nerve ending exploded in a shower of pleasure. He stopped moving as my name ripped from him in a series of whole notes that lasted for at least four bars. A couple of jerky thrusts later, he collapsed over me, his hands covering mine as he kissed the corner of my mouth.

"Fuck, Olivia. You have fucking wrecked me."

"Ditto, Garrett," I whispered.

Our bodies started to cool, and he pulled out. Gently, he tucked my girls back into my bra and reached around me to reclasp it. With excessive concentration, he rebuttoned my shirt and tenderly pushed my skirt back down my thighs. When his eyes found mine again, emotion as hot as the sex we'd enjoyed blazed from his.

He cupped my cheek, his thumb gliding along my jaw, as he held my eyes with his. "In case you have any other ideas, what happened between us just now wasn't sex. What happened here transcended sex by an astral plane, and I'm not letting you deny that."

I covered his wrist with my hand. "I won't deny it." With a squeeze of my hand, I added, "But it changes nothing."

His other arm came around me. "It changes everything. For a decade, I've searched for what I lost when we gave each other up. It was here with you the whole time. I'm not giving you up again, O. I can't."

"Garrett."

"You can lie to yourself all you want, but what you told me in so many ways after I arrived here tonight, that was the truth. And the truth is, we belong to each other. We have since the day we met."

He tugged me into his chest, and I went willingly, holding him as close as he held me. For a minute, I didn't have to fight. For a minute in his arms, I could just be. I wanted his truth as much as he did. But I couldn't see a way forward for us without one of us giving up everything we'd worked for, which wasn't fair to either of us. One of us giving up our dream would doom our relationship every bit as much as when we followed our dreams. Though he wasn't ready to admit it yet, ours was an untenable situation from the get-go. Not even off-the-charts love-making could change that.

"It's late, and I have to be on set hours ahead of the band."

"Come on, then. I'll walk you to your car."

Out of nowhere, I heard myself say, "Do you want to come home with me?"

His smile said he was waiting for my invitation. "Yes."

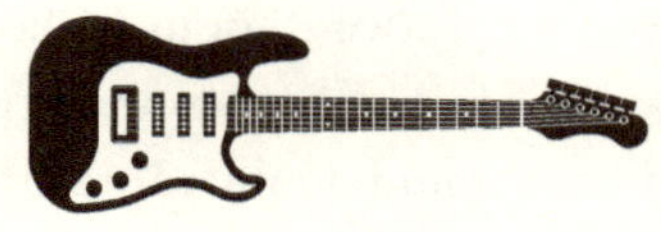

Chapter Twenty-Two

Garrett

IF ONLY I could break him of his insistent use of "sir" when addressing me, Landon Berg would be the world's best fucking assistant. He showed up on set almost at the same time Olivia and I did, carrying my messenger bag with my iPad and notes as well as a change of clothes. While I would have preferred a Balefire T-shirt with the charcoal Armani slacks he brought rather than the cream-colored polo he apparently picked up from some store on the way over, beggars couldn't be choosers.

As I changed into clean clothes in the band's dressing trailer, visions of Olivia and me in her bedroom fresh from a shower filled my thoughts. When I had to work at zipping my fly, I rolled my eyes at myself. How I was supposed to keep my head in the game with that sexy woman running the show, I had no idea.

When I stepped out of the trailer, I nearly bumped into the woman in question. With one hand holding her phone to her ear, she wrapped the other around my waist to maintain her balance before she swung around me with a quick smile and kept right on moving. I had to jog a few paces to catch up to her before I fell into step beside her. Her free hand gestured to the air as she informed whoever was on the other end of the call that they most definitely would arrive on time, traffic be damned. Maybe they should have left the warehouse on schedule. The thing was, she didn't shout or lose her cool, but I wouldn't have wanted to be on the receiving end of that tone of voice.

After she clicked off, I snagged her hand, smoothing the pad of my thumb over her soft skin and enjoying the hitch of her breath at my touch. "Anything I can do to help?"

For a second she let out a sigh and gifted me a dreamy smile. Her eyes strayed to our clasped hands, and she smoothed her thumb over mine, neither of us needing words to know we were both remembering last night after we returned to her surprisingly tiny apartment. Damn, did I like knowing I'd put that expression on her face.

Then her head came up, her expression telling me work interrupted our stolen moment. "Unless you can magic a truckload of lights that should have been here before we arrived this morning, there's nothing you can do." As we walked beside the flight simulator, she stopped and glanced around, her forefinger absently tapping her chin. After a couple of seconds, she pulled up a number on her phone and shot off a quick text.

"When the band arrives, have them suit up for the simulator scene, would you please?" she said.

"We're starting with the flight simulator?" I had no idea what shape the boys would be in when they arrived, so starting with that scene sounded a bit risky.

Her tone was all business. "Without the lights, we can't film the second opening, but we don't have time to waste waiting around for them to arrive either. We're filming the flight simulator at some point today anyway. Might as well start with it."

"Right." I shot off my own text to Landon to have a pitcher or two of hangover cure at the ready. The original plan for filming the flight simulator scene after lunch wouldn't have been a problem no matter how the boys spent last night. Starting with it first thing this morning? Yikes.

Before I could hit Send on my phone, Olivia was all the way across the set checking on camera tracks and consulting with the cinematographer who kept sneaking drags off her vape pen. As I admired my woman doing her thing, raucous laughter growing in volume alerted me the band had arrived.

I hustled back over to their trailer, meeting them at the door. "You sound pretty chipper this morning. Early night last night?" I asked with more hope than belief.

"Earlier than yours," Blu said with a smirk.

"What's that supposed to mean?"

"It means, Landon was seen leaving your room early this morning carrying your gear," Tron said, his brow waggling. "If that's the case, then where did you sleep last night?"

"Not a question I've ever asked *you*," I shot back.

"Touchy, touchy," Dakota said, an teasing gleam in his eyes. "I wonder if a certain director knows anything about it."

"None of your fucking business, Dakota."

"Sounds like a confirmation to me." Jack too? What the hell?

As he stepped past me to enter their trailer, Tron clapped me on the shoulder. "About time, man."

Blu nodded as he passed me. "Don't fuck it up."

"What he said," Dakota added as he joined the others.

Jack gave me a knowing grin but said nothing as he stepped up into the trailer.

I scrubbed a hand over my face and sighed. Olivia kept her private life private. Always. I doubted that had changed from back in the day, which meant she wouldn't appreciate all this speculation about us. For once, I hoped the boys could keep their observations to themselves. Then I followed them inside.

"We're starting with the flight simulator scene," I announced as I joined them. "So dress for that."

"Why?" Dakota demanded.

"Supply chain problems. A truckload of lights hasn't arrived. But we only have this area for the day, so there's no time to waste while we wait for it." I glanced around at the guys who appeared uncharacteristically clear-eyed for the morning after a day off. "You up for it? If you need 'em, I've got smoothies coming."

"Annie and I stayed in and watched movies last night. We didn't even think about Parker's excellent liquor cabinet," Dakota said with a smirk as he shucked off his T-shirt and tossed it over a chair.

"Cristy and I hit up her favorite party bar, but I was only there as arm candy." Tron grinned. "We called it a night hours before the bar closed."

Jack headed over to the rack where their costumes hung. "Clio and I gave the nanny the night off to enjoy LA. For once, baby-girl let us sleep. Not giving that up when I can get it."

Blu coughed into his hand. "Like you, apparently, Garrett, I don't kiss and tell." But the cheeky slant of his mouth said it all.

Ignoring his innuendo, I confirmed, "You're telling me I can cancel the pitchers of hangover cure I have coming." My tone was dry as toast.

"Or we can drink that nasty green shit as a preventative, cuz tonight is going to be a whole different deal." Dakota laughed as he shucked his jeans and stepped into his formfitting flight suit.

"Yeah? Why is that?"

"Olivia promised to join the party after we finish the shoot. I'm looking forward to the lady doing shots with us." His smirk dared me to contradict him.

Knowing my lady as well as I still did, I thought Olivia would do one, maybe two shots with the boys and find an excuse to sneak out of the party early. But Dakota didn't need that info. I found a chair and checked my emails while the boys dressed. As I scanned one from Emory, our rock star office manager back at Balefire's studios, a thought struck me.

Addressing Blu, I asked, "When was Ashleigh going to be on set? We're going to need her earlier now that we've switched up the shoot."

He shrugged. "She and the other women are probably in her trailer drinking mimosas, I'd guess."

"Could you text her and tell her to get ready, please?"

He finished buttoning his dress shirt to his sternum and fished his phone from the pair of jeans he'd showed up in. After he shot off a text, he pocketed his phone and slipped the red tie over his head to hang loosely from his neck, Ashleigh's prop later in the scene.

When the hair and makeup team arrived, I made myself scarce. Out on the set, the crew methodically set up the shots, everyone doing their jobs like cogs in a well-tuned machine. But I didn't see Olivia anywhere.

Landon suddenly materialized beside me. "Sir? Shall I deliver this to the band's trailer?" He held a pitcher of green smoothies in one hand and four Solo cups in the other. I grinned at the joke of him using Solo cups to deliver a hangover cure.

"They don't need it, but Dakota mentioned they'd take it anyway."

At his furrowed brow, I added, "As prevention."

"Ah." He gave me a sage nod and headed for their trailer.

"For the love of God, would you stop calling me 'sir?'" I called after him.

He nodded again, but I could swear I heard him chuckle under his breath.

I headed in the direction of the flight simulator where, at last, I discovered Olivia. For a couple of minutes, I quietly watched her in her element. Her ability to handle people and situations with calm firmness made her formidably sexy. Damn, it was all I could do to hold back from marching right up to her, bending her over my arm, and kissing the hell out of her.

As though she sensed my naughty thoughts, she glanced over her shoulder to catch my eye. A wink so quick I almost missed it flashed my way, and then she returned her attention to her assistant who didn't even pause in his conversation with her.

Stepping over cables and around cameras and equipment, I made my way over to her.

"How are the guys?" she asked.

"Surprisingly sober and ready to go."

"I texted Ashleigh, but she was already in her trailer. Looks like we'll be able to rearrange the shoot and remain on schedule." A tiny sigh escaped her, her only nervous tell.

Bailey Saunders, the band's head road engineer, showed up right then. "Hello, Miss Carter. Where should I set up the band's equipment?" he asked.

"We have an area over there by the boom." She pointed to a spot directly behind us. "If you could stage it all there, they'll have easy access to it."

With a quick salute, Bailey headed off to oversee the rest of his crew taking care of the band's equipment. About then, the guys strolled out onto the set. In their tuxes, Blu and Jack looked the part of suave spies coming off a night of undercover shenanigans at the local casino while Dakota and Tron cut dashing figures in their camouflage flight suits. Their cocky strut told the entire crew they knew how good they looked. I hid a smile. In moments like this, I couldn't help how proud I was of these guys and what they'd accomplished in the ten years since we'd started working together. In so many ways, they were like the little brothers I never had but always wanted.

Not far behind them, the band's ladies arrived on the set. Ashleigh wore a robe over her dress, while Clio, Annabelle, and Cristy were dressed as usual—hot. The guys stopped showing off for the crew and focused their attention on their women instead.

"You like the suit, Anna-baby?" Dakota said as he sidled up beside her.

"Mmm-hmm. Do you get to keep it afterward?"

"If you like it, I'm keeping it."

Somewhere along the way, Tron must have shared with Cristy what he was wearing for this scene because she showed up in a matching flight suit. Only hers was unzipped to the belt at her waist, exposing a bright pink sequined top with a plunging vee beneath it. Matching platform sandals with massive bows on them gave her the illusion of height until she stood next to Tron who tucked her under his arm. Giving her a squeeze, he leaned down and said, "Too bad you're not in this scene too. I'd like to fly you into space in that outfit."

She shot him a sexy side-eye and hugged him back.

As always, Clio rocked the girl-next-door look in a tight pair of jeans and a silk T-shirt. At first glance, one might think she dressed down, but I'd bet a week's wages that everything covering her body was designer. The woman had impeccable taste, something her husband appreciated judging from the expression of pure love that rested on his features when she walked over to him and gave him a saucy once-over as she smoothed a hand over his lapel.

"You gonna show me what's under that robe, my beauty?" Blu asked Ashleigh, addressing her with the title of a song he wrote for her back before he put that giant glittering rock on her finger.

"When the time's right," she flirted back at him.

Usually, all the flirting and private innuendo between the guys and their women nauseated me. Today, I found it sort of entertaining. Why the hell that would be, I had no idea.

Then Olivia interrupted all the commentary, and I had my answer.

"Now that you're all here, we can start. I want to do a run-through for practice without your instruments, then one with them to make sure everything will go according to the script." Her voice was all business, which set the tone for the morning.

Without a word, the band headed to their marks while Clio, Annabelle, and Cristy stepped back to join the crew behind the cameras and Ashleigh made her way to her staging point. Olivia slipped a headset over her head and motioned for me to sit in the chair next to hers. Jeremy handed me a headset as well, and the team ran through their checks to make sure we were all cued and miked up.

With one small glitch when Dakota's hydraulic lift stuttered for a second on its way up—and Annabelle audibly sucked up all the available air watching its slight wobble—the practice run was flawless. When the band added their instruments, the scene came alive.

"Please tell me camera five is recording," Olivia said into her mic.

"As you asked, every camera is set to record, ma'am," the camerawoman running that track replied.

Olivia nodded, satisfied, and made a note on her script.

My boys did me proud, playing and moving through the script as though they'd practiced it for weeks rather than a few days ahead of the shoot—without props. No matter how hard they partied, no matter how irreverent they acted, when it came to the music, they were always professional. At the appointed time for Blu to sing his lines to the "lady in red," if I hadn't known better, I could have sworn both he and Ashleigh were trained actors. She played the femme fatale like she'd been born to it. Though surprise flickered in his eyes for anyone who knew him well, Blu didn't break character at all—until he kissed her before she let go of his tie.

"If he does that when he believes the cameras are rolling, we can edit it out," Olivia said.

Sarah, her cinematographer chimed in, "Or not. That was sizzling hot."

Olivia shot me a side-eye, and I shrugged. Whatever she decided to do in post was her call. I was only along for the ride.

♪

The guys ran the scene four or five times with a tweak here, a change in camera angle there, an emphasis on a shot or two, before Olivia called a break to review what we had. Everyone crowded around the monitor, so I stepped back, giving the director and the band their chance to review the shoot so far.

"Fuckin' A! Even with only a green screen behind it, that shot with you banging out a rhythm in space is awesome!" Jack said, addressing Tron. The smile on his face mirrored the enthusiasm in his voice.

The normally rock-steady Adam Tron was almost beside himself with delight. "That flight simulator is the fuckin' bomb, O. Thanks for letting me play in it." He wrapped her in his arms and smacked a fat kiss on her cheek.

For several seconds, she stood stock still. Then she gave Tron a genuine smile. "Glad you enjoyed it."

The part of the scene with Blu and Ashleigh came up on the screen, and Blu wrapped a hand around her waist and pulled her in to his side. "You're a natural, babe," he said as he brushed a kiss over her temple. "Hotter than hell."

Olivia added a note to her iPad and glanced over at the two of them. "We may need to reshoot that groupie scene you surprised me with the other day."

"Why?" Dakota asked as he shot me a narrow-eyed stare.

"I have an idea for setting up the woman in red part of this scene." Her eyes glowed with whatever she had in mind. "You guys want to do this again?"

"Any excuse to play in that simulator," Tron said with a grin.

"Any excuse to look this good in a flight suit," Dakota added, high-fiving Tron.

"Okay, everyone. Places," Olivia called out.

She'd just called "Action," when a commotion at the back of the set interrupted the shoot.

Jennifer Hartwell stomped out into the middle of the scene. A couple of assistants tripped after her and glanced around sheepishly like they'd rather be anywhere else.

"What the hell is this, Garrett?" she sneered. "You thought you could get out of our deal by talking the director into shooting this scene first? How did you think that was going to play out?"

CHAPTER TWENTY-THREE

Olivia

GARRETT GAPED LIKE a fish sucking air when Jennifer Hartwell arrived unannounced on the set. I'd ferreted it out of Jeremy that the impromptu scene with the groupies during the previous shoot had been the band's idea. For some reason, Garrett had piggybacked their idea with the invitation to Jennifer even after he'd said he didn't really want to work with her. After the stilted way the band played when she joined them onstage, I'd had the distinct notion that experiment was a one and done. I'd believed him when he'd said he didn't have anything going on the side with the woman.

Guess I was wrong.

But what was she talking about the two of them having a deal? With the exception of advocating for her as the woman in red if Ashleigh didn't want to do it, he hadn't mentioned including her in the video again. Never once had he even mentioned her when we'd worked on the script together. From the expressions on the guys' faces, this development was a total surprise to them too, and not a welcome one.

Dakota spoke up first. "What the fuck is she talking about, Garrett?" He included the rest of the band in his glance. "We agreed this is our video, which means no *actresses*." Pure loathing marred his handsome face when he shot a look in Jennifer's direction. The emphasis on the word told an additional story of what he thought of her acting.

After sticking her nose up at Dakota, Jennifer cocked her hip and planted a hand on it, challenging Garrett. "Are you going to tell them, or shall I?"

He set his headset on the chair he'd vacated and stepped toward her, a warning in his voice. "Jennifer, you don't want to do this."

"Don't I?" she sniffed. "This video is all about publicity for *my* movie. It only makes sense that I star in it as well. You promised," she whined.

Closing his eyes, he pinched the bridge of his nose and sighed. The defeated set of his shoulders was my first clue that I wasn't going to like what happened next.

"I didn't promise anything. I said I would push to have you included, which I did. Ask Olivia."

"That's true. More than once, he's mentioned putting you in the video," I said. How I'd landed in the position of backing him up when it was becoming clear he'd tried to end-around me about putting the woman in my video pissed me off. My eyes never left his when I added, "He invited you to crash the shoot the other day." Before this moment, I'd forgiven him that fib. Now my guts roiled at what else he'd lied to me about. Like last night. Had that all been a lie too? The way he'd made love to me had felt oh-so-real. Genuine. True.

Bile rose in my throat.

Color rode his high cheekbones when it dawned on him that I knew he'd lied to me. His physical response and his silence didn't make me feel any better.

"All of this begs the question of why you're shooting my scene without me," Jennifer pressed.

My heart hurt at the implications of the whole ugly scene, but I'd had enough of Jennifer. "Last I checked the call sheet, you don't have a role in this video."

"But I do," she insisted. Her attention swung back to Garrett. "Unless you want me to share what I know about Cristy Valor and Mali Tatum."

Wait. This didn't sound like a conversation between lovers, or even former lovers. No, this sounded more like blackmail. Color drained from Garrett's face, confirming my suspicions. Throughout the entire exchange, the four members of Balefire had trained their glares on Jennifer. Now four pairs of hostile eyes swung to their manager.

"What about Cristy and Mali?" Tron demanded.

Garrett put up his hands, a defensive gesture. "It doesn't matter. It was almost a year ago, and everything worked out." His words were aimed at the band, but his eyes pleaded with me.

Tron repeated through gritted teeth. "What about Cristy and Mali, *Garrett?*"

"Mali asked questions. I answered." That defeated slump to his shoulders became more pronounced.

"You gave Mali the ammunition to potentially ruin Cristy's career?" Tron was halfway to Garrett before Jack and Blu could restrain him. "Why would you *do* that?"

"I didn't know any particulars, but Mali asked the right questions. She drew her own conclusions and ran with them. All I knew was that Cristy's hold on you, Tron, had the potential to wreck the band." Garrett ran a hand through his hair and dropped it to his side. "I couldn't let that happen."

The pain stacked up brick on top of brick on my heart. More than anything else, the band would always be everything to him. "You tried to break up Tron and Cristy?" I asked. "Why would you want to do that?" None of this made any sense. "Their chemistry on stage is explosive. It's why I suggested her for the woman in red in the first place."

"Except for her being with the wrong band member in that scene," Garrett reminded me. Turning back to the band, he added, "See? I've learned my lesson. I didn't let Olivia create a PR mess for you by filming a scene between Blu and Cristy."

Now he threw me under the proverbial bus?

Brick after brick. I had a death grip on my iPad to keep myself from wrapping my arms around my middle to hide my heart from all the hurt Garrett's words inflicted.

"But you wanted me to do the scene with Jennifer?" Blu's eyes blazed with anger. "So much better. Not."

Jack, who'd stayed silent to this point, spoke up. "I stood up for you when you tried to break Dakota and Annabelle up even though Annabelle is Clio's best friend. And I pushed for you to have a second chance when you tried to bring Mali on board the last tour to break Tron and Cristy up." He shook his head. "But sharing Cristy's awful secret with her worst enemy? That's low, man. How could you do that?" Crossing his arms over his chest, he added, "Now you make deals with this bitch who made a run at each of us when she tagged along on our last tour. What the fuck are you thinking?"

"Decisions made with your little head, Garrett?" Dakota taunted.

Garrett shot a look of anguish in my direction, but he talked to the band. "Jennifer is the reason you guys have a song in the movie. She pushed the other producers for it in spite of the amount I asked for on your behalf."

"Because you had a mutual agreement. You stick us with her so she doesn't out you," Dakota snarled. "We don't give a shit about the money, Garrett, and you know it. We wanted to do the video for the challenge"—his eyes strayed to me—"and to work with Olivia. We thought—"

"Skip it," Blu interrupted. "Our manager is never going to grow up."

"Now that we've cleared the air, shall we get to work shooting my scene?"

Wow, for being an A-list actress, the woman didn't have the first clue about reading a room.

Blu said, "Catch up, Jennifer. Didn't you hear Olivia say you're not on the call sheet?"

"But Garrett promised—"

"Like he said." Dakota hooked a thumb in Blu's direction. "Catch up. Garrett's not in charge of this gig. Whatever he promised, you're not getting it."

"Especially after you tipped your hand. Garrett's done a shit-ton of damage the last couple of years, but we're not letting him compound it by putting you in our video." Tron turned his attention to me. "Are we, O?" It wasn't a question.

Garrett took a step toward me, fear and anguish taking turns crossing his features. Still, he said, "Remember who her dad is, Olivia."

Of course I knew who her dad was, but that didn't answer why Garrett was still advocating for Jennifer. At one time, interning for Hartwell Studios had been high on my wish list, but I'd moved far beyond those days. Surely, he wasn't still back there?

"Do you have something else to share with the class?" Dakota sneered.

As the conversation had continued, the band had subtly moved until they'd all but circled the wagons around me—us against them, Balefire and me against Garrett and Jennifer. Though hours had passed since I'd enjoyed a lovely breakfast—with Garrett—it was currently in serious danger of making a comeback.

In the short time since Jennifer Hartwell had barged onto my set, Garrett aged ten years. He blew a stream of air skyward and faced the band. "All the bombs have been dropped. I just don't want Olivia to pay the price for me making a deal with the devil."

"Garrett, you can't back out of this. I won't let you," Jennifer screeched as she charged toward him.

"That's what you get from sleeping with her. Why do you

suppose the rest of us stayed the fuck away from that?" Dakota shook his head.

"Once. I slept with her *once* on the last tour." Garrett glared at Jennifer who stood in front of him, her chest heaving in anger. "The second biggest mistake of my life."

I couldn't decipher the look he shot me, but it didn't matter. He wasn't the man I'd loved so deeply back in college. I could accept that, had accepted that. Life experiences changed all of us. But the man I'd reconnected with over the last few months, and especially over the last few weeks of working side-by-side, wasn't the man I thought he was. The man who'd made love to me all night, who'd made me believe we had a chance in spite of the goals that drove us, wasn't this man. This deceiver who could betray his friends and throw me under the bus? How could I have let myself fall for him again?

"You know what? I'm done," I announced.

"Like done, done? Like you're not going to see this project through?" Blu asked in alarm.

A sigh escaped me. "I'm done with all the drama. We'll take a break while security escorts Miss Hartwell from the set."

"You can't do that! Do you know who I am?" she shouted.

I glanced around for my assistant and located him beside Sarah, my cinematographer who was now openly smoking even though it broke all my rules. "Jeremy," I said.

"On it." He spoke into his radio.

"I will be in this video!" She advanced on Garrett again. "Garrett!"

"You heard the director."

She changed her tactics and her trajectory. "I'll have the song struck from the movie. You won't be able to use any of the footage you have from it. If you won't put me in this video, there won't be a video."

"Fortunately in business, contracts trump tantrums, Miss

Hartwell," I said with a calm I was far from feeling. She and her dad could—and likely would—ruin my fledgling studio. But I wasn't going to be forced into working with this diva who made the band look bad when she joined them in front of the camera. More importantly, I refused to work with the woman who stole my most coveted dream from me with her ugly revelations.

My security team didn't waste time arriving on set. "Please escort Miss Hartwell from the premises and see to it she doesn't return."

"Yes ma'am," the team leader said.

"Also, she's persona non grata at the studio. Make sure to put her name and photo on the list so the whole team knows. Thank you."

He nodded.

Jennifer jerked her arm from the team leader when he took it to lead her off the set. "You're going to be sorry. All of you!" she screamed. Two guards flanked her and all but dragged her away.

Widening my eyes and glancing around at the band and their ladies who now stood with them, I said, "Well. That was exciting." I sat down hard in my chair.

From one side, Garrett came running while Blu and Dakota rushed to me from my other side. I waved a hand at them. "I'm fine. Honestly." I looked Blu and Dakota in the eye but couldn't maintain eye contact with Garrett. Gathering myself, I said, "I won't waste your time or your money. We'll finish the stage shots after lunch. Would it be possible to invite the friends who joined you the other day to today's shoot on such short notice? I don't want to use anything from the surprise the other day." With a nod in the direction where Jennifer had been escorted out, I added, "You know, since I don't have much footage before she interrupted."

"How long do we have?" Blu asked.

Pulling up the schedule on my iPad, I said, "It's going to take a couple hours to remove the flight simulator and put up the portable stage. Will that be enough time to gather your friends for an impromptu concert?"

The band and their ladies talked it over for a few seconds.

"Shouldn't be a problem," Dakota said. "So you liked our surprise, huh?" His tone was decidedly playful. After the trauma following the shoot, it was hard for me to keep up with his sudden mood change.

"It was a great idea. We should have thought of it from the start." Inadvertently, my eyes strayed back to Garrett who stood aloof from the rest of us, his shoulders hunched, his hands jammed deep in the pockets of his trousers.

Dakota's mood change didn't extend to Tron who held Cristy close to his side and glared at Garrett. "I forgave you when you invited Mali along with the clear intention of fucking things up between Cristy and me. But I don't think I can overlook you sharing Cristy's pain like that."

"At the time, none of us knew about Cristy's past. Mali asked if you two were still together." He shrugged. "I said I didn't know, but Cristy's manager was as determined to keep you apart as I was. Turns out, my reasons were more altruistic than hers, which didn't matter to Mali or to you." He held out his hands in a pleading gesture. "But I've been atoning ever since the shit hit the fan when Mali outed Cristy's secret. I've worked nearly as hard on the Be Valorous Foundation as the two of you—and with as much sincerity. That has to count for something, doesn't it?"

"I don't know, Garrett. This time I have to think about it," Tron said.

Garrett pulled his lips between his teeth, an obvious attempt to hold his emotions in check.

Hearing the lengths he'd gone to in order to keep the band together when he thought it might break up hurt me so much. From what came out during Jennifer's interruption and meltdown, he'd done a number on the band too. I shouldn't have felt any kind of sympathy for him, yet my chest burned at the pain radiating from him.

"Team meeting?" Jack asked.

"With our women," Tron said.

The others nodded.

"Team meeting? What is that?" I asked.

"It's when the band wants to talk among themselves—without me." Garrett's dejection aged him another five years.

The four band members and their significant others walked off the set to discuss whatever it was they needed privacy to talk about. When they were out of earshot, Garrett wandered over near me. After he cleared his throat, he said, "I imagine this time they're going to fire me." A self-deprecating snort slipped out. "Funny thing is, this time I don't deserve it." His eyes found mine. "My mistake was in trying to straddle the line—play Jennifer until the shoot was over and it was too late for her to do anything about it." He shoved his hands back into his pockets. "I didn't want you to know the things I'd done, and I didn't want to force you to work with someone you clearly loathe. But I should have known better when it came to her. This is probably the first time in her life she didn't get what she wanted. And I'll pay the price."

"You left me for them." God, I hated how small my voice sounded on those words. "Why would you deliberately hurt them the way you did?"

He blew out a breath. "I was window dressing for my parents' marriage. They were a unit, but *we* were not a family. They trotted me out to show to their friends on occasion then put me away with babysitters, and later, they just left me on my own. Then I met you." His hands closed over the back of his neck as he stared at the ground. "When I walked away from you—from us—I fell into a black hole. I tried to fill it with groupies and alcohol and ingratiating myself with the band, but nothing ever made me feel better. I never felt like I belonged anywhere to anyone. The only time I ever belonged anywhere was when I was with you." His eyes found mine. "But in the end, you jettisoned me too. Your dream was more important than me."

"Pot, kettle, yeah? You followed your dream and left me behind."

"You know what my dream has always been, Olivia? To belong to someone. To be so important to them that they can't overlook me, ignore me, walk away. Turns out, that's a pipe dream. Falling for you was my biggest mistake because you're a loner."

His words stung so much, I couldn't catch a breath. But he wasn't done.

"You don't need anyone. No wonder I could never belong to you or convince you to belong to me. You were right all along. We were never going to work out."

He signaled to Landon who stood beside Jeremy, their heads turning from watching the conversation between the band members to us. After aiming a shrug at my assistant, Landon loped over to us.

"Looks like you're going to be able to put all those notes to work"—Garrett indicated the iPad in Landon's hand—"sooner than you thought. Tell the band they can have their lawyers draw up the severance papers and leave them at the Denver studio. I'll stop in sometime soon and sign them."

Landon almost choked. "What are you talking about?"

He nodded in the direction of the band. "I'm sure you'll figure it out as soon as they're done meeting." Closing his eyes, he shuddered in a breath like the air he drew inside himself was composed of tiny knives. Blowing it out, he turned to me. "When the boys announced they wanted to work on this project with you, I thought it was fate giving us a second chance. After last night, I was sure of it. But I was wrong. So fucking wrong. About everything." He reached toward me, his hand close enough to my skin for me to sense his heat, then he dropped it to his side without touching me.

I missed that touch like missing a limb.

"The video will be incredible, O. Once you distribute it, every band in the country will want to work with you, which will open other doors." A sad smile tilted his mouth. "Don't worry about the

Hartwells. Josh has more sense than his daughter. He knows a moneymaker when he sees it. You'll be okay."

"Garrett, what are you saying? You're not leaving, are you? We haven't finished the shoot…" My words trailed away at the sad half smile on his face.

Without another word, he turned on his heel and walked off the set, taking my heart with him.

CHAPTER TWENTY-FIVE

Garrett

"JESUS, DUDE. YOU look like death warmed over," Nick Parker said as he opened the door to my knock. He wrinkled his nose. "Kinda smell like it too. What happened?"

"Mind if I tell you inside?" I asked.

My friend opened the door to his beachside bungalow wide enough to let me pass. "You know where the guest room is. Hit the shower and meet me on the deck," he instructed.

I nodded my thanks and carried my suitcase down the hall to the right of his spacious living room. A shower sounded like paradise after days of sleeping in the car.

After I'd walked away from the implosion of my entire life, I'd gathered my shit, checked out of the hotel, and rented a sweet red Mercedes convertible. Then I hit the road, driving the Pacific Coast Highway north from LA. More than once, I'd pulled off the road to sit on the beach and stare at the ocean for hours. The steady wash of the waves on the shore soothed me, centered me, let me breathe for a minute. Time escaped as I lost myself in memories. Oddly, most of them featured Olivia more than the band, even though I had more memories with Balefire.

Spending time with her again had only dug up emotions I thought I'd buried too deep to ever let resurface. But by our last night together, I'd had to come clean with myself—I'd never stopped loving her. Of course, that explained why no matter how much sex I'd had with groupies following the band over the years, some of it even pretty good, none of it could ever fill the hole that walking away from her had left inside me. After the events on my last day of the shoot, I had to come to terms with the fact that hole would never be filled. Olivia couldn't see a way forward for us that didn't involve her giving up her dreams. She couldn't give me a chance to show her I loved her enough to compromise for her.

As hot water sluiced away days of road grime, sand, and sweat, I thought about how I hadn't shown her what I was willing to give up for her. For too long, I'd pushed hard for what I wanted. But even before the end with the band came during the video shoot, I'd been working on ways I could be with her and still run Balefire's business.

When I joined Nick on his deck, I smiled at the pitcher of martinis sweating on a low table between two deck chairs. As he gazed at the waves crashing on the shoreline below his house, he sipped his drink. I filled the empty glass waiting beside the pitcher and sat in the opposite chair.

"Damn. I needed that," I said as I set my half-full glass back on the table and stared out at the ocean crashing on the rocks bordering his private beach.

"Thought so." He raised a brow. "You want to tell me what the hell is going on?"

"Only if you promise to let me stay the night after I tell you." I sipped more martini in anticipation of the humiliation I faced in disclosing my behavior for the past two years to my friend.

He laughed. "Can't imagine I haven't heard worse than you're going to tell me."

I drained my glass and poured another. Nick sobered up in a blink.

"But there's a first time for everything, I guess." He poured himself another too and settled back to wait.

"I betrayed the boys."

"Already knew that. They've been making you pay for it for about a year." He glanced at me over the rim of his glass. "They've been a bit rough, if you ask me."

"Yeah, well, you didn't know all of it. Though I didn't overtly mean to—but who knows what my subconscious was up to—I gave Mali Tatum the ammo to go to the tabs about Cristy at the end of the last tour." Settling into the Adirondack chair, I rested my head against the back and closed my eyes. "The boys didn't know that part until Jennifer Hartwell figured out I hadn't been successful in convincing them to put her in the 'Dangerous Life' video." I turned my head to look my friend in the eye. "She shared that info in the most public way possible during a diva fit on the set when Olivia told her she wasn't on the call sheet."

"Let me guess. The band had one of their team meetings."

Saluting him with my glass, I said, "Got it in one."

"Because you've been walking on eggshells since last fall, you figured this one was the end of the line." He sat forward in his chair, his drink in his hands between his knees.

"I see you came to the same conclusion, and at about the same speed."

"Even if I hadn't produced their last five albums, they wouldn't be that hard to read." He leveled me with a look. "Those boys took a long time to fall in love, but when they did, exactly like with everything in their music, they went all in."

I snorted out a laugh. "That they did, my friend. That they did."

"You, of all people, should have seen that coming."

The mournful scree of a seagull flying along the surf caught our attention for a second. Nick drank more of his martini and glanced back at me.

I shrugged. "I did see it coming. That was the problem. I tried to get in the way of it when it wasn't any of my business. It was selfish and shortsighted, and now I get to pay for it." I blew out a breath. "After Jennifer dropped her bomb and the band stepped out for their team meeting, I said goodbye to the director and her crew. I didn't want them to witness another scene when the band sacked me." The slug of alcohol I tossed back burned my throat. Thinking about Olivia and how I'd let her down, had always let her down, burned through me right along with the booze.

For several minutes, we listened to the calming sound of the waves rolling onto the sand.

When I had myself marginally back together, I continued. "The thing is, Nick, I've atoned for what I did. For ten years, I worked my ass off for Balefire. Since the end of the last tour, I've doubled down, trying to prove to them that everything I did was for them, for their success."

"What about Olivia Carter?"

I sat up so fast, I sloshed a few drops of martini on my clean pants. Swiping at the moisture with my free hand, I said, "What do you know about Olivia?"

A smile ghosted over his features. "Only that the band specifically wanted to work with her."

"Who told you that?"

"Touchy subject?" He threw back the rest of his martini, poured another, topped mine up, and waited.

"Look, you know I had a history with her," I began.

"Your history might have been part of the reason the boys wanted to work with her so much." His eyes glittered in the light of the setting sun.

"What the *fuck* do you know that you're not telling me?"

"Dakota might have mentioned that working with Olivia might

be good for both of you." Leaning his head back against his chair again, he said, "Guess he got that wrong."

I downed another martini and poured a what? A fourth? A fifth? Didn't matter. For once, the alcohol wasn't doing its job. At. All. Thinking about Olivia brought on pain that burned through my veins like lava. Unlike ten years ago, this time I wouldn't be able to dull it enough with music and groupies and, apparently, alcohol to forget about it sometimes.

"When the band announced they wanted to work with Olivia on this project, for the first time in a long time, I was genuinely excited about a video. When she threw up roadblocks to the two of us spending time alone together, I played that challenge." A self-deprecating snort slipped out. "The night before Jennifer ignited her explosion, I thought Olivia and I had reached an understanding that we could work out some things she thought were insurmountable." I tossed back my drink, frowned at the now empty pitcher, and set my empty glass on the table.

For several long minutes, we were quiet together as we watched the sun start its slow descent into the sea.

At last, Nick broke the silence. "What's in the way of you two making things work?"

"Before that last day on the set, I would have said logistics."

He finished his drink, stood and picked up the empty pitcher. With a nod toward the door, he headed inside. Picking up my glass, I followed him.

"Logistics aren't insurmountable." Standing at his island, he measured alcohol into a shaker.

I stood across from him, watching him mix another batch of martinis. "Says the man who had problems with logistics."

His brow went up. "So?"

Swallowing over the burn at the back of my throat, I finally choked out, "Logistics were never the real problem."

"Ah."

The whole that-explains-everything tone of his voice pissed me off. But he was pouring a fresh batch of martinis into the pitcher, and I needed numbing, not an argument. The smirk on his face told me he got that.

We settled back in the Adirondack chairs on the deck, and he gave me another minute before he started in again. "What is the real problem?"

"Olivia doesn't need anyone. She likes being alone."

For the first time since the Olivia inquisition began, he stopped with the smirks and side-eyes and sage tones. "Shit, mate. Not a hell of a lot you can do with that."

"Nope."

"Except…"

"Except what?"

He ignored the irritation in my tone. "What are the logistics she thinks stand in the way of you being together?"

"Besides that I'm an asshole who tried to keep the band to myself?"

"The fucking pity party isn't going to help you here, mate."

I sipped my drink and stared at the dark water lapping at the shoreline. "She's trying to build up a studio in LA. Balefire's home base is in Denver. Long-distance relationships are wicked hard to maintain." Shooting him a look, I added, "As you know."

Nick's wife had divorced him when he relocated from London to LA, long before he started producing Balefire's music. His marital status made me question why I'd come to him with this, except for him being my only true friend outside of the band. Well, my only friend at all, now.

"Well, if you're sure Balefire's jettisoned you—"

I ran a hand through my hair, closed my eyes, and leaned back into the chair. "The whole mess with Jennifer was the last straw, no doubt."

"You don't know that." Something weird was in his tone.

"Why else would they call a team meeting after Jennifer's nasty revelations?"

"Still not convinced the band is that stupid after everything you've done for them." He shot me a look. "But nothing's holding you back from returning to LA and Olivia. With all your contacts—and perhaps me making suggestions to a few of mine—combined with her reputation for excellence, she could outplay anything the Hartwells might pull and build a damn fine studio." He sipped thoughtfully at his drink. "Or you could talk her into relocating to Denver. Thanks to Balefire and a few other bands who don't to follow the LA trends, Denver is creating its own music scene. Could be a good move for her."

"You haven't listened to a damn thing I've said, have you? The expression on Olivia's face when she heard what I'd done to hold the band together—" I shook my head. "I've totally shit in my bed."

His smirk at my expense irritated me.

"You think it's funny that I've detonated my life? Fuck you, Nick." I tossed back another drink and scowled at my glass. Clearly, none of my choices lately were worth a shit.

"Nah, mate, it's not funny. But in all the time I've known you, I've never seen a situation you couldn't think your way out of." He lifted the pitcher and indicated my glass. "Drink up. No sense in wasting good alcohol."

For some reason, his words buoyed me. Guess that's why I'd found my way to his doorstep after days on the road by myself.

♪

I woke up in Nick's guest bed with the mother of all headaches. Right about now would be a great time for Bailey Saunders's famous hangover-curing smoothie. Too bad I'd never pried the recipe out of the guy. Squeezing my eyes shut against the muted light coming through the window open to the ocean, I had to smile. The chances of Nick having any of the green shit that went into that smoothie tucked away in his fridge were about as good as me having a fairy godfather come along to magic away the last ten days.

With a groan, I rolled my ass out of bed and headed to the shower. I might have appreciated the beauty of white marble shot through with veins of dove gray that made up the vanity, walls, and shower of the bathroom more if they hadn't reflected the light coming through the high window above the toilet so well. Though I worked to keep my mind blank, as the hot water pounded over the back of my neck and between my shoulder blades, images of Olivia smiling up at me through wet lashes as she lathered soap over my chest and stomach kept pushing in. Like some kind of fever dream, this Olivia shimmered in and out of focus with another Olivia from long ago, one with rounder cheeks and longer hair. Jesus, I missed her—like losing half of myself.

Even after drinking almost all of Nick's booze last night, I hadn't erased one iota of the pain of losing her again before I'd had a chance to prove myself to her. All I'd ever wanted was someone to love who loved me back as much I loved them. I'd had that once with her, but being young and full of myself, I thought I could have it all—the girl, the band, the career. The love. All I had to do was work for it. I'd make a big success of the band—and by extension—myself, and she'd see how valuable that was and how much I could do for her. And she'd want that, want me.

It was selfish and single-minded of me and left no room for her to grow and become the person she wanted and needed to be. Too late, I saw that now. I also saw how even more incredible a person she was when she went after her dreams. If anything, I wanted her more because of that. Olivia was the whole package: brilliant, beautiful, creative, driven.

And she didn't need me.

"Eh, you look about the same as when you arrived yesterday, but you smell better." Nick chortled as I wandered into the kitchen a while later. "Breakfast is in the warmer." With his thumb, he indicated the oven. "But you'll probably want this first." He reached into the fridge and produced a pitcher from which he poured a glass of thick green nastiness that had a miraculous resemblance to Bailey's hangover cure.

"How the hell do you have this?" I asked as I took the glass from him.

"Bribed your head road engineer with Metallica tickets—in Prague." He grinned at my raised brow. "Worth every dime I paid for his vacation on one of Balefire's touring breaks."

Holding my breath, I drank down half the disgusting concoction. "Doubt I'll ever acquire a taste for this shit, but I can't argue with how it works." I held up the glass and stared into its contents. "You gonna share the secret recipe with your old pal?"

"What the hell? You don't know how to make this stuff? After all this time with the band?" He shook his head. "For a smart man, you're terribly good at missing the important stuff."

"Yeah, I'm getting that." I finished off the smoothie and rinsed the glass in the sink. It would have been great to rinse my mouth as well, but I knew better. Instead, I sat my ass in a chair at the table in the breakfast nook and waited for the smoothie to do its job.

Nick busied himself heating a pan with a thin coating of oil on the stove. When it was hot enough, he cracked in a few eggs and popped some bread into the toaster. He set two plates on the countertop beside the stove and filled them with sausage links, beans, and broiled tomatoes that he pulled from the oven. After topping them up with the fried eggs, he set both plates on the table, one in front of me, the other in front of the chair opposite. He cut the slices of toast in half, slid them onto a rack, and set it in the middle of the table between little pots of butter and jelly.

"Can take the boy out of London, but you can't take London out of the boy, huh?" I said as I surveyed the full English breakfast in front of me.

"Only thing missing is fresh scones. No one out here can make a decent one, so I've given them up." He helped himself to a slice of toast he slathered generously with butter and jelly—or what he called it—jam and then went to work on his breakfast like he hadn't eaten in days.

Guilt gnawed at me when I glanced over his shoulder at the clock on the wall and noted we were having brunch rather breakfast. "You could have eaten without me."

"What sort of host does something so crass?" he asked, truly offended.

For a few minutes, we ate in silence, the food going down surprisingly well after I'd ingested that hangover-killing concoction. I was just mopping up the last of the juices on my plate when Nick soured my stomach.

"Emory called me the day before yesterday, wondering if I'd seen you or heard from you. She sounded pretty desperate."

"Landon, the assistant who's been working with me since last fall, has all the notes and my blessing to share them. Besides, Emory is the true backbone of the operation. Everything runs through her. Can't imagine her ever sounding desperate." I walked my plate to the sink, rinsed it, and put it in the dishwasher. Having spent time with Nick on touring breaks in the past, I knew where everything was and helped myself to a mug from the cupboard above the stove. I set it beneath the Keurig and perused the coffee choices in the basket beside it, selecting a plain coffee I resolved not to doctor up with cream.

"She's been trying to contact you for almost two weeks. You're not answering your phone or checking emails."

I leaned back against the counter and sipped my black coffee. "Can't imagine a reason for doing either."

"You know, you're not the only one at fault here. The band hasn't been lily-white in everything that's happened this last year." He put his plate and utensils in the dishwasher then cleaned the pan from the stove. "You've beaten yourself up over what you did because you feared them splitting up, but they've been harder on you these last months than you deserve."

I stepped aside to let him grab his own mug for coffee.

"Did it ever occur to you they might have figured that out?" he asked as he filled his mug from the coffee maker.

Sitting back down at the table, I stared out the window at the ocean, its waters glowing turquoise in the late morning sun.

"Tron and Jack were the two who made sure Dakota didn't fire me in Florida last fall. When Tron heard what went down with Mali, he would have decked me if Blu and Jack hadn't stopped him." I swallowed some coffee. "Jack's the one who called the team meeting this time, so I'm pretty sure Jennifer's parting shot cost me my job." Clearing my throat, I amended, "She didn't cost me my job. I did that all by myself." Rolling my mug between my hands, I chose my next words carefully. "I didn't have particulars about Cristy's past, but the fallout from Mali going to the tabs was ugly. No one deserved how the fans and the press treated her." I leveled my friend a look. "Tron truly loves her. Anyone could figure that out even without the rock he put on her finger blinding them. Finding out that I had anything to do with that mess beyond attempting to bring Mali on tour with us would understandably set him off."

Nick stared me down for an uncomfortable minute. "Call Emory. Today."

Chapter Twenty-Six

Olivia

WORD LEAKED OUT that I was producing the next Balefire video, and Dana was complaining about how answering the phones was infringing on her other duties running the front office of my studio. It was a good problem to have. I guess.

So far, I hadn't heard anything from Hartwell Studios about pulling the footage they'd given me to use in the "Dangerous Life" video, so I was cautiously optimistic cooler heads had prevailed over Jennifer's diva tantrums on my set. But that wasn't why I didn't sleep at night. No, what kept me tossing and turning and buying industrial-size concealer was one MIA band manager. Garrett had blown back into my world, made me see what we could have had if I'd had more faith, and exposed me for the chicken I am. He'd told me he loved me and walked away.

The throbbing pain in my heart blinded my vision for the rest of the day of that shoot. After the band returned from their "team meeting," their shock at Garrett's absence set us behind. None of us had our head in the game as we worried about where he was and what it meant that he'd just walked away—from the shoot, from the band. From me. We'd ended up doing takes way into the night, over and over before we finally had something I could work with.

Several times as I sat in the production room viewing the footage, I'd lost myself in thoughts of his opinion on this take or that part of the script. Jeremy anxiously watched me, cautiously asked me how I was and was there something specific I was looking for in the part I'd run over and over for the last hour or so? By the end of the first week after Garrett walked out, I ached for him so bad, all I wanted to do was burrow deep into my bed, curl up, and will the world to stop turning. By the end of the second week, my stomach had migrated to my throat as scenario after horrible scenario invaded my mind, each of them ending with me never seeing him again.

I'd checked in daily with the band and the front office of their studio in Denver. No one had a clue where he was or if he was safe. His last words gnawed at me: "The only time I ever belonged anywhere was when I was with you. But in the end, you jettisoned me too. Your dream was more important than me." But that had never been true. Letting him go to follow his dream of becoming the manager of the biggest band in the world had been an act of love. I'd thought then that if I tried to hold on to him, I'd lose him anyway. He'd hated his old job so much, hated his parents' corporate world with all its rules and protocols. Managing the band allowed him to flex his creativity in a way he could never have done in finance, even as he made piles of money.

Making it easy for him to walk away from me to have that rock 'n' roll life he'd craved so much tore my heart out. Ten years later, nothing had changed.

"Olivia, are you okay?" The concern in Jeremy's voice jerked me back to the present.

The computer in front of me had frozen on a clip of the "groupie" scene we'd reshot. I tapped out a couple of commands to bring it back to life and swung my chair a quarter turn to face him. "Yeah, sorry. Got a little distracted there for a minute." My laugh sounded hollow to my ears.

The expression on his face said I might have been "distracted" for a while.

"So what do you think of splicing this scene in behind the shot with Dakota and Tron with the flight simulator when they hit the line 'How far can we run?' then jump-cut to the fight scene from the movie on 'Can't escape the damage done'?" I asked. With a couple of commands, I showed him what I had in mind.

His mouth rounded in a comic *O* before he turned to me and said, "This is why I fought so hard to work for you. I never would have thought to make those connections, and they're brilliant." He put up his hand for a high five, and though I thought it silly, I didn't leave him hanging.

"Great. We'll go with that then." I sat back in my chair. "I think that's the last tweak I wanted to make."

Dana tapped on the door and walked in behind us. "I *really* need you to look at the schedule." Guilt washed over me as her long-suffering tone told its own story of my emotional absence from work. "Flyboys and Cristy Valor have new music they want to share, and their people are insisting they work with you even after I told them you're booked solid through the summer."

"Can you make sure this version is set, please?" I asked Jeremy as I stood to follow Dana to her office.

"Yes, ma'am." He tossed me a crisp salute, but his eyes looked troubled.

As I hustled to keep up with my assistant clipping down the hallway to the reception area, I mentally berated myself for letting my team down. Though I'd texted him a few times and even broke down late one night and left a message when he didn't pick up, I had to accept that Garrett's radio silence meant this time it was truly over with us. Time for me to focus on what was in front of me and take care of the people who depended on me to run my business like a professional rather than a woman with her heart shattered into a million tiny shards.

Dana slid into her chair and pulled up a calendar spreadsheet for the next few months. I blinked at the lack of white space on it.

"Wow. That's…" I blew out a breath. "Wow."

The sardonic look she threw over her shoulder told me to focus.

"Are we contractually obligated to the dates with Jam Band next month? Or can we push them out another month?" I pointed to the screen, and Dana highlighted it.

"No, they're 'penciled' in there for now. From their manager's insistence, you'd think they were Balefire rather than someone whose highest chart so far is twenty-five." She rolled her eyes.

I bet Garrett pushed exactly like this, I thought then shook my head. *Stay in the game, Olivia.*

"They all start somewhere." I pointed to a few open days in the next month's calendar. "Let's move them to here and tell their manager we'll firm up the contracts if they agree to a two-day shoot. Slide Cristy Valor into the slot that change opens up and send her manager confirmation today. As for Flyboys, I've heard some not-so-good stories about how they behave on set. Tell their management I'll need reassurances in writing that they'll behave like professionals before I agree to work with them at all."

Dana nodded and made some notes on a separate screen.

"I imagine that will put them off, and they'll find someone else who wants to work with them."

She sat back in her chair and shot me a grin. "Well, well, well, look at you, hotshot. A month ago you would have said yes, crossed your fingers, and hoped for the best."

I smiled back. "A month ago, our calendar didn't look like that." I swept a hand toward her screen.

"By the way, Emory Murakami from Balefire's studios left a message. It seems their manager is alive and well and never left California."

It was all I could do to remain upright from the sucker punch of those words. Garrett was still in California? Yet he hadn't even acknowledged my texts? Whoa. He was well and truly done with us. No matter that he'd said he only felt whole, like he belonged, when he was with me. Apparently, he was the loner after all.

"Uh-huh," I finally managed. "Guess the band is happy to hear that."

Dana narrowed her eyes at me. "I had the impression she thought you would be happy to hear it."

"If you could let Balefire know the video is ready for them to view and approve, that would be great." I turned toward the door to my office. "I have some paperwork to finish and then I'm taking the rest of the day off."

She opened her mouth—undoubtedly to remind me of all the calls she'd fielded and how maybe I should take care of them. Tilting her head, she peered closely at me, shrugged, and returned to her computer. Whatever she thought she saw on my face didn't matter. I needed time alone, and I didn't care how that looked to the staff.

For a second after I closed it, I sagged against my office door. Then I pulled the blinds to the window facing the reception area and sank gratefully into my plush leather chair, my one indulgence when I set up the studio. Pinching the bridge of my nose, I willed the tears to stay inside. Garrett remained in the state, probably somewhere near or even in LA, yet he still didn't want anything to do with me, which left me with pain so deep, it hollowed out my chest, leaving a hole where my heart used to beat.

White noise filled my head as I willed my mind to go blank. I discovered that if I held myself super still, I could pretend to be weightless, allowing my body and my brain to become blessedly numb. When my phone jangled in my pocket, I nearly carried my desk and chair with me when I leaped into space. The sun's rays slanting through my exterior windows told me hours had passed since I'd escaped into my office. After I clumsily retrieved my phone from my pocket, I saw Tron's name and photo filling up the screen.

"Hello, Tron." My voice came out scratchy. Swallowing a couple of times, I tried again. "What can I do for you?"

"Your assistant left a message the video is ready. You got time tomorrow to show it to us?"

"I can email it via an encrypted server, and you can watch it tonight in the comfort of your own studio, if you like." Though I kept swallowing, my voice sounded like I'd cried a river of tears. That's when I became aware of the dampness on my chest. Glancing down at my blouse, I saw wet stains on the silk clinging to my skin. Touching a hand to my face, I discovered the tracks of tears I hadn't even known I cried.

"Yeah, we'll just hop on the jet and come on down late tomorrow afternoon. We'd rather see it for the first time with you."

"Sure seems like a lot of time and expense to approve a four-minute video," I hedged. Honestly, I'd had enough trouble watching the guys perform on screen over and over after everything that went down in the middle of the shoot. Garrett left me for them once. This time, he left all of us. Having to spend time with them when my feelings were still so raw was level with a stint in a medieval torture chamber.

"Garrett thinks this song has Oscar potential. Your production can help keep it on the Academy voters' minds every time it shows up in the queue on YouTube and when they flip on their late-night video shows." The boyishness of his laughter left me wondering if winning an Oscar truly mattered to him. Then he sobered. "If we're going to have a chance to win hardware to decorate Balefire's studios, we all want input on the final product."

He said something else, but I was still stuck on the part where Garrett had weighed in on the song's potential. Was he in Denver with the band, now?

"Nah. He's still holed up at Nick's place on the beach outside of San Fran."

Guess I asked the question aloud. I blew out a breath. At least he hadn't stayed nearby.

Tron interrupted my thoughts. "So we good for tomorrow afternoon?"

"Uh, sure. I'll have Dana put it on the schedule."

But when I stepped out of my office, the reception area was dark. "What the hell?" A glance at my watch said my private pity party lasted far beyond quitting time. I stood in the quiet and shook my head.

After I left a sticky note on Dana's computer to add Balefire to the ever-growing to-do list for tomorrow, I headed back to the projection room. Selecting a new chair, shenanigans with Garrett in my old favorite had forever ruined it for me, I cued up the final video and tried to watch it in the way a casual fan would rather than as a director-producer who'd seen it at least a thousand times. Even with a concentrated effort to keep my mind open, the scene with the groupies exuded a sort of melancholy. No matter how creatively I'd tried to infuse it with the excitement of a live show, that scene screamed Garrett walking out. Jeremy had assured me it was arguably the best scene in the video, but I still couldn't see it in the right light.

Something had to give. I shut down "Dangerous Life" and cued up the raw footage of a Turnkey video we'd shot earlier in the week. After the stern talking to I gave myself, I still sat through the footage without the first clue about what we had with it. When I glanced down at my notes, I saw they'd inexplicably switched from the Turnkey script to the Balefire one with Garrett's notes attached. It had taken years for me to move on from him the first time. How long would I live in this purgatory without him this time?

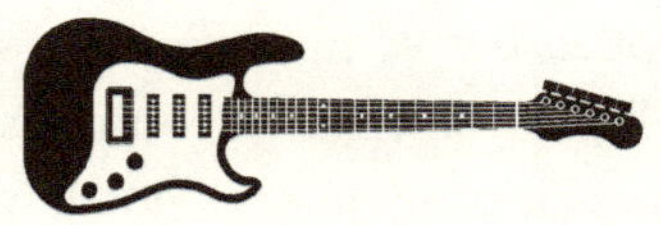

CHAPTER TWENTY-SEVEN

Garrett

I WAS CONTEMPLATING A Jameson, neat, for lunch rather than the spread on the table in front of me as I waited for the band in the private dining room. Instead, I sipped ice water and nodded over the rim of the glass when the four of them filed into the room. Their usual boisterous screwing around didn't precede them, and I couldn't decide if I should be nervous about that or not.

According to Emory, after I finally gave in to Nick's badgering and called her, there was never any hint the band intended to fire me. Instead, they needed me back at the office to plan and set up the Midwest leg of the "Dangerous Life" tour we'd discussed when I was trying to deflect them from other, less pleasant conversations. Turns out, the idea had stuck with them. They especially liked how I'd taken their ladies' needs and desires into consideration with my suggestions.

I'd spent last night in a stripped-down suite at the hotel. No balcony, no Jacuzzi tub, no fancy wine and fruit basket waiting on the bar. In a weird sort of way, it was a refreshing change from how I usually traveled with the band. Of course, the minibar was well stocked, but in the end, that hadn't helped me sleep at all. Being within a couple of miles of Olivia's apartment gnawed at me. Then I'd remember the horror on her face during Jennifer's nasty revelations, and I knew I could never make that up to her. She'd never needed anyone, so how could I explain to her how terrified I'd been of losing her? Of losing the band?

The irony now was I'd made peace with that possibility. Didn't mean I wanted to experience it, but after talking some things through with Nick, I believed I could survive if Balefire decided to cut me loose.

I'd asked Emory about the team meeting they'd had on set. Emory danced around it until it came out the guys had wanted to devise new punishments for what had gone down with Cristy and Mali. To teach me a lesson, apparently. When I walked off and didn't return their calls and texts, they'd had a little rethink. Today, we were clearing the air.

Or they were well and truly going to fire me. I couldn't tell for sure from their expressions. Every one of them looked far too serious for the players in the biggest rock 'n' roll party band on the planet.

"It's not Chef Jeff—or your mom"—I nodded at Blu whose mom ran the best restaurant in Denver. "But I've been assured it doesn't suck," I said, indicating the covered platters of food in the middle of the table.

A tiny smirk lifted the corner of Blu's mouth, but otherwise, no one in the band reacted to my opening salvo. So I occupied my mouth with another sip of ice water.

"You wanna tell us what that was all about?" Dakota asked, his tone filled with disgust as he sat opposite me and smoothed his napkin over his lap.

"What was what about?"

"You ditching the video shoot and going MIA?" With a glare in my direction, he reached for the pitcher of water in the middle of the table and poured himself a glass. "You're our manager, for fuck's sake. It's your job to take care of that shit."

"Instead, Tron's been the point man with Olivia and her studio. Not. His. Job," Blu added as he took the pitcher of water from Dakota and poured himself a glass.

I folded my hands on the table beside my plate. "Huh. Guess I thought I was out of a job, what with the way you all reacted to Jennifer's nasty revelations."

Blu rolled his eyes. "It was a team meeting, Garrett. Jesus."

At the risk of making my situation worse, I said, "Last time you had a team meeting, one that included your ladies too, you put me on probation. This time, I connected the dots all by myself."

Tron pulled a face. "For fuck's sake, Garrett. Stop acting like a diva."

"Look, we can see how you might reach that conclusion," Jack cut in, aiming a dad expression at his bandmates. "But that's not what went down at all." He sat up tall, commanding the other men's attention. "We talked about this, guys. We aren't blameless in what happened between us and our ladies. Some of our messes were our own, not Garrett's."

Three pairs of eyes immediately took a tour of the table, the room, anywhere but at Jack—or me.

Jack leveled his eyes on me. "Everyone in this room knows that half of our success comes from our music and half from your management of it. None of us is ready to break up the band." His brow went up. "That includes you."

Tron let out a sigh. "Landon told us some of what you said to Olivia that day, about believing you don't belong, that you're not part of the team." He pushed a hand through his hair. "I can see how you might feel that way these last couple of years, but ever since you started managing us, you've belonged with the band."

Blu shot Jack a look and slumped back in his chair. "Yeah, we've kinda been assholes too. Guess when you're a family, sometimes you take each other for granted and forget that family should always come first."

"I put you guys first. Always," I whispered, not trusting my voice not to crack if I spoke up.

"We're aware," Dakota said. An unholy light came into his eyes. "That was part of the reason we insisted on doing the video with Olivia."

My head came up. "What does Olivia have to do with any of this?"

"You gave her up for us," Dakota said matter-of-factly. "At the time, we thought that was a good idea. We could all be wild and single together."

"We were teenagers. We didn't know diddly-squat about what we truly asked of you," Blu added.

Like they'd rehearsed it, Tron chimed in. "Now we know. Finding women who make us better men maybe made us grow up a little."

Narrowing my eyes, I said, "I take it you think I should grow up too?"

"Nah. You were always the grown-up." Tron smirked.

Jack leaned his arms on the table. "We all saw the way you mooned after Olivia at the Grammy after-party."

"I did not 'moon after' Olivia," I shot back with air quotes.

"You kinda did," Blu said with a grin.

"We all saw it." Dakota waggled his brows.

I wanted to deck the whole damn bunch of them. So I noticed how gorgeous Olivia looked that night in her slinky dress with her hair all swept up, so what? I wasn't "mooning" over her.

"She's a kick-ass music video director and producer. She proved that with her production of the Grammys, which by itself would have been enough for us to want to work with her. Insisting you help with the script? Well, maybe the two of you would remember old times…" Blu trailed off.

"The video was a setup." Dread fell over me at how Olivia would react if she ever found out.

"Kinda. Kinda not. It depended on how you two feel now." Blu tossed back his water and refilled his glass.

"From the sparks flying between the two of you every time you were in the same room together, it looked like the old flames were banked, not out," Tron said.

The other guys in the band were right. Tron was too damn observant.

I sucked in a long breath and blew it at the ceiling. "Yeah, well, I poured gallons of cold water on those flames the day I walked off the set. Doubt Olivia wants one damn thing to do with me now."

Dakota drew patterns on the table cloth with his knife, his tone nonchalant. "That's not what Landon says he heard from Jeremy."

"Yeah, from what Landon says, Jeremy has had his hands full keeping Olivia focused. Jeremy told Landon she's been kind of a zombie ever since you walked out." Jack tossed his thigh over the arm of his chair, a tiny smirk teasing the corner of his mouth as he swung his foot back and forth.

"Gossip runs rampant in this business, Garrett. You know that," Tron added.

Four pairs of eyes danced as they stared at me, and for the first time since I walked into a coffee shop and caught sight of the most beautiful girl in the world, something like hope warmed my chest. After everything that had gone down over the last couple of years, the band still wanted me to be a part of them. More than that, they wanted me to have what they had—the love of a good woman. The sneaky way they went about it should have pissed me off, but as I looked at the faces around the table, I had to admit, their tactics were pure Balefire. Make a production out of falling in love.

I laughed.

"For the record, I'm the one who's doing the punishing this time." I tapped my finger to my lips. "One of you is going to have to 'fess up to her. Hope whichever one draws the short straw is man enough to withstand the explosion." Not bothering to hide the smirk on my face, I reached out and uncovered a platter of mini sliders. Miraculously, after waiting on the table for nearly an hour, steam arose from them along with a mouthwatering scent of perfectly cooked meat.

My pronouncement broke the tension that hovered beneath the smirks and smiles and shared looks since the band arrived. Within minutes, platters of quesadillas, mini pizzas, and homemade jalapeño poppers steamed alongside the sliders. I shot off a quick text, and a minute later, a couple of bartenders arrived with a cart well stocked with the band's favorite spirits. But all they wanted was shots of Jameson, which they raised to toast our renewed status as one cohesive unit.

I coughed over my shot, and the four of them wasted no time calling me out.

"What the fuck?"

"Whiskey virgin?"

"Jesus, Garrett. Didn't take you long to fall out of practice."

"I call you're on Dakota's team for shot races."

Covering with a laugh, I dabbed at my watering eyes with my napkin and played along that the burn in my throat was from the alcohol. Then I signaled the bartender for another round, and this time without the toasts, I held it together. By the time every platter on the table was empty, as well as a fifth of Jameson, the five of us were in high spirits. Only then did they drop the bomb: we were headed to Olivia's studio to view the finished video.

CHAPTER TWENTY-EIGHT

Olivia

ALL DAY, JEREMY acted especially weird, sliding me sidelong glances when he thought I wouldn't notice, making sure my coffee never cooled before he replaced it with a fresh cup, being Johnny-on-the-spot with the best clips, in his opinion, for the Turnkey video I'd decided to work on. By afternoon, I'd had enough.

Sitting back in my chair, I crossed my arms over my chest and narrowed my eyes at him. "It's not like I'm going to send you on an errand or something when Balefire arrives. You were part of the production team, and you're included in the screening. You'll have plenty of opportunities to fan-boy all over the band. So maybe you can stop hovering and go make sure there are refreshments in the projection room or something."

The tops of his ears fired up as always, and he ducked his head. "Sorry. I only wanted to make sure you—" He stopped, his neck and cheeks doing their best to match the tips of his ears.

"I—"

I rolled my hand in a go-on gesture.

His Adam's apple bobbed a couple of times. "You seemed tired this morning, so I only wanted to be sure"—he swallowed again—"you had everything you need."

"From the weird way you've acted all day, I think it's something else." I sat forward and leaned my forearms on my desk. "Spill it."

He bumped into the door in his haste to back out of my office. "Just noticed you've been tired lately and wanted to do a good job for you." Reaching behind his back, he grabbed the doorknob and opened it. "I'll head on over to the projection room and make sure everything's ready for when Balefire arrives."

As if his feet had caught fire, he ducked out the door, stopping a fuzz short of slamming it behind him. For a long moment, I stared after him. Something was up, no doubt something the band had cooked up and enlisted Jeremy's help with. Hard telling with Balefire what that would be, but at least I could brace for the surprise this time. After the whole groupie surprise during the shoot, my money was on a full entourage of celebrities joining us in the screening room for the big reveal.

Of course my mind wandered to Garrett and if he'd be with the band. Rumor had it that after Jennifer's bombshell on the video set, the guys seriously considered firing him. After everything he said to me that day, I couldn't imagine them doing anything more short-sighted for themselves. Garrett loved those guys like the brothers he never had and always wanted.

During the long sleepless nights I'd spent since that awful day, I'd had time to reflect. All my life, I'd thought I had something to prove. Growing up with an older sister who wowed our parents with every accolade she earned from sports to academics to her vast network of friends, I always felt I had to do more just to be seen. I dreamed that earning my JD and going to Hollywood to run a major studio one day would finally shine a light on me where I stood in my sister's shadow. With single-minded focus, I'd pursued that goal—and paid a price.

My sister was happily married with preteen twin daughters for my parents to dote on. When I'd taken a couple days off from work last summer for a screaming trip to Denver to celebrate the twins' tenth birthday, my mother had pulled me aside and asked if I was happy. She'd never asked me that before, and her eyes were troubled when I told her I was happy enough. But I wasn't. I was lonely. I'd been lonely ever since Garrett and I called it quits.

He accused me of being a loner, someone who didn't need other people, but he was wrong. Twice too late, I'd never told him.

I needed him.

Rolling my head and shoulders, I refocused on my task.

The pity party wasn't editing video clips. Turning back to my screen, I scrolled through the scenes Jeremy had cued up for me, a tiny self-deprecating smile curving my lips. Wonder Kid did know me. Every one of his favorite shots found their way into the "use" folder. It wouldn't be long before I'd have to advertise for another assistant when he decided he wanted to show up sooner in the credits.

Dana knocked once and stuck her head around my door. "Balefire is here. They're waiting in the projection room."

A glance at my watch told me they were early. Furrowing my brow, I said, "We did schedule this for six, right?"

She rolled her eyes. "After working with them on this shoot, you still haven't figured out they do everything on their time? Shut down your computer and hurry yourself over there." She clapped her hands a couple of times. "Don't want to keep the paying clientele waiting."

I gifted her with a long-suffering stare from beneath my brows and returned to my screen, shutting down open folders and leaving myself a note for where I'd left off. Knowing the band, I wouldn't be back in the office tonight.

When I arrived at the projection room, I saw that Balefire filled the seats near the projector, leaving two open, my usual spot, which I didn't want, and the one beside it. With a blink of surprise, I noted that no other celebs had joined them. At the back of the room, Jeremy busied himself pouring fingers of Jameson over ice. I didn't see Garrett anywhere, which worried me about those rumors of his departure from the band.

"Hello, boys. I see Jeremy is taking good care of you. How was your flight?" I asked them in general.

"Too early for alcohol, which means we have to make up for it now," Dakota said with a smirk as he helped himself to a glass from the tray Jeremy held.

"Which reminds me. Why were you here two hours early? I thought we agreed to do this at six." I said as I walked over to the seats beside the projector.

"What can we say? We're super-excited to see the finished product," Blu said with a laugh that didn't quite meet his eyes.

I gave my attention to Tron. "I told you when you called that I could send the video via an encrypted server. You could have watched it last night from the comfort of your own place."

"Yeah, but we wanted to watch it with you." The sneaky side-eye he slid the rest of the guys put me on alert.

Something was up.

"Olivia, we always watch our videos with the directors," Jack said with a straight face.

"Riiight." I'd done my homework. Nothing about the way we'd shot this video was anything like the work the band had done with other studios in the past. But when the four of them hid behind their drinks, I knew they weren't spilling whatever surprise they'd cooked up. I shot the heavens a glance and turned to Jeremy with a sigh. "Better pour one of those for me."

Avoiding the memories of another screening of the video made up for the awkwardness of running the projector from the other chair. Jeremy furrowed his brow at my choice as he handed me my drink, but he didn't ask. Thankfully. I sucked down a fortifying sip then booted up the machine. After checking volume levels and presets, I dimmed the lights, pushed Play and sat back to gauge the guys' reactions to seeing the project for the first time.

At the two-minute mark, where the third verse introduced the groupie scene, a familiar citrusy scent with an undertone of musk alerted me to a certain man joining us. As he took the seat beside me, Garrett kept his eyes trained on the video playing on the screen. But his hand found mine, and I didn't know what to do except to turn my hand up to grasp his. Tight.

At his touch, sensations bubbled and fizzed through me, leaving my body on pins and needles. After the way he'd walked out and didn't return my texts and phone calls, I should have been furious with him, should have told him to find someone new to play. Yet I was so relieved he was alive and well, I didn't bother with attitude. I lost track of the end of the video until the band erupted in cheers and high fives as the closing credits rolled.

"Fuckin' A, Olivia!"

"That's fucking brilliant!"

"Great job, O!"

"Yeesss!"

"Pour another round, barkeep!" Dakota said to Jeremy.

"Let's watch it again," Blu added.

"If we weren't rock stars already, that video would make us rock stars," Jack said, his face lit up like Christmas.

Blu merely grinned, but his expression was aimed at where Garrett's hand covered mine.

While Jeremy gathered glasses for Jameson refills, Garrett leaned in to whisper, "We have a few things to discuss."

My brow shot up in question, but he only gave me an enigmatic smile.

I reset the video as Jeremy distributed another round of drinks. After I dimmed the lights and pushed Play, Garrett stood and tugged on my hand. At my questioning expression, he nodded toward the door at the back of the room, and I followed him out.

In the hallway outside the door, he pushed me against the wall, lowered his head, and kissed me like kissing me was all he'd thought about in the weeks he'd been MIA. Fisting my hands in his shirt, I held on and kissed him back with all the need of him I'd held inside for a decade. When at last we came up for air, his mouth looked as bruised as mine felt.

"I'm sorry," we said in unison.

We exchanged a smile and dove in for another kiss. I twined my arms around his neck as he flattened me to the wall with his body. Who ground against whom didn't matter as we explored each other's mouths, teasing and tasting, sharing air, and delighting in each other. I have no idea how long we kissed each other stupid in the public hallway of my studio, but we were both panting when the door to the projection room burst open, and the exuberance of the band spilled into the hall and interrupted our homecoming.

"Get a room," Dakota said with a light punch to Garrett's shoulder.

"What he said," Blu added with a smirk.

"Party's at Cristy's place if you want to join us later." Tron winked as he sauntered by.

Jack punched him in the shoulder hard enough to unbalance his step. "Do they look like they want to party with us tonight?" Grinning at us, he added, "Have fun, you two. Don't do anything we wouldn't do."

Dakota's laughter rang back down the hall. "Well, that leaves it wide open then, yeah?"

The four of them continued to cut up as they made their way to the lobby. Jeremy poked his head around the door of the projection room. "I'll just clean this up and head out, if that's okay, Boss Lady." For the first time all day, my assistant looked relaxed.

"Don't worry about cleaning up, Wonder Kid. I'll have the night staff take care of it. Enjoy your evening."

He smiled and said, "Looks like you already have a head start enjoying yours."

"Jeremy!"

Though the tops of his ears pinkened, he chuckled. "Just sayin'." He closed the door, stuffed his hands in his pockets, and whistled the tune of "Dangerous Life" as he followed the band out into the lobby.

Garrett gazed at me, the expression in his eyes so soft I could have fallen into their gray depths like resting on a cloud bank. "Your place or mine?"

"Seriously? You're leading with that cheese?" I couldn't decide if I wanted to laugh or cuff him.

His expression turned serious. "We need somewhere private to talk, Olivia."

"My office is private," I offered.

"I'm hoping that once we've talked about some things, we'll want to do other things. In a bed." The wicked smile that accompanied those last three words turned my knees to jelly.

"My place," I managed to say over the desire riding me hard.

He kissed the corner of my mouth—a promise for later—took my hand, and walked me down the hall.

♪

The drive to my apartment was quiet. I led him inside and headed to the kitchen and my stash of alcohol in a tiny side cupboard beside the fridge. I pulled out a bottle of Jameson and one of Patrón, which was pretty much all I had besides a bottle of white chilling in the fridge. Before I could even ask which he preferred, he said, "We don't need that." He made himself comfortable on my couch and patted the cushion beside him. "Come here."

I wasn't so sure we didn't need something to make this easier. For several seconds, I debated with myself before I finally joined him empty-handed on the couch.

"Why did you leave like that? Why didn't you answer my texts or return my calls?" I didn't see the point in hiding my hurt, my tone proclaiming it in the quiet of the room.

"If you had seen the look on your face after Jennifer dropped her bombs, you wouldn't have stuck around for the dressing-down either."

"Garrett—"

He covered my lips with the pad of his finger. "Let me answer your questions first, then you can say what you need to say."

I nodded.

Leaning his head back against the cushions, he stared up at the ceiling for a long minute. Then he sat up, his hands folded between his knees, and he started talking. "We were so young and single-minded." He shot me a side-eye. "Both of us. But we could have worked out a way to stay together and still chase our dreams. In the last couple of weeks, I've thought a lot about how we can do that together now. But before that can happen, I have to come clean about how I tried to sabotage each of the guys' relationships. If you can stand me after that, we might have a chance."

"You sure you don't want a drink first?"

He snorted out a self-deprecating laugh. "Won't make this any easier." Looking me in the eyes, he said, "I was afraid if the guys hooked up in serious relationships, they'd want to stop touring, stop being a megaband. If they chose that, where did that leave me?" His eyes pleaded with me to understand. "I'd given up everything to manage them, so if there was no more Balefire, I had nothing left."

His gaze slipped back to his hands. "It started with keeping Jack on the road and away from Clio. Then I made a half-assed run at Ashleigh that turned them all against me. Next, I whispered in Dakota's ear about a phantom affair between Annabelle and Bailey Saunders where I learned that the class clown has zero sense of humor when it comes to his lady. Finally, I attempted to add Mali Tatum to the tour to replace Cristy and split her and Tron up. That one blew up spectacularly and almost cost me managing the band." Flexing his hands once, he rubbed his palms up and down the expensive fabric of the trousers covering his powerful thighs.

Once again, his eyes found mine. "I've atoned for it. All of it.

But when Jennifer told the band the part I played—it was inadvertent, but that doesn't matter for the result—I was sure their team meeting was to fire me. I didn't want that to happen in front of the one person in the world whose opinion matters most to me. So I walked away before you could witness another ugly scene."

I pulled up a knee and rested my chin on it. "From the way they acted today, you're still their manager though, right?"

He nodded. "I didn't return your texts because I didn't have an answer. First, I think I was numb. Then I was a wreck. Losing you and losing the band all at once sent me down a bad path. I drove for days, spent hours on the beach, drank enough booze to supply a tour, lived out of a rental car until I ended up at my friend Nick Parker's place up the coast. Though I was physically safe, emotionally, I was all over the place."

Seemingly by itself, my hand found its way to his forearm, where I reassured him with a squeeze. His gaze somewhere in the middle distance, I couldn't be sure he even knew when he covered my hand with his.

"Emory reached out to Nick, and between them, they convinced me the band wanted to keep me on. The team meeting that day was to exact more atonements from me. When I walked away, the guys started to figure out that maybe they hadn't been entirely fair either."

A smirk tugged at the corner of his mouth. "They flew in early today to meet with me. We spent a few hours hashing out how all our behaviors could use some work." It was his turn to give my hand a squeeze. "When they told me we were headed to your studio, I panicked. Especially after they confessed that part of the reason they wanted you to direct and produce this video was because of your work on the last Grammys production." His thumb rubbed the back of my hand in a soothing way. "But mostly, they were meddling in my private life—in a more altruistic way than I meddled in theirs."

My eyes flew to his.

He grinned, but trepidation colored his tone. "They were

matchmaking. Somewhere along the line after I put all my effort into making the Be Valorous Foundation a major force in changing perceptions and laws concerning child marriage, they decided I needed someone special back in my life." Raising his hand to my face, he cupped my cheek and held me. "They wanted to atone for taking me from you in the first place."

"But what if I had been in a relationship? It's a long time since any of us have even seen each other."

"Don't worry. They did their homework." His lips thinned. "They had no intention of hurting you to help me."

I slid my foot back to the floor and angled myself to face him. "So how do we move on from here? You're still managing the band, and I still want to run my studio."

Smoothing his other hand down my arm and back up to my shoulder, his thumb gliding along my collarbone, he said, "We have a few choices. We can try long distance."

I pulled a face and he laughed.

"I can work remotely from LA and travel with the band on tour."

I tilted my head.

"Or you can move your studio to Denver." Now both of his thumbs were moving over my skin, soothing me even as he tipped my plans on their head. "As Nick pointed out while I was staying with him, Denver has quietly become a music hub. Lots of musicians are recording there. You could open a studio, start a trend the way Tyler Perry abandoned Hollywood for Atlanta and created a viable alternative for film production." His eyebrows bobbed up and down.

"Whichever idea appeals most to you," he went on, "that's the one I want too." The love shining from his face warmed all the places inside me that had been cold for so long. Twining our fingers together, he told me with touch and eyes that he meant every word. "As long as we're together, the rest is details. I belong with you, and you belong with me."

"So I'm not a loner who doesn't need anyone?" I said over the lump in my throat.

"I never should have said that." He tucked a strand of hair behind my ear. "We both know that's a lie. I'm sorry."

For long minutes, our gazes locked. Only when he cupped my cheeks and smoothed the moisture away with his thumbs did I notice the tears running unchecked down my face.

"I need you, Garrett. I've always needed you."

In one smooth motion, he hauled me up to straddle his lap, his arms coming around my waist to pull me to him. "I need you, Olivia. More than anyone else in the world. I love you so much."

The kiss was slow, lingering, gentle. A quiet promise that this time, no matter what, we were together—and staying that way.

Epilogue

Garrett

Six months later

THE DAY THE Oscar nominations were announced, we put the finishing touches on Olivia's new Heart Dreams Studio in the center of downtown Denver. The core members of her staff—Jeremy, Sarah, Dana, four of her lighting techs, and all of the sound engineers—agreed to move with her rather than accept a severance package and remain in LA. When that happened, no one was more surprised than the Boss Lady herself. Turns out, people like working for people who treat them well.

Olivia treated everyone well.

Except for Flyboys who refused to agree to her terms for behavior on set so she turned down their request to work with her. As a result, they tried to blackball her—with a bit of help from Jennifer Hartwell who had sicced them on Olivia in the first place. About that same time, Balefire released "Dangerous Life" with the video, and the rest, as they say, is history.

Inside of three days, the video had over a million views on YouTube. By the end of the first week, it was the most watched music video of all time. There were so many downloads on Spotify that it almost crashed the site. It set viewing records all across the world.

Now it was up for an Academy Award for best original song in a movie. Just like I promised.

Balefire catered the party on the main soundstage. What started out as a kind of housewarming for the new studio turned into a celebration of all things Olivia Carter and Balefire with all our Denver friends along with some Hollywood buddies in attendance. As usual, the boys were doing shots of tequila from their ladies' navels—all except for Jack since Clio's pregnancy prevented him doing shots on her belly. From the besotted way he stared at her, I don't think he cared.

"You going to let me do shots from your navel, Boss Lady?" I teased Olivia as I pulled her in close.

"Sure."

My brows shot up.

"At home in the privacy of our bedroom." She glanced down at her bright turquoise formfitting dress. "Unless you want me to show everyone here the pretty lingerie you gave me for today's special occasion."

I smacked a kiss on her mouth. "I do *not* want anyone but me to see you in that lace thong." Sliding a hand over the firm globe of her ass, I held her tight against the evidence of how much I appreciated her wearing my gift.

"Thought so."

"Congratulations on your new place," I said, my lips a breath from hers. "From what Dana says—"

"Complains." She grinned.

"You're booked until this time next year." I brushed a kiss over her mouth. "After today's big news, you'll probably be booked into the next decade."

She smiled against my lips. "Thank you. For everything."

Shaking my head, I said, "I didn't do this. This is all you, babe."

"Not what I meant. We took a too-long hiatus, but we were never truly over. You had that all figured out before I did. Thank you for not giving up on us." Nibbling at my lower lip, she silently asked for more.

I sealed my lips to hers, our tongues sliding and gliding over each other the way our bodies would when the party broke up and we returned to the mountain cabin we'd bought together, the one Olivia had always dreamed of owning.

Swaying to the sound of "Dangerous Life" blaring from the overhead speakers, we kissed each other like we had all the time in the world.

"I love you, Olivia Carter. Always have. Always will."

"I love you, Garrett Phillips. For always."

DANGEROUS LIFE

Music and Lyrics by Blu Connolly, Jack Whitehorse, Dakota Perri, and Adam Tron

Heart pounds, time races
Live fast, the past erases
Outrun all the faces
Get out now, leave no traces.

Chorus:
It's a dangerous, dangerous,
A dangerous life.
Angel lust, dangerous
Savor this life.

Wanted out, but she's there.
Can't escape the warfare.
No promises life's fair.
Can't escape this nightmare.

Chorus:

It's a dangerous, dangerous,
A dangerous life.
Angel lust, dangerous
Savor this life.

Bridge:

How far can we run?
Can't escape the damage done.
Live fast. Race the sun.
Escape the flash of a gun.

Chorus:

It's a dangerous, dangerous,
A dangerous life.
Angel lust, dangerous
Savor this life.

Dance along the edge of a knife
No justice in this dangerous life.
Salvation wears a red dress,
If we can escape this.
Dangerous, dangerous life.

Chorus:

It's a dangerous, dangerous,
A dangerous life.
Angel lust, dangerous
Savor this life.
Savor my life.

***Stay For Me* Playlist**

"Shoulders"—Coheed and Cambria
"Passive"—A Perfect Circle
"Picture"—Kid Rock (feat. Sheryl Crow)
"Broken Pieces"—Apocalyptica (feat. Lacey)
"Breathe"—Through Fire
"Teardrinker"—Mastodon
"No One Like You"—Scorpions
"Hero of the Day"—Metallica
"Someone You Loved"—Lewis Capaldi

Acknowledgements

I never meant to write *Stay For Me*. As far as I was concerned, Garrett Phillips was a first-class jerk for his own twisted reasons, and that was that. But my critique group—LindaRae Sande, Sara Vinduska, Jacque Cobourn, and KJ Gillenwater—KJ especially, wanted to know Garrett's backstory and why he tried his level best to keep the boys in the band single throughout the previous books in the Balefire Series. The more my writer buddies nagged me, the more I wanted to know what his story was too. Which explains how you're holding in your hand the unexpected, unplanned-for fifth book in the series. ;)

Since I hadn't planned on writing this one, it didn't come easily. Then in the middle of writing it, I lost both of my parents to illness in the space of three weeks, which put my writing on hold for an extended period. My editor, Nikki Busch, saved this book when she gave me not one but two extensions to finish it. In addition to her kick-ass skills as an editor, Nikki is a rock star of a human being, and I'm forever grateful for her understanding and patience with this story.

I also want to shoutout my lifelong best friend and partner in crime, Coleene Torgerson, who, in the middle of her own struggle with breast cancer, encouraged me to keep going and went out of her way to be there for me when my parents were dying and afterward. You are the best friend anyone could ever have. I love you so very much.

None of this happens without the love and support of

CruiserMan who reads all my books and tells all the people to read them too. It's not always easy being married to a writer. Grady, your patience when I zone out to follow my characters and when I talk your ear off about my latest plan for my career and when I ask you to entertain yourself when I pull out my laptop while we're on vacation shows me your support. You have no idea how much that means to me. I love you more.

Ultimately, my books do not exist without the support of readers like you. Thanks so much for reading *Stay For Me*. If this is your introduction to the Balefire Series, why not give the other books in the series a read too? They are standalones with the events of *Play For Me* and *Sing For Me* happening simultaneously. The events of *Wild For Me* and *Hot For Me* happen simultaneously as well, so if you read them out of order, I promise you won't be lost.

If you've read the series, a massive thank you!

If you want to know what's coming next, sign up for my newsletter. The link is on my website. You can also keep up with me on the socials. I'm most active on Instagram, but you can also find me on Facebook in my reader group, and I'm dipping my toes into TikTok, so look for me there as well. Finally, your follows on BookBub and my Amazon Author page help me so much, and I appreciate you following me there.

Website:
https://tamderudderjackson.com/
Instagram:
https://instagram.com/tamstales32
Tam's Romance Warriors on Facebook:
https://facebook.com/1531651733710243
BookBub:
https://bookbub.com/authors/tam-derudder-jackson
Goodreads:
https://goodreads.com/author/show/19849371

Tam DeRudder Jackson's love of all things Celtic led her to write the Talisman Series. Steeped in Celtic mythology, these steamy, fated mates, paranormal romance adventures are set in the mountains of Tam's native Montana and the Highlands of Scotland. *Rogue*, the most recent book in the series, was named a best romance of 2022 by the *Independent Book Review*.

An avid fan of rock music, Tam never misses a chance to see a live show, especially if it's Shinedown, one of her favorite bands. Her love of rock music inspired her contemporary rock star Balefire Series, a sexy fun ride following the lives and loves of the members of a fictional megaband. Readers of this series consistently give the books five-star reviews.

Tam earned her BA in English from Montana State University and her M.Ed. in literacy from Lesley University. After a short teaching stint in Bath, England, she settled in the wilds of Wyoming where she taught adolescents all about the Celts and a bit about writing before she stepped out of the classroom to pursue her writing career full time.

When she's not writing, you can find her working her way through her mountainous TBR piles, alpine skiing, or traveling to some new place on her ever-expanding bucket list. To stay up to date on her adventures, connect with Tam on her website *www.tamderudderjackson* where you can subscribe to her newsletter.